"I told them the truth…" Xander said.

"The truth?"

"Yeah, that I was investigating McQuarry's death."

"From what angle?"

"I was vague on that point, but they took the bait without much more needed."

"Interesting. All right, what time?"

"In an hour with the widow, lunchtime with the mistress."

Scarlett nodded with approval. "Good. Let's make it happen. Time is ticking."

Grabbing her coat, she swung it around her shoulders but was surprised when Xander pulled her close by her lapels.

"What are you doing?" she asked, wary.

"Just reminding you what's between us," he answered, brushing his lips against hers, igniting heat with the slow slide of his mouth. She didn't need reminding. Her mouth opened and his tongue accepted the invitation, dancing with hers. A dangerous fire burned between them but they didn't have the time to play. It took extreme force of will to break the kiss but she did. Xander released her and she left everything unsaid, choosing to spin on her heel and walk out the door.

* * *

If you're on Twitter
think of Harlequin R
#harlequinro

Dear Reader,

I love writing stories with incredibly high stakes, impossible situations and intense passion—and, boy, I hit the jackpot with this one!

A word of caution while reading this book: don't forget to breathe! There were so many times while writing this story that I found myself holding my breath because there was so much happening, and I hope you find it just as exciting as I did.

I love hearing from readers. Connect with me on Facebook or Twitter, or drop me an email. You can also write me a letter at PO Box 2210, Oakdale, CA 95361.

Happy reading!

Kimberly

SOLDIER FOR HIRE

—

Kimberly Van Meter

HARLEQUIN® ROMANTIC SUSPENSE

Recycling programs
for this product may
not exist in your area.

ISBN-13: 978-1-335-45669-4

Soldier for Hire

Copyright © 2018 by Kimberly Sheetz

This edition published by arrangement with Harlequin Books S.A.

For questions and comments about the quality of this book, please contact us at CustomerService@Harlequin.com.

Printed in U.S.A.

Kimberly Van Meter wrote her first book at sixteen and finally achieved publication in December 2006. She has written for the Harlequin Superromance, Blaze and Romantic Suspense lines. She and her husband of seventeen years have three children, three cats, and always a houseful of friends, family and fun.

Books by Kimberly Van Meter

Harlequin Romantic Suspense

Military Precision Heroes
Soldier for Hire

The Sniper
The Agent's Surrender
Moving Target
Deep Cover
The Killer You Know

Harlequin Superromance

Family in Paradise
Like One of the Family
Playing the Part
Something to Believe In

The Sinclairs of Alaska
That Reckless Night
A Real Live Hero
A Sinclair Homecoming

Visit the Author Profile page at Harlequin.com for more titles.

This book is dedicated to all the hardworking, dedicated women out there making things happen in their universe; those not afraid to be strong, to be leaders, to be role models. We need more of you in the world today as we face an uncertain future.

Strong women: may we know them; may we raise them.

And finally, to my daughter...you are already everything I ever wanted to be, but you're doing it ten times better and with more grace. I don't say it enough but I love you more than you'll ever know.

Chapter 1

"You know how this is going to end, Xander."

Xander Scott melted against the wall, clinging to the shadows as his former Red Wolf team leader, Scarlett Rhodes, tried to convince him to come out peacefully, knowing full well that wasn't going to happen.

Naw, everything had already gone sidewise; Scarlett knew he wasn't going to go meekly to his own destruction but, hey, he gave her props for tenacity. The woman wasn't known for her soft and fuzzy side—hell, that was one of the things Xander liked about her— but right about now, he wished Scarlett was a little less rigid so she'd listen to what he was trying to tell her instead of hauling his ass in over some bullshit frame job.

"I didn't do it, Rhodes," he said, quickly assessing his position within the abandoned building, stalling for time. Scarlett had found him faster than he'd anticipated, zeroing in on his location like a bloodhound, but he knew her tactics, which was his only saving grace, otherwise she would've had him trussed up like a Christmas turkey ready for the table.

Well, that and the fact that while Scarlett played by the rules, Xander didn't.

"Looking pretty guilty from my end. Innocent people don't run," she replied, the sound of her changing position pricking Xander's ears. "But turn yourself in and we'll talk about it."

Xander chuckled grimly. *Yeah, we'll talk about it. Sure.* "Think about it, Rhodes. It doesn't make sense. I'm being framed and you know it."

"Turn yourself in."

"Screw you, Rhodes," he muttered, his gaze catching on the dirty window. They were on the third floor. A jump from that height would break bones at the very least. He was partial to his limbs remaining intact. Besides, Scarlett would have all exit points covered. She'd have a guy stationed in the stairwell, at the fire escape and all back doors. Scarlett was nothing if not efficient. "Why would I have any reason to hurt innocent people? Granted, politicians are scum but I had no beef with McQuarry. You're barking up the wrong damn tree."

"Cut the crap, Xander. You're wasting time. You know you're surrounded. Don't make this harder than it needs to be. If you're innocent, you've got nothing to worry about. But right now, you're just making things worse by running."

Xander blew out a short breath, still trying to figure out how he'd gotten to this moment.

One minute he was going day to day—maybe a little rough around the edges, maybe playing fast and loose with a few rules but for the most part, things had been good.

Manageable.

Sure, sometimes he still woke up, drenched in cold sweat, heart hammering like a meth head after a fresh rail, hands curled in fists ready to swing to the death, but who didn't, right?

Okay, so maybe not everyone had a psych eval that read like a cautionary tale but then not everyone had seen or done the things he had in the service of the good ol' US of A.

Did he set the pipe bomb that killed Senator Ken McQuarry three months ago at a political rally in Tulsa? Hell, no.

At least, he didn't think so.

Yeah, and that was the problem. He couldn't actually remember that day so well.

Sweat popped along his hairline. "You know whoever's framing me for this has done their homework. They knew I had a background in the bomb squad. I was cherry-picked. A little too convenient, though, don't you think? I had no motive, Rhodes."

He was trying to appeal to that stubborn logic locked inside Rhodes's skull, but the redhead was like a dog with a bone—single-minded and hungry for the marrow behind the crunch. "You know me, Rhodes," he said in one last attempt to get her to see she was fighting the wrong fight. "I mean, you *really* know me. Ask yourself if any of this bullshit sounds legit."

Xander was playing with fire. No one knew about him and Rhodes. They'd both agreed to keep it that way for the sake of their careers.

But he had to play any card he could.

A pregnant pause almost gave him a glimmer of hope until Rhodes said, "Doesn't matter. It's not my job to determine if you're guilty or not. It's just my job to bring you in."

Well, it'd been worth a try. He inched a tiny pocket mirror out so he could peer around the corner. Scarlett, looking dangerous as a coiled viper, covered in SWAT gear, her red hair pulled back in an efficient bun, her gun drawn, waited for him to make his move.

God, she was hot.

Even when she was determined to deliver his head on a platter.

Sorry, Rhodes. That's not happening today.

Xander tucked the pocket mirror away and quietly pulled the pin on the flash bomb, lobbing it in Scarlett's direction. The short bang and immediate smoke created cover, but it would only last a moment. Xander rolled under the smoke and popped up behind Scarlett, jerking her to him, his elbow hard across her windpipe, while the barrel of his gun pressed into the narrow opening exposing her rib cage.

"Damn you," Scarlett growled. "I should've known you wouldn't fight fair."

"And why would I do that?" he asked. "Especially given the fact that whoever is trying to drag me down for a crime I didn't commit isn't exactly playing fair, either?"

"What's your move now? The building is surrounded. Your little smoke show didn't do anything but clog up my sinuses. Congratulations, snot."

He chuckled. "You know, someday your sarcasm is going to put you in hot water. You're lucky I'm not a psychopath or at the very least, a sociopath without a sense of humor."

"Your jokes aren't funny."

"Ouch. Kitty cat has claws, but then I remember that from the scratches you left on my back."

"Screw you, Xander," she bit out, her muscles tensing. He would only be able to hold her like this for a few minutes longer and she knew it. He'd sparred with her enough times to know Scarlett was deadly with her hands and feet.

"Maybe later," he quipped, but now wasn't the time to trade witty banter. "Look, if you're really interested in finding out who set that bomb, start looking in the opposite direction of where you're being told to look. It's the oldest trick in the book—sleight of hand—and you're falling for it. You're better than that, Rhodes."

"I don't need you to tell me how to do my job," she growled, and he knew his time was up. As much as he hated to do it, he couldn't very well let go of the tiger's tail and just hope for the best. With one quick motion, he brought the butt of his gun down hard on her head, knocking her out cold.

Her pride might sting and she was going to have one helluva headache but after a few days of rest, she'd be fine.

Lord help him if she managed to catch him after this incident. Scarlett would likely lop off his balls just for fun.

Scarlett opened her eyes to a fog, her vision swimming and her head in an excruciating vise. She struggled to regain her equilibrium but Xander had gotten her good.

Damn asshole had nearly caved her skull in.

Through her bleary vision, she realized she was being loaded into an ambulance, which meant Xander had used her as a distraction to get away.

She swore under her breath, struggling to get up but the EMTs started saying things like "Whoa," "Hold on, be still," "you've sustained a concussion," and she knew she was stuck with an ambulance ride to the hospital, which would only give Xander an even bigger head start.

"I'm fine," she protested but no one was listening. Zak Ramsey, part of her team, crowded into the ambulance beside her and she closed her eyes to stem the spinning. She didn't want the company but that was only because she was fuming mad that Xander had gotten the drop on her and she was embarrassed.

She was the team leader, not a rook.

And yet, Xander had practically waltzed free from the building they'd had completely zipped up.

Until he'd used her as bait to get away.

"What happened?" she asked, her voice little more than an aggrieved croak.

"We heard a single shot and came up to your location. We found you on the ground, bleeding from the head and Xander gone."

In spite of herself, a smile formed. "SOB fired off a shot so you'd break off to provide support, which left the exits wide open. Brilliant, actually."

"Well, yeah, that's what we figured, too, once we saw that you weren't actually shot."

"Xander wouldn't have shot me," Scarlett said. It seemed counterintuitive to say she knew Xander wouldn't gun her down in cold blood, yet she was determined to bring him in for allegedly setting the bomb that'd killed a US senator and a handful of civilians a few months ago. She couldn't explain it but she just knew that Xander wouldn't do something like that to her.

She reached up to gingerly touch the spot where he'd clocked her and she'd no doubt end up with a goose egg for her failure.

"Why the hell are you grinning, TL?" Zak asked, confused. She didn't blame him. The whole damn situation was confusing. Going after one of their own? Yeah, it was confusing as hell.

"I'm smiling because he's good," Scarlett admitted with a rueful chuckle. "If he'd wanted to hurt me, I wouldn't be here suffering a useless ambulance ride to the hospital. He knows protocol will demand tests to ensure I'm okay. The tests will show a minor concussion and I'll be pulled off the case for a few days, giving him time to get that much farther away. Like I said, brilliant."

Zak grinned, too. "Yeah, that sounds about right." He gestured to Scarlett's bandaged head. "I bet that hurt like a son of a bitch."

"It didn't tickle," Scarlett retorted, wincing as a wave of pain almost made her nauseous.

"You need to try and relax," the EMT warned, but Scarlett just rolled her eyes. She'd had worse than a bump on the head.

To the EMT, she assured him, "I'm fine. This is just protocol. I'll be out in a few hours."

The EMT disagreed. "You took a pretty hard knock."

"I got this," Scarlett said, waving away the EMT's

concern to the man's disgust. She didn't care about hurt feelings. Returning to Zak, she said, "Xander knew just where to crack me in the head to get the job done without knocking my lights out permanently."

"Talent. Did he say anything to you before taking you out?" Zak asked.

"Yeah."

"What'd he say?"

"That he's innocent."

Zak frowned, shaking his head. "Do you believe him?"

"Not my job to believe him," Scarlett answered, closing her eyes again when the vertigo became unbearable. "Just my job to bring him in. The attorneys can sort the rest."

"Yeah, but you gotta admit this whole case stinks of rotten eggs. I mean, Xander's an asshole, sure, but we both know he's not the kind of guy to kill innocent civilians. Maybe he's right… Maybe someone is framing him."

"Well, we're not PIs, Ramsey," Scarlett retorted, if only to remind herself as well. Something was tugging at her brain, aside from the constant and excruciating thud of her heartbeat inside her head, and she didn't like it.

Smart criminals had a way of getting inside people's heads—and Xander was smarter than most. Hell, he had a ridiculous IQ, not that anyone would know by his baffling penchant for reality television. The man could binge-watch episodes of *The Bachelor* for hours on end when the same programming would make Scarlett put a gun in her mouth if she had to suffer more than ten minutes of the crap.

Xander also had the worst eating habits she'd ever seen of a former army ranger. Xander treated his body like a dumpster rather than a temple and yet somehow, he still managed to beat her PT times.

And it had nothing to do with muscle mass or any of that shit. Somehow, Xander had figured out how to convert processed sugars and carbs into high-octane fuel for his body when the same diet would've sent normal people into diabetic comas.

"Where's the rest of the team?" she asked.

"I sent them back to the hotel to await further instructions."

Red Wolf Elite was based out of McClean, Virginia, which was a veritable hotbed of special forces, FBI and military personnel, so when Xander's trail hadn't left the state, she'd been surprised. Not that he would stick around now that the welcome wagon had almost managed to catch him. It would take a few days of R&R before she could be cleared for the field again, but she wasn't about to send the team home, not when they'd come so close to catching him.

As much as she hated to entertain the bent of her thoughts, questions that'd sprung up the minute his file had crossed her desk, rose with sharper clarity.

Xander had been right about one thing—there were details in this case that made no sense.

But then when did terrorists ever make sense?

Was she willing to believe that Xander Scott, a highly decorated former army ranger, was capable of killing innocent people to get to one politician?

A politician who Xander claimed he didn't know shit about until Red Wolf had been hired as security detail for the rally?

Xander had been the first to scoff at the detail, saying they weren't babysitters.

True, they were a highly skilled, elite force of former military badasses working for a private military company.

PMCs were making big money right now with the US government hiring out details in the Middle East instead of sending troops to deal with any problems left in the wake of military conflicts.

The money was good, and it gave retired soldiers a place to feel useful when civilian life wasn't in the cards for them.

So yeah, when the detail came across her desk, she'd rolled her eyes in private but she wasn't the one signing checks so she went where she was told.

Except Xander had voiced what they'd all felt.

Playing security guard to a pampered, doughy, left-wing senator trying to get the conservative vote for his re-election campaign was definitely below their pay grade, but Scarlett packed up her team and they went as ordered.

Now she wished she'd conveniently discovered a schedule conflict for that detail.

You're better than this, Rhodes...

Xander's voice urged her to dig deeper, to look beyond the flash bomb creating the sound and smoke to find who'd actually thrown the thing in the first place...and why.

Damn you, Xander.

Chapter 2

The thing about knocking boots with someone you aren't supposed to see naked—say, your boss—the sex was damn electric.

So electric that it haunted your dreams and left you with a need so aching you'd do anything to make it stop.

Yeah, so that happened on the regular.

It wasn't so bad when he'd been home, in his own bed. But now, on the run, sleeping in a rattrap motel, on sheets that smelled of bad choices and infrequent washings, an erection was damn inconvenient.

He wasn't much in the mood for lovin'.

He closed his eyes but Scarlett was there.

Naked Scarlett.

That night had been epic—whether that fell in the good or bad column, he still wasn't sure—but damn, it sure left behind a scorch mark.

Basically, they'd been celebrating a successful completion to a complicated detail and they'd all headed down to the local pub to blow off some steam. Usually, Scarlett broke off from the team when it came to slugging back shots—said it looked bad for the TL to get sloppy with the team—but that night, she'd agreed to have a beer with them.

Maybe she hadn't liked the idea of celebrating alone, or maybe it'd been something more personal, but when she'd said yes, Xander had been just as surprised as everyone else.

As it turned out, their TL could hold her liquor pretty damn well and that led to a friendly competition—which then turned into a liver-destroying expedition.

Ahh, tequila, why are you such a harsh bitch?

While everyone else tapped out, Xander and Scarlett kept at it.

Until... Well, suddenly, they were done with shots and they were in Scarlett's apartment, naked and making even worse choices.

But, *hot damn*, those choices had led to some seriously awesome sex.

Xander pushed at his stubborn erection, irritated by its refusal to calm down.

He didn't care how amped up he got—he wasn't about to jerk off in this disgusting place. A guy had to have his standards.

As the TL, Scarlett was rigid, by-the-book, hard-ass, hard-nosed, with zero-tolerance for bullshit.

As a lover, Scarlett was wild, insatiable, dangerous and intoxicating as hell.

Basically, it'd been like having sex with Scarlett's black-sheep twin with daddy issues.

There'd been biting, scratching, howling, grunts, sweat and the smell of raunchy sex.

Like he'd said—epic.

Until morning.

Then things had gotten awkward…fast.

"I think we can both agree this was a mistake," Scarlett had said stiffly over her coffee mug, her rumpled hair sexier than anything Xander had ever seen, even if her expression had returned to that of his hard-nosed TL. "You're welcome to a cup of coffee, but then you're going to need to go home."

Usually, he was the one giving that speech. Felt different being the receiver. "Either the sex was that good…or that bad. Do I want to know where I landed on that scale?"

"The sex was good."

"Just good?"

"Are you looking for a medal, because I'm fresh out of those."

"Too bad, I'm sure a medal for sex would look pretty good against the ones Uncle Sam gave me for meritorious service." He waited while Scarlett poured coffee into a mug and pushed it across the counter toward him. He grabbed the mug and took an exploratory sip. The hot bracing liquid was black enough to put hair on his chest but he choked it down, not wanting to look like a pussy by asking for cream. "So, out of curiosity…if it was so good, why the one-and-done?"

"Because I'm your superior and it's inappropriate. Sex last night was a lapse in judgment and I'd appreciate it if we could keep this private."

"Yeah, sure," he agreed, realizing she was right. Scarlett was a good TL and he didn't want to do anything that would jeopardize her position within Red Wolf. But he wasn't going to lie, he would've been down for a few more rounds. "It's a shame, though. We are pretty good together. Between the sheets, anyway."

That tiny smile she allowed told him she agreed but Scarlett wasn't one to mess with the rules. Her bones could've melted from pleasure but she'd still stick to her guns. Xander respected her attention to detail and the way she held the line but damn, his ego would've lapped up the cream if she'd swayed even the slightest in his direction.

Xander shook off the memory as a yawn cracked his jaw. She wouldn't stop chasing him. He'd have to keep watching over his shoulder while trying to figure out who the hell wanted him to take the fall for the bomb.

Scarlett would only be out of commission for a few days. He had to go underground if he was going to shake her off his tail.

A part of him wished she would've listened to him. It would've been nice to have her on his side. It also would've felt good knowing that she believed him. He supposed that was immaterial but it meant something just the same.

Xander wasn't a sap, hated mush and generally thought feelings were as tolerable as a case of hives.

His addiction to *The Bachelor* didn't mean he secretly pined for love. *Hell, no.* He watched *The Bachelor* because he knew that love was bullshit and secretly he was always hoping for them all to fail.

Yeah, he was an asshole, but at least he was honest.

He liked that about Scarlett, too.

Her blunt honesty was refreshing. Even though she'd tossed him out of her apartment, he'd respected her straightforward approach. No posturing, no dancing around feelings—just straight up truth.

We can't keep screwing each other because I could lose my job.

Couldn't get plainer than that.

And now she was chasing him like a fox after a rabbit.

Was he a little bit messed up in the head that he found that sexy?

Of course he was.

Xander sighed, mildly surprised when he found himself still rock hard. For crying out loud, he wasn't going to get any sleep like this.

Curling his hand around his shaft, he closed his eyes and gave into the memory that never failed to do the trick.

It was just so he could get some sleep, he told himself.

Not because he missed her or anything.

Scarlett was released from the hospital and she returned to headquarters where she found her core team.

Zak Ramsey, CJ Lawry and Laird Holstein were playing poker when Scarlett walked into the room. "Glad to see you've kept yourself busy," she said. "We've lost valuable time. We need to find a way to get back on track."

When no one readily agreed, she could feel what was coming, mostly because she was dealing with the same questions as everyone else.

"Look, I get it," she said, addressing the elephant

in the room. "Xander is one of our own. We are a tight group, but the facts are clear—he broke the law—"

"Allegedly," CJ cut in with a shrug. "I mean, innocent until proven guilty, right?"

"Of course, but that's for the courts to decide, not us. Here's the deal—either we bring him in or the FBI does. The only reason they're letting us handle this is because we've assured them we can get the job done on the DL. That's what we do. We get shit done. This job is no different."

"It's plenty different," Laird disagreed, tossing his cards, folding. "Look, something ain't right about this deal. You know it, we know it, and we're just supposed to toe the line against one of our own? A man who'd give his life for any one of us in this room, including you, TL?"

"That was before," Scarlett said sharply. "Things are different."

"It's bullshit," CJ said, tossing his cards, too. "It's a goddamn frame job. There's no way in hell Xander did what they're saying he did."

Scarlett felt the rising tide of animosity and she didn't blame them. They weren't pissed at her, just the situation. But what the hell was she supposed to do? Break the law for the sake of a man who may or may not be guilty?

"As much as I hate to do this, we all know that Xander's got demons. How are we supposed to know whether or not those demons got the better of him?"

"We all got demons," CJ returned, casting Scarlett a flat stare, daring her to go down that road. She knew they were all damaged goods in some way or another. "I ain't saying that Xander wouldn't consider taking out a politician if the wind conditions were right but he'd never take down civilians. That shit ain't right." CJ rose and grabbed his jacket. "If we're done here, so am I."

Scarlett let him go. CJ had a temper. She didn't need him going off over something as stupid as this. Emotions were running high in the room, the tension thick enough to slice through. She needed time to think and her head hurt. If she pressed her team right now, they'd push back and that would get them nowhere fast. "We'll reconvene at 0700 hours tomorrow," she said. "Don't let your emotions call the shots. I don't have time to deal with any of you hotheads getting into trouble."

Scarlett watched as her team filed out and as soon as they were gone, she swallowed a few Excedrin for the excruciating pain in her head.

Maybe she ought to be thankful for the drum beating her brain. Seemed pain was the only thing keeping other thoughts at bay. She talked a good game but the truth was, Xander had gotten under her skin.

Had been since that night.

She hated the clichéd "there's just something about him" but damn, if it wasn't appropriate for what she couldn't quite explain about her attraction to Xander.

The energy between them snapped and crackled like a downed power line, whipping about, wreaking havoc and mayhem with its promise of destruction.

Destruction was an apt description for what would happen if word of Xander and Scarlett's indiscretion got out.

It wasn't like her to lose her grip like that.

But Xander, *goddamn*, that man was unlike any she'd ever come across.

Oh, she'd known it, too. The minute their eyes had

met, there'd been a powerful zap at the base of her spine and that electrical current had traveled the length of her body like a bullet train straight to no-man's-land.

The tequila had just been a convenient excuse to do what she'd wanted to do from the beginning—bang the ever-lovin' shit out of that hard, chiseled, scarred and beautiful body.

Eyes closed, it was easy to remember every moment of that night.

Scarlett groaned at her own weakness, grinding at the pain behind her eyeballs. It would take a week to be back to 100 percent but she didn't have that kind of time to waste.

She grabbed her laptop, logged into the encrypted Red Wolf interface and pulled Xander's file. She knew it by heart, but she went over it again just to be sure she wasn't missing anything.

Her gaze skimmed the basic blotter information: name, highest active rank, MOS, commendations, etc.

The psych evals were her favorite—to sum up: the guy had issues, but who didn't in their line of work? Scarlett didn't hold that kind of stuff against her team members. She judged them based on their performance, their skills and their ability to walk unflinching into a shit storm.

Xander was the best of all of them when it came to looking danger straight in the eye and laughing.

From the outside looking in, one might say Xander was bat-shit crazy.

But Scarlett understood Xander on a different level than most. She recognized that need for danger that flowed through Xander's veins, that hunger to face death and win.

It wasn't hero-syndrome. It was something far darker.

It was the need to feel worthy of being alive.

Each successful mission appeased that insatiable desire for redemption, even though they all lived with the knowledge that redemption wasn't in the cards for most.

They'd all done things in the service of their country that had left scars, nightmares and broken off a piece of their souls.

But hey, that was the job.

And they accepted it.

Scarlett closed the laptop, knowing she wasn't going to find the answer there. In spite of her gut instinct telling her to screw the evidence, she had to trust the process. If Xander was innocent of the charges, the courts would exonerate him.

It wasn't her job to prove his innocence.

It was her job to bring him in—and that's exactly what she was going to do.

Chapter 3

Xander kinda wished he could call up his buddy Zak and rub it in his face that a certain level of mistrust in banking institutions had worked out in his favor.

When you were on the run, cash was king. Seeing as Xander had kept his money in weird little stashes around his apartment, when he'd made the decision to cut out and run before Scarlett could bring him in, being able to stuff his bag with cash had been a plus.

It wasn't like he could've waltzed up to an ATM to pull out his money because then his face would've shown up on the Big Brother spy network. And yeah, if people didn't believe that all their shit was on display in some techno-nerd's deep web, they were naive.

And the government was the biggest techno-nerd around.

But Xander was prepared. He had a wad of cash, a

burner phone and a laptop with the latest encryption software that zing-zanged around the globe for IP addresses so if he needed to nose around for intel, he could do so without risking a trip to the city library to use their public terminals.

Still, being on the run wasn't chill.

It sucked.

Not to be a wimp about it, but he missed his bed. Too many tours on the ground had turned him into a crotchety old man when he didn't get a good night's sleep on his expensive Tempur-Pedic.

He chuckled, hearing in his head how the team would've busted his balls for being such a baby. God, he missed those guys already.

He'd give his life for any of them. Even Scarlett.

Irony, right?

Xander wasn't going to hold it against them that they were following orders. Although, he kinda wished they'd given him more of the benefit but that was selfish, and it went against their ingrained training. Soldiers followed rules or people died.

He wanted to shake some sense into Scarlett so she'd recognize that Red Wolf was being used to do someone else's dirty work.

But until he could show her that he was right, she was going to chase him down. Simple as that.

The neon light of the dive bar beneath the seedy motel gave the room a reddish glow, appropriate for the rattrap but it served his purposes.

The place reminded him of a roach motel he'd crashed in once in a while in DC. At the time he'd found the parallel between the place where self-important men made decisions that affected everyone, except themselves, was a seething cesspit of political bullshit where people smiled right before they plunged the knife in their so-called allies' backs and the shitty motel amusing. Xander couldn't take the hypocrisy any longer, which was why he'd gotten out of the Rangers, but found, like most Red Wolf team members, there just wasn't a place for guys like him in society.

Red Wolf had been his sanctuary, his lifeline.

Once again, he'd found purpose. And, not gonna lie, the pay was pretty sweet, too. But then the private sector had always been superior on the pay scale in comparison to government work.

Unless you were so far up the chain you could sniff what Uncle Sam had for dinner the night before. Xander had known that he'd never be cut out for that kind of work, so getting out and doing merc work with a private company would've been his only option.

Until Red Wolf had approached him.

Yeah, Red Wolf wasn't a place that advertised on Craigslist for job opportunities. No, they sought out their targets carefully and then made a surgical strike, quietly and efficiently.

Xander sighed, giving into a moment of self-pity before reaching into his shirt pocket for his meds.

He grimaced as he shifted in the bed, his back clenching in an angry spasm, reminding him who was in charge. He washed down the potent painkiller with a generous swallow of his beer.

He was no different than most in his position. His body was screwed and tattooed. Literally. *But chicks dig scars, right? Yeah, but did chicks dig drug addicts?*

His body had been broken and mended back together again one too many times. The pain was just a part of who he was now. The painkillers were part of his management.

That was the story he told the docs and they'd bought into it for a long time, but then government regs changed and the lockdown on narcotics got downright militant.

He'd gone from getting his shit the legitimate way to paying an exorbitant amount to a man named Pablo who sold him Oxy by the tab.

And he needed more and more just to get through the day.

Okay, and maybe sometimes he took a little more than he needed but who didn't play fast and loose with prescription drugs these days? Hell, college kids lived off Adderall during exams and that was perfectly fine when everyone knew it was just legal amphetamines. *But hey, it's all good...until they get caught and then mommy and daddy throw a fit, demanding to know how little Johnny got his hands on something so addictive.*

Maybe the doc should've warned Xander how addictive Oxy could be; maybe it would've made him look for an alternative.

Hell, there were a lot of what-ifs but what good did they do? Didn't change the facts of what'd happened in Tulsa.

Scarlett wanted to know why he'd run?

Because he was guilty.

Not of setting that bomb— No, he'd never do something so cowardly as to kill innocent people.

But make no mistake, he was guilty as hell.

And whoever had set him up knew of his little problem.

Former bomb-squad, Army ranger and current drug addict.

Yeah, his life read like a damn play-by-play for how to draw a direct line toward the easiest chump to take the fall.

The evidence may be circumstantial but Xander would make a terrible witness.

They'd take one look at the evidence—Xander couldn't account for his whereabouts when the bomb went off because he couldn't remember shit about that day—and they'd lock him up tight.

The people wanted a head on a spike for what'd happened in Tulsa.

And someone had already prepared Xander's skull for the presentation.

His eyelids started to drag, his head to bob.

First thing tomorrow, he'd…

And he was out.

The team stared, some frowning, some bewildered.

Zak was the first to break the stunned silence. "No. You're not going alone. We're coming with you."

Scarlett hadn't slept at all last night. She knew what she needed to do, and she didn't want anyone else to end up as collateral damage if things went south.

She'd spent the night trying to talk her way out of this one decision but by morning, she'd known there was only one way this situation could go down.

"Look, here's the situation. I can move faster without a detail slowing me down. Xander is on a ticking clock. If we don't bring him in, the FBI will take over and any chance Xander has of beating this will disappear."

Zak narrowed his gaze. "You believe he's innocent."

"I don't know that," Scarlett said, shaking her head. "But there are questions that I can't answer and my gut is saying... Hell, I don't know but I can't let someone else bring Xander in. If he's guilty, I need to be the one who brings him in. He's one of our own."

"All the more reason why we should help."

"I need you back at headquarters being my eyes and ears. You're going to need to run interference if too much attention swivels Xander's way. Trust me, this is going to be a bitch for everyone involved but I can't deny that something doesn't feel right."

It took a lot to admit that to her team when she'd been the most adamant that they weren't there to uncover any hidden truths about the case.

She'd learned a long time ago that ignoring her gut was a bad idea, which meant she was about to do something either really stupid or really dangerous—either one would probably kill her career or put her in the ground but she knew it was the right decision.

However, she wasn't going to put her team at risk. "I don't need any of you in the direct line of fire. If Xander is right and someone is framing him, that means we could have a snake in our home. If Xander is lying and he's just trying to save his ass, I need to be the one to bring him down."

"That's what I'm talking about, let's shake out the traitor," CJ said with a gleeful smile because CJ was a little crazy. "Holyyy shit, I'm ready."

Zak cast CJ a warning look before returning to Scarlett. "We need a timeframe. How long?"

"FBI is going to start sniffing around after a week. If I haven't found him by then, there's nothing else we can do. But until then, you've got my six here at HQ. No communication through our regular phones. We'll use burners for any intel on this mission. Any questions?"

Laird piped in. "Yeah, what happens if he's actually guilty?"

Scarlett allowed a grim smile. "Then, I'll do what I do best… Bring the asshole down."

"Simmer down. He's not guilty," Zak said to Laird, then to Scarlett, "I don't like it. You need backup. Anything could go wrong."

"Xander isn't going to hurt me."

"Well, he did nearly crush your skull," CJ pointed out with a shrug. "I mean, that was pretty savage."

"He didn't nearly crush my skull, CJ. He knocked me out to gain time to get away. It was my stupid mistake to let him get the tactical advantage. I swear, I'll never live this down."

The team chuckled in spite of the serious situation but that was their MO. Make jokes before heading into a screwed-up situation.

"Fine. I don't like it but I see your plan," Zak said, sighing as he straightened. "We'll get burners and hold down the fort, make it look like business as usual."

"Good." Scarlett released a pent-up breath, relieved. With Zak on board, he'd get the rest of the team in line. "So, from now on, this mission is locked down, eyes only. Code name Double Down."

CJ grinned. "Yeah baby, 'cuz it's all or nothing in this game."

"Exactly," Scarlett said, nodding. "Any questions?"

"Yeah, are you sure you can handle Xander if he's guilty? I mean, I'm the last person to even want to think that it's possible, but we've all seen people we trust go bad for whatever reasons. I love the guy, I do. But Xander has always been a wild card," Laird said.

Laird was right. They'd all seen the ugly side of humanity at one point or another because combat situations were hell and greed was an insidious evil. But there was something in her gut that told her Xander wouldn't hurt her.

Even if he was guilty. "I can handle Xander," she assured Laird but she hoped to God her intuition wasn't wrong. She was putting her career and her life on the line for the dipshit and he'd better be straight about the facts or she'd happily throat punch him.

Plan in place, they broke off like a well-oiled machine. Scarlett had been the TL for this team for three years. She knew them well and trusted them more.

Even Xander.

Trust was a funny thing, though. Either it was strong as steel or fragile as glass, but you never knew how well it was going to hold up until tested.

Well, she was about to find out if she was standing on steel or falling through glass.

Time to double down, baby.

Chapter 4

Xander knew concussion protocol would require Scarlett go through bureaucratic hoops to ensure her brain was okay after he'd knocked her out, which meant he had a finite amount of time to put some distance between them.

He had to get to Tulsa, back to the scene of the crime, to see if anything jogged his memory about that day. Thank God, he had a duffel of cash; otherwise, he'd be driving nineteen hours instead of taking a four-hour flight.

Admittedly, he was taking a risk flying, even with a fake ID, mostly because Scarlett knew his aliases and once she was cleared for duty she'd find his destination pretty quick, but he didn't have the luxury of taking things safe.

He had to hope that Scarlett didn't tell those bu-

reaucrats to shove it and hop back on his tail like the
maniac she was.

God, that woman… If she weren't so damn hot, he'd
say she was crazier than him.

Not his kind of crazy—no, Scarlett was more controlled—but still, you couldn't lead a Red Wolf team
without being a little left of center. None of them were
right in the head, which was how they were able to do
the jobs they were assigned without batting an eye.

But it also made believing that he could blow up a
bunch of civilians to get to one politician totally plau-
sible.

Hell, no one was looking twice at that story.

Messed up vet with a checkered past and a previously unknown prescription drug addiction—yeah, he
knew just how perfect he was for this frame job but it
pissed him off that Scarlett was playing into the game.

She knew him.

She, of all people, should've been able to see through
that smoke screen and then he wouldn't have had to
knock her lights out.

Although, if he managed to clear his name and get
his job back, he was totally going to rub Scarlett's nose
in the fact that he'd gotten the jump on her. Actually,
that thought gave him the warm fuzzies. Lord knew
he had precious little of those to pass around.

He grabbed an Uber to the airport, made quick work
of buying a ticket on the first flight out of Virginia
and settled into his seat, prepared to sleep through the
four-hour plane ride. With any luck, his resting asshole face would deter any eager Chatty Kathys from
striking up a convo. He wanted to shut his eyes, slip

into dreamland and wake up in the dreary nothingness
that was Oklahoma.

His lids had only just closed when he heard a familiar voice.

"You're getting sloppy, Scott."

His eyes opened slowly to find Scarlett standing in
the aisle, looking pissed and deadly as hell. He wanted
to say she wouldn't shoot him in front of all these passengers but he was willing to guess her trigger finger
was damn itchy after what he'd done.

Damn it. He should've rented a car. "You going to
stand there all day? You're gumming up traffic."

Scarlett smirked as she swung into the seat beside
him, flashing her ticket at him. "Looks like we're travel
buddies."

He eyed her warily. "Yeah? And how do you figure that?"

Scarlett leaned toward him, her voice lowered to a
sexy rumble. "Well, it seems this is your lucky day,
Scott. I'm going to see for myself if your story is total
bullshit. If it turns out you're innocent, I get a valuable member of my team back. If it turns out you're a
damn liar, I get to put you away. Either way, it's a win
for me. So yeah, buckle up, baby, you've got yourself
a travel buddy."

Awww hell. He didn't want Scarlett riding shotgun
with him on this adventure but the way he saw it, he
didn't have much of a choice. Either he accepted Scarlett's dubious help or he tried to ditch her again and
spend the entire time looking over his shoulder for one
angry TL who was a crack shot.

Yeah, seemed better to play nice.

Xander chuckled and shrugged. "Guess it is my lucky day. The team on board with this?"

"I wouldn't be here if they weren't."

He didn't want to seem like a sap but it meant something that the team was willing to take a chance on him. He jerked a nod and sent his gaze out the small window, needing a minute to collect himself. He wasn't usually a crier but this hit all the feels in all the tender spots.

"You going to cry?" Scarlett asked, frowning. "Pull yourself together or I'll put a bullet in your kneecap."

He laughed, not entirely sure that she was joking. "How's that head of yours?"

"Pounding like a mother. You clocked me good and don't think for a second that I'm not going to pay you back for that one."

"Oh, I know you will."

"Good."

Maybe he was an asshole but he took a certain amount of pride for getting the jump on Scarlett. She was TL for a reason—shrewd, smart and always on target—Scarlett didn't mess around. "Admit it… I got you good," Xander couldn't resist teasing, even though he knew poking at Scarlett was like poking at an angry bear.

She leveled a short look his way and changed the subject. All business. "What's your plan?" she asked.

"My plan? Well, presently, I plan to sleep. In case you've forgotten, I've been on the run for the past week and a half and it hasn't exactly been a vacation filled with rest and relaxation."

"Boo-hoo. You shouldn't have run in the first place." She had zero sympathy. "If you would've trusted your

team, we could've handled this the right way. Now we
have to do things the wrong way and that means it's
going to be ten times harder than it needs to be."

"Yeah? So turning myself in would've been the right
way? What makes you think that I wouldn't have met
an untimely end while in custody? Something tells me
that whoever is framing me isn't real keen on having
me around for long. Dead men tell no tales and all that."

She conceded his point. "Still, you made it worse
by running. You could've at least told me."

There was something behind her curt response that
tugged at his conscience. Did Scarlet *have* feelings?
And if so, had he inadvertently stepped on them? To
be real, that was more disconcerting than the idea of
being framed. "Yeah well, hindsight and all that. Kinda
hard to think rationally when you're being framed for
a crime you didn't commit."

"Copy that," Scarlett acknowledged with a solemn
nod, then added, "But you have to believe in your team.
You know that without the strength of your team behind you, a mission is bound to fail. You panicked—
and that's exactly what a rookie would do."

He disagreed. "You call it panic—I call it calculated
self-defense. I wasn't about to give up my control and
walk into a potential ambush like a lamb to slaughter.
Sorry, it is what it is, but that ain't happening."

The idea of walking meekly into anything remotely
close to what Scarlett had been suggesting made his
balls shrivel up.

Scarlett could tell he wasn't going to budge and she
wasn't going to waste the energy, which was good because he was done talking about it anyway. Pulling his

ball cap down low, he folded his arms across his chest and closed his eyes.

"You're really going to sleep?"

"Mmmhhmmm."

"Damn it, Xander. We need a strategy."

"No, I need sleep. It's two and a half hours to Oklahoma. Cool your jets until we land. Read a magazine or something."

Scarlett exhaled in irritation, muttering under her breath, "You're making it real hard to remember why I'm putting my ass on the line for you."

He smirked from beneath his ball cap. *Because I'm the best dick you've ever had, baby.* In the interest of self-preservation...he kept that comment to himself.

Scarlett was fuming.

She narrowed her gaze at Xander—who, by the way, was already lightly snoring as if he were sacked out in the Hilton and not folded into an economy seat two sizes too small for his solid frame—and wanted to shove him out the plug door.

And if she took a moment to enjoy the image of Xander flailing from the plane at thirty-thousand feet elevation, she didn't feel an ounce of guilt, mostly because her head hurt and that was squarely Xander's fault.

She'd purposely purchased the seat next to her so that no one else would be sitting in close quarters to them; the last thing she needed was some yahoo eavesdropping on their conversation.

But as it turned out, the extra seat was unnecessary. Well, Xander was going to pay her back for that extra seat, seeing as she'd purchased it with her own money.

Almost three hours to kill and Xander was off to la-la land, sleeping like the dead. Scarlett grabbed the in-flight magazine and thumbed through it, not really looking at anything in particular, just using it as a distraction.

But her mind was difficult to distract.

Part of the reason she suffered from insomnia.

Her brain didn't recognize the "off" switch.

And one of the memories her brain liked to chew on was that night with Xander.

First, it had been an epic mistake. Let's just get that out of the way right now.

Second, it had been the best sex of her life.

Third, she had been pretty drunk so it was possible her recollection of the event couldn't be trusted.

Yet, knowing that she'd been sauced didn't seem to water down what she *did* remember.

Xander, his body crisscrossed with scars and tattoos—she was a sucker for both—with muscle cording that solid frame like he'd been carved from stone and his hands, calloused and rough like a real man's should be, touching her bare skin with urgency.

Yeah, that kind of loving was hard to forget.

It didn't help that she'd been in a bit of a drought, either—did three years qualify as a drought or a cry for help?—and she'd been about ready to hump the table leg.

The liquor had only made that need for human contact worse.

Most people didn't understand their job, how ending an assignment successfully is an adrenaline rush unlike any drug and if that adrenaline wasn't channeled, it turned restless, which with their demons, was dangerous.

Blowing off steam was a necessity, not a luxury. Usually, she went off on her own but that night she'd needed companionship.

She'd known better than to drink with the guys, especially Xander, but she'd been weak. There was no way to pretty that up and she hated that she'd succumbed to her baser needs with barely a fight.

But there'd always been something between her and Xander, that tiny spark that was hard to ignore. The way his eyes sparkled with mischief most days made her stomach tremble and when that intensity swiveled her way, she about melted in the most feminine way imaginable.

And it freaked her out.

Scarlett was more comfortable with the prospect of shooting people than opening up to another human being. Being vulnerable—*no, thanks.*

So why'd she let down her guard with Xander? Hell, she wished she knew. Maybe if she'd gone home that night, she would've spent some quality time with her vibrator and then gone to bed alone. Maybe if that'd been her course of action, she wouldn't be threatening her career for a man who may or may not be guilty.

She glanced over at him. He seemed pretty chill for a guy who was on the run but that was Xander's gift. He never crumbled under pressure—a quality she admired—but would it kill him to show just a smidge of human emotion. His life was on the line, for crying out loud.

Not even a thank-you for risking her ass for his. Typical Xander, but she couldn't complain too much.

He hadn't asked for her help or for her involvement. She bought tickets to this shit show all on her own.

Scarlett blew out a short breath, shaking her head as she replaced the magazine in the mesh compartment on the backside of the seat in front of her.

The thing about alcohol, it did more than drop panties… It dropped walls.

Walls that were there for a reason.

Scarlett shifted in her seat, uncomfortable with her memories.

How much had she told him about her past? The night was an erotic blur for the most part but she remembered lying in his arms afterward, a feeling of safety overriding her usual need for distance.

It had left her with a vague sense of disquiet, wondering if she was missing out on something potentially great. But by morning, all that had remained was the intense need to forget any of it had happened.

Shaking off the memory, Scarlett returned to her present situation.

She didn't have access to the internet or her notes on the Tulsa case. Maybe she ought to follow Xander's lead and take a short snooze.

Right after she downed some whiskey and a few aspirin for her pounding headache. She rubbed at her temples, casting a dark look at her snoozing travel companion. How was it even possible that Xander slept like the dead as if nothing were troubling him?

She'd need a horse tranquilizer to achieve that level of relaxation.

Signaling the flight attendant, she ordered her whiskey, tossed a few aspirin to the back of her throat and settled in for a quick catnap.

When she opened her eyes again, Xander was already bright-eyed and bushy-tailed, preparing for the landing. Damn, had she really slept hours in a blink? Scarlett wiped at her eyes and tried to get her bearings.

"Hey there, sleeping beauty," Xander teased. "I thought you were going to sleep through the landing."

"It must be the head injury," she groused, sending him a dark look. "How close are we to landing?"

"About ten minutes."

Scarlett checked her watch to confirm. "A few minutes off schedule but not bad."

"We hit some turbulence and wind resistance."

She nodded, secretly glad she'd slept through that. As many times as she's flown and jumped from an airplane on missions, she wasn't a fan of flying and always white-knuckled the bumpy spots.

Whenever Scarlett felt out of her element, she clung to training. "When we land, we'll rent a car and get a hotel off the main path. Somewhere without a lot of traffic."

Xander leveled his gaze her way. "Look, I appreciate you willing to come and see this thing through with me but you're off the clock."

"Meaning?"

"Meaning, you're not my TL right now. This is my detail and I call the shots. If you can't do that, you might as well take the next flight back to McClean."

"So you're saying you're in charge," Scarlett summed up, amused and a little wary. "You're the boss."

"Exactly."

Scarlett wasn't on company time, so technically Xander was right. Although on the flip side, she was

doing him a favor by not clapping him in iron bracelets, so a little respect wasn't out of order.

She supposed it was better to work side by side than
against one another, especially if they had the same
goal, so she conceded with a nod. However, she didn't
hesitate to add, "If it turns out you're guilty, I'm going
to take you down."

"I would expect nothing less, but I'm not guilty so
I'm not worried."

"I guess that's what we'll find out."

Xander shrugged. "Yep."

As the plane began its descent, Scarlett wondered
if she was putting her faith in a really good conman or
a man who had demons but was ultimately innocent.

The clock was ticking.

*Please be innocent. I don't want to have to arrest
or kill you.*

Chapter 5

He hadn't planned on a travel buddy, but he was happy to have Scarlett with him while he figured this cluster out. Scarlett was a worthy adversary. The last thing he needed was her chasing after him while he tried to save his own ass.

"So how long do I have before the FBI starts sending in the goons?" he asked as they climbed into the rental car.

"A week."

"How'd you manage to get a week?" he asked, impressed.

"I pulled some favors."

"For little ol' me? I'm touched."

Scarlett cut him a wry look. "Don't be. This is about Red Wolf, too. This situation makes all of us look bad. Especially me. People are already questioning my skills because of this situation. How'd I not know that one of my own was a psychopath? All anyone had to do was pull your psych eval and it was all over. Your file reads like a tragedy waiting to happen."

Xander remembered his last evaluation. He hadn't exactly been cooperative but then the doctor hadn't exactly been warm and friendly. "That doc was an uptight prick. I wouldn't trust anything in that report as fact."

Scarlett shrugged with mild disagreement as she ticked off a few of the bullet points. "I don't know... Unsociable, problem with authority, adrenaline junkie... Sounds about right."

"Some might say those are my good qualities."

"Only an idiot would say that."

Xander scowled. "Yeah? Well, nowhere on that report does it say I'm a danger to society. There's no law against being an asshole."

"True enough. So let's just get to brass tacks... Why would someone want to frame you for McQuarry's death?"

Xander wished he knew. Unfortunately, the list of people who might hate him was probably longer than the list of people who would throw some water on him if he were on fire. A sergeant had once told him, *You got a way of pissing people off*, and he hadn't been wrong.

"I don't know," he answered, navigating downtown Tulsa traffic. "But I aim to find out and when I find the bastard, I'm going to show him the error of his ways."

"What makes you think it was a man?" Scarlett retorted and Xander had to admit, it could be a woman screwing him over. "Got any disgruntled lovers?"

"Do I know of any woman pissed off enough to kill

innocent people just so I would take the fall? No. Contrary to what you may think... I'm not an asshole to everyone I come into contact with."

Scarlett chuckled. "Okay, well, someone wants you to take the fall and we better find out who and fast. So what's the plan?"

"First, I need to find out who hated McQuarry enough to want him dead. That'll give me a direction to head in. I figure the best way to find out the skinny on a politician is to ask the press."

"You can't talk to the press," Scarlett protested, flabbergasted at his idea. "Word has probably already spread that you're on the run and you'd make a juicy story. No, forget it. No press."

"Look, everything you just said is probably true but journalists have a way of sniffing out the dirt faster than anyone can. I don't have the luxury of asking around myself. I need a shortcut to information—which means asking a reporter who was familiar with McQuarry and his work."

Xander knew he'd made his point when Scarlett buttoned her lip, even though she still wasn't happy. "Fine," she bit out, her scowl darkening. "But we're not just going to walk into the *Tulsa World* office, bold as you please, and start asking questions. We should meet somewhere private and you should wear a disguise."

He barked a short laugh. "A disguise? Like a hat or something? Or maybe a Rastafarian wig?"

"I'm being serious, Xander. My ass is on the line, too. You shouldn't take any unnecessary risks."

Xander knew she was probably right but he didn't want to wear a disguise. "I'll swap my ball cap for a cowboy hat," he said. "Does that work for you?"

"How have you lived this long?" Scarlett grumbled in irritation. "You're just bound and determined to do things all your way, aren't you?"

"Sorry, darlin', that's just how I roll."

"Oh, shut up and don't call me *darlin'*. I might not be your TL right now but I'm not your sugar-tits, either."

His brow climbed and there was no mistaking where both their minds went.

That night.

Did she have to bring up her breasts? Like it wasn't hard enough already to forget how it felt to have those dusky rose nipples pearled in his mouth. Of course, he wasn't about to tell *her* that. She was likely to turn him from a rooster to a hen just for bringing up the subject they'd both agreed to forget ever happened.

But funny thing about that… He couldn't seem to honor his end of the deal.

That night with Scarlett was all he thought about in private moments.

Judging by the warning in her expression, Scarlett wasn't interested in a repeat of that night. More's the pity. He could use the tension relief of a good orgasm, and so could Scarlett if that pucker between her brows was any indication of her stress level.

"Since I can't stop you from being completely reckless, why don't we just book a hotel at the Ritz and see if we can get our mugs on the evening news for fun?"

"Now you're just being sarcastic, which I can appreciate, but I've already got lodgings figured out. You'll be happy to hear that I already had a motel picked out that's off the beaten path, as you suggested."

Scarlett nodded with silent relief. He wasn't a complete idiot nor was he trying to take unnecessary risks,

as she put it, but he knew in his gut that talking to a
journalist was the right way to get fast answers.

If nothing else, it would give them a direction to
go in.

He knew Scarlett was probably grinding her teeth at
taking marching orders from him but that was too bad.

This was his rodeo, not hers, and they were going
to do things his way.

There was something hot about the way Xander
took control but being the TL was too ingrained in her
blood to take a back seat without chafing.

She still thought he was being stupid talking to the
press but that could pan out with a lead so she stopped
raising a ruckus about it. He was right in that they
needed leads—fast—and sometimes big gains required
bigger risks.

True to his word, they drove to a motel in an older
part of the city, not quite as maintained and definitely
not on anybody's radar.

In short, it was a roach motel.

"This meet with your satisfaction?" Xander asked,
smiling as he shouldered his duffel bag. "I don't even
think they have Wi-Fi in the room."

Scarlett chuckled, shaking her head. "Don't gloat.
It's not attractive."

"Is that where I've been going wrong all these
years?"

"That's just the tip of the iceberg, I'm sure."

"Dating tips from my TL. I'm sure there's a cautionary tale in there somewhere."

They checked in under assumed names, Xander paid
cash and they found their room. Xander did a perimeter

check, they mapped exits and set up an escape plan in case they were spotted by anyone feeling adventurous enough to turn Xander in.

The room wasn't winning any awards anytime soon.

One big bed covered in a 1970s-era-paisley-printed comforter dominated the small room and a small round table with two rickety chairs was pushed against the grimy window. Cobwebs dressed the corners— housekeeping could use a pointer or two—and the floor was stained with various spots of dubious nature.

Oh, yeah, this was a shithole.

Perfect.

"This is the place where dreams go to die," Scarlett said, the corner of her mouth lifting. "How'd you find it?"

"I just Googled one-star hotels in Tulsa. This gem popped up. I have to be honest, it was between the Nesting Hen Motel and The Flycatcher Inn. Naturally, I went with The Flycatcher Inn because the flycatcher is the Oklahoma state bird. Seemed appropriate."

She didn't want to laugh. Nothing about their situation was remotely funny but her insides tickled at the absurdity of Xander's thought process. Scarlett sobered as her gaze focused on the one bed. "I know you weren't planning on a traveling companion so I'm not going to bust your balls about the single bed, but let's be straight with each other right now… I'm not sleeping with you."

"You're going to be very tired."

"Ha ha. You know what I mean."

Xander seemed to force a rueful chuckle, saying, "Yeah, I guess I do. Okay, no sex. I get it. Keep things professional. Probably better that way."

"Of course it is."

"Just for argument's sake, what if we could both use a little stress-reliever? I wouldn't hold it against you if you wanted to use me for my body."

Xander's earnest expression was totally fake and yet, Scarlett flushed with heat as memories of how good they were together crowded her head. Recovering with a scowl, she reiterated, "No, we need to keep things straight. You and I both agreed sex the first time was a mistake. Now is not the time to start repeating bad decisions."

Xander sighed and flopped onto the bed, the old springs protesting loudly. "That's one way to look at it," he said, folding his arms behind his head. "Or you could look at it this way. It makes sense to deny our chemistry when you're my boss but technically, right now, we're equals so what's the point in denying what we both want? You're a logical woman. Chew that over for a minute or two and you'll come to the same conclusion."

Scarlett didn't care how he packaged his offer—she wasn't budging. "Stow it, Scott. This isn't a damn vacation and you'd best remember that simple fact. You're walking a fine line and if you don't start taking this seriously, I'm out. I'm not going to jeopardize my career for a numbskull who doesn't have the brains God gave a goose to recognize that it's time to stop messing around."

That poked a nerve. Xander lost the laughter in his eyes and sat up, his gaze hard. "I don't need you to tell me that I'm in a screwed situation. I'm the one with his ass in a vise. I didn't ask you to come along. You

did that all on your own so don't lecture me on consequences. I'm well aware of what's at stake."

"Then start acting like it."

"Jesus, Rhodes, just for once could you pull that
damn stick out of your ass? I get it, things are ugly
and I'm staring down a good chance of being thrown
in prison for a crime I didn't commit—*I get it*—I sure
as hell don't need you shoving that fact down my throat
just for shits and giggles." Xander grabbed his coat and
stalked from the room, slamming the door behind him.

Scarlett let him go. It was her job to hold the line,
to be the cool head in a situation, even if that meant
sacrificing her feelings and needs.

This was no different.

Yeah, sure, in a perfect world where there weren't
any consequences for sex with a subordinate she'd be
riding that bad boy all day, but they didn't live in a
perfect world and the consequences were too severe
to mess with for a few moments of pleasure.

Moments. Ha! Of course, she meant figuratively.
Xander was no one-pump chump or minutes-only man.

A shiver tickled her skin. She rubbed at the goose-
bumps rioting along her forearm. *Enough of that.* Grabbing her burner phone, she texted Xander.

Bring food when you come back.

No sense in starving. They needed fuel to power
their brains and bodies.

Maybe if she satisfied her physical hunger with a
loaded cheeseburger, she'd mute the dull roar of desire
that was a serious distraction for them both.

Maybe.

Chapter 6

"The arrest warrant was issued two weeks ago. Why aren't we going after this guy?"

FBI Special Agent Conrad Griggs knew this had been coming but he'd hoped for a little more time. He owed Scarlett but he didn't know how much longer he could keep the heat off Scarlett's team while they handled things on their end.

"Red Wolf asked if they could handle the situation internally. Out of professional courtesy, we agreed to let them have time to bring in Xander Scott on their own."

Senior Director Paul Platt wasn't known for his leniency or his compassion so his irritation wasn't unexpected, but Conrad was surprised that Platt was even aware of this case.

"Terrorists don't get professional courtesy. The man

is guilty of killing a US senator and a handful of civilians. He gets no quarter from this agency or any other agency employed by the US government. Am I clear?"

Conrad shifted in his seat, uncomfortable. "As far as I know, Xander isn't guilty until a court of law determines him to be."

"Don't play word games with me, Agent. This situation looks bad for everyone. There's a lot of heat coming down and people higher up than me want this man's head on a plate. McQuarry was a respected and well-loved senator. Someone's feet are going to be held to the fire and right now, those feet belong to Scott."

Reading between the lines, Conrad knew that meant it didn't matter if Xander was innocent. He fit the bill for the crime and people wanted this to go away, neat and tidy.

"And if he's being framed?"

"Who the hell would want to frame some nobody for a crime like this?" Platt asked, his tone incredulous. "Have you read Scott's file? He's a ticking time bomb. Honestly, I'm surprised it took him this long to snap."

Conrad didn't know Xander well but he trusted Scarlett and Scarlett never would've allowed a loose cannon on her team.

"Maybe that's the point," Conrad suggested with a shrug. "He looks good for the crime…maybe too good. Things usually don't fall together that easily."

"Easy? Have you lost your ever-loving mind? This case has been a goddamn nightmare from day one. An embarrassment to the United States government and cleaning up the mess falls to us, so stop dicking around and bring that man in." Platt adjusted his girth, straining the limits of the leather belt encircling his hips and said, "No more talk about Scott being framed. We don't need that kind of contamination on the investigation. Bring him in so we can prosecute. End of story. You hear me?"

Conrad nodded, but everything about how Platt was acting felt off. But Platt was his boss so he couldn't risk losing his job over Scott. Maybe Scarlett was wrong and her man was guilty.

Hell, he knew it sucked to find out that someone you trusted was a bad apple—been there, done that—but sometimes it happened and you just had to roll with it.

Still, Conrad couldn't help but mention, "You know Xander Scott is a highly decorated veteran, and he served multiple tours in Iraq and Afghanistan. Did you read that in his file?"

Platt flushed and his gaze turned shrewd. "Yeah, it's a shame. Sometimes even the best of us screw up or snap."

The words rang hollow. Conrad knew better than to keep poking at this particular spot but he was feeling reckless. He nodded, seeming to accept Platt's answer, adding, "True enough. Just a pity, though, you know? He served our country with honor. Seems wrong to chase him down like a rabid dog."

"Guilty men don't run."

"I guess you're right." *Or men who know they're being framed don't stick around to negotiate.* "I'll make the necessary calls to put a team together."

"Good. That's what I want to hear."

"However, I should remind you that Xander isn't going to be easy to find. He's good at disappearing, going off the grid. He doesn't use a bank so he's traveling with cash."

"No one truly goes off grid in this day and age. He'll leave behind bread crumbs and you'll find them."

Conrad would have to call Scarlett and let her know he was out of options.

"And keep me in the loop."

That last part surprised Conrad. Platt rarely took this much interest in cases like this. Arrest warrants didn't usually trip his meter. "Sir?" Conrad questioned with a frown. "How deep would you like to be in this case?"

"All the way," Platt answered, moving to the door. "We all answer to someone, Griggs. That includes me."

Platt let himself out of Conrad's office, leaving behind a wealth of questions. Something felt off.

He picked up the phone and called Scarlett's office but got voice mail. He tried her cell with similar results.

Conrad left a quick but vague message for Scarlett to call him back and then he grabbed his coat. He needed to satisfy the questions in his own head before he sent a team off to bring in Xander.

Listening to his gut had saved his life more times than he could count.

Right now, his gut was saying dig deeper.

So that's what he was going to do.

Scarlett realized her phone was dead and plugged her charger in. She never let her phone get so low that it completely died but then Xander had thrown off her game.

She wasn't in a habit of breaking rules but here she was, sharing a roach motel with a federal fugitive. Funny how things changed in a blink of an eye.

Grabbing the burner phone from her bag, she called Zak to check in.

Zak answered on the second ring. "It's about time. I was starting to freak out. Did you find Xander?"

"Yeah, he caught a plane to Tulsa. I snagged the same flight. Tell CJ he owes you a beer."

CJ had been sure that Xander wouldn't fly, that he'd grab a rental or better yet, an old sedan from a used car lot. But Zak had agreed with Scarlett that Xander would take the most direct route, given the time crunch. The two had argued and then bet against one another.

Zak chuckled. "Damn straight he does. So are you with Xander now?"

"Yeah, I convinced him that it was better to work together, not against one another. He agreed. We're holed up in a shitty motel in Tulsa. It's a good defensible space but the accommodations are worse than that hotel in Basra."

"That bad?" Zak asked, shuddering. "I must be getting old because that no longer sounds like an adventure to me."

"Same." Scarlett was going to miss her bed but she just had to keep reminding herself she'd slept in worse. "Xander wants to meet up with a local journalist to find dirt on McQuarry. He thinks that might be the best way to find out who's framing him."

"Not bad. Journalists always have the dirt. Even if they can't print it, they know it."

"It's risky, though."

"No argument there but this gig isn't going to be a cakewalk no matter how you slice it. Risk is part of the detail."

"You're right. So here's what I need you to do. I

need you to make contact with Special Agent Conrad Griggs over in the Washington, DC, FBI office. He's the one keeping the heat off Red Wolf while we figure this out. I need to know if there's anything he can send to me about this case that might not be common knowledge. Seeing as this is the FBI's case, they should have more intel than we do."

"And you think he's just going to hand it over, nice and sweet?"

"Conrad is a good guy. He and I go way back. He'll help if he can."

"All right, if you trust him…" Scarlett heard the question in Zak's voice but he moved on. "How's Xander holding up?"

"He's fine." *Damn man acts like he's on vacay, not fighting for his life.* "Nothing gets under Xander's skin for too long. Remember, don't use my regular cell for anything related to Xander. Also, go ahead and give Conrad my burner number. I have my personal laptop so he can send any files he's got to my Dropbox."

"Be careful, TL. Assuming Xander is innocent— which I'm sure he is—the fact that someone is willing to go to such lengths to frame him means they won't stop at killing to get what they want. Don't step into the crossfire."

"Head on a swivel," Scarlett assured Zak. "In the meantime, keep me in the loop but watch your surroundings. You never know who could be watching and listening."

"Paranoia is my favorite pastime," Zak drawled, coaxing a smile from Scarlett. "Don't let Xander do anything stupid."

At that, Scarlett laughed. "That's like asking the wind to stop blowing during a hurricane."

"True, but if anyone can stop him, it's you."

Scarlett's smile remained even as she clicked off. Xander showed up five minutes later, no longer scowling, holding two bags of fast food.

"Sorry for being a dick," he said, tossing a bag her way. "You're right. We need to keep things professional."

"Glad you see things my way." She opened the bag. A giant bacon cheeseburger. Her favorite. "Loaded?" she asked with a hopeful grin, to which Xander nodded. Scarlett lifted the burger out, inhaling the aroma of grease and fries with delight. She tried not to put too much store in the fact that he remembered how she liked her burger, but she wouldn't deny the warm spot beneath her breastbone. Focusing her attention on her food, she said, "You're forgiven," and tucked into the heart-attack special.

Xander chuckled, unwrapping his own burger to say, "It's probably a good thing we're not smashing. There are enough onions on that burger to kill a moose. Your breath will be epic."

"You're one to talk about bad breath. You go days without brushing your teeth. You've probably got fungus in your mouth from when you were a kid."

"Brushing isn't so much important as flossing and I always floss," Xander said, tossing back a French fry. "A dentist told me that."

"Your dentist was a quack."

"Possible. He only took cash and had a lot of stories about the Mexican mafia. I'm not sure he has a license to practice any longer, but he always gave me a good discount."

"You're lucky you still have teeth in your head," Scarlett returned around a big bite. "If we get out of this situation alive, do yourself a favor and see a real dentist before your teeth fall out and you're left with the need for dentures. Trust me, chicks don't dig toothless guys."

Xander waggled his eyebrows. "I don't know... Could be fun. Imagine what I could do..."

Scarlett threw a fry at him with a laugh. "You're disgusting," she said, leaning back in the chair, enjoying the simple pleasure of delicious, greasy food and the company of a fellow soldier.

Tomorrow would happen soon enough and anything could change within a few hours.

So yeah, she'd enjoy a burger and leave everything else at the door.

A beat of companionable silence followed as they finished their dinner. Scarlett changed into something more comfortable to sleep in—cotton shorts and a soft long-sleeved top—and climbed into the bed while Xander spent some time surfing the net, looking for information.

Xander would probably still be boyishly handsome when he was an old geezer—chasing the ladies in his wheelchair and winking as he gummed his applesauce in the old folks' home—because that's just who Xander was and always would be.

If Scarlett were to draw her complete opposite, Xander's face would be the one she drew.

And if she were being honest...she liked that about him.

Xander yawned and finally closed his laptop to disappear into the bathroom. When he reappeared, he was only in his boxer briefs.

She wasn't going to make a big deal out of it—she'd seen him in less—but her body flushed and she turned on her side away from him as he climbed into the bed.

Closing her eyes, she willed sleep to come but complete silence had always been her enemy. Too much quiet made for easy listening to the noise in her head.

Plus, she wasn't accustomed to sharing a bed with anyone.

Irritated, she flopped onto her back, trying to find a comfortable position.

"Are you going to do that all night?" Xander asked.

"Sorry. I'm not used to having company in my bed," she groused. "And you take up more than your share."

"I promise I don't have cooties."

"I know that."

He chuckled. "Then relax."

"It's not that…" She risked a glance toward him. "It's because…there's history between us."

"One time does not history make," Xander said. "Or so I'm told."

She wasn't going to argue the point. Exhaling, she deliberately closed her eyes and rolled to her side, plumping up her pillow and settling once again.

A long beat of silence followed until Xander said, "Do you really regret that much what happened between us?"

That was a loaded question—one she didn't want to answer. She regretted being messed up in the head, which made it impossible to trust, which in turn made her a nightmare to be in a relationship with. Not that she wanted anything real with Xander.

Or anyone.

Her silence seemed an answer in itself. "I guess so," Xander replied with a sigh. "That's an ego-buster."

Scarlett turned to glare at him. "Did you ever think maybe it has nothing to do with you?" she said, unable to just let him think whatever he liked. For some reason, it mattered with Xander. "Look, aside from the fact that I'm your boss...I'm just not the type to form unnecessary attachments. Trust me, it's better that way. For everyone involved."

Every time she'd ignored her instincts and allowed something to happen, it ended badly.

"I'm not cut out for relationships."

"Me, either."

His simple agreement coaxed a reluctant chuckle out of her. "Yeah? Two peas in a pod, I guess."

"Or two broken people with too many sharp edges to be allowed around normal people."

"Ain't that the truth," she agreed, the tension lifting a little. She turned to face him, tucking her arm under her head. "Maybe that's why we're so good at what we do... We can compartmentalize like Olympic athletes without blinking an eye."

"Mental boxes for everything," Xander returned with a half-grin. They were joking but only sort of. That was the sad reality that they both recognized. "I know why I'm broken, but what's your story, Rhodes?"

This was around the time she usually shut down. But that feeling of safety had returned and she found herself sharing, even when she didn't want to. "Jacked-up childhood. When my dad wasn't beating me...he was doing other things." She gave a self-deprecating chuckle and added, "He wasn't exactly in the running for Father of the Year."

"He ever get caught?"

Scarlett shook her head. "Small town bullshit. No one wanted to get involved. There was no one to rescue me so I rescued myself." A lump rose in her throat. She hated talking about her past. "Anyway, he's dead but he was dead to me long before that. His going into the ground was just a formality."

Xander nodded. She was relieved to see nothing but respect in his eyes at her admission. There was no pity, no "you poor thing" judgment in his expression, just plain respect for having the balls to do what no one else had been able to do for her.

And because of that, she admitted quietly, "I don't regret what happened between us, Xander. There are just reasons—solid ones—to make sure it doesn't happen again."

Xander accepted her answer with another nod because he got it, even if he didn't agree. She knew he was down for more but he would respect her decision because no matter what that psych eval implied—Xander was a damn good man.

"Goodnight, Scott," she said, closing her eyes.

"'Night, Rhodes."

At just like that, suddenly Mr. Sandman decided to stop being a prick—and she slept.

Scarlett was asleep beside him but sleep was a long ways from finding Xander. If Scarlett's father weren't already dead, he'd have liked to have been the one to permanently knock his lights out.

How could a father do that to his own daughter?

He'd seen a lot of messed up shit in his time but he'd never get used to the knowledge that some people were just bad eggs.

His own father was a royal asshole but he'd never been buggered by him.

Beat him within an inch of his life, but the man hadn't touched him like Scarlett's father had touched her.

He wanted to pull Scarlett to him and hold her close, but he knew that would go over as well as giving a cat a bath so he kept his hands to himself.

But aside from Scarlett's revelation, he had other things keeping him awake. More immediate issues than Scarlett's messed-up childhood.

With Scarlett with him, his secret wasn't likely to remain a secret for long. He didn't want her to know how addicted he'd become to his pain meds. It was his private shame, his weakness, and he loathed the idea of Scarlett thinking less of him.

But there was another reason he needed to keep his pill-popping from her—it created motive.

He couldn't account for the time when the bomb went off. He'd passed out and woken up after the fact, but he couldn't exactly tell his TL that he'd been high as a kite during an operation so he lied.

He'd told Scarlett that he'd been on the opposite side of the plaza when the bomb had gone off.

Truthfully, he'd been damn close. It was a miracle he hadn't been caught in the blast. It was pure luck that in the chaos no one seemed to notice the minor cuts and abrasions on his face.

But the lie weighed heavily on his conscience. He

hated lying to Scarlett, but it'd been a split-second decision that he'd had to make and he couldn't take it back.

Now his statement was on official documents. To admit that he'd lied about his whereabouts would only seal his guilt.

And Scarlett would never trust him again.

He exhaled and rolled to his side, quietly watching her as she slept. It was surreal to be in the same bed once more. He could honestly say that he figured the only way that was ever going to happen again would be in his dreams.

Xander knew he was being a friggin' sap but he wished he could pull her into his arms and hold on for dear life. It'd been a long time since he'd wanted anyone in that role and he hadn't expected it to be Scarlett but, damn, she was his equal in every way.

But he was going to respect Scarlett's wishes and keep it professional. Of course, she was right. It made sense to keep things straight because neither knew how this was going to shake out in the end, but lying beside her and keeping his distance...was a special kind of hell.

Rolling away, turning on his side, he tried to focus on what he knew about the McQuarry bombing.

Thanks to his little blackout—he didn't know much.

The operation had been simple: provide security for Senator Ken McQuarry as he did his little rally speech in downtown Tulsa. McQuarry had been a typical white male politician sort—trying to hide his soft and doughy gut in expensive suits, his mouth full of rhetoric—and he hadn't been running any particularly controversial platforms so the job should've been a cakewalk.

They hadn't expected someone to rig the amphitheater and blow up the senator.

Hindsight.

The bigger question was how did someone put Xander's fingerprints on the plastic explosive when he sure as hell didn't rig that bomb?

Scarlett groaned softly in her sleep. He didn't dare try to comfort her. Force of habit, they were all light sleepers. He could only imagine the demons she entertained. Maybe his and hers could have a playdate.

A part of him wanted to know what made her twitch at night, what secrets were locked away in that complex brain, but he would never pry. That was the thing between fellow soldiers, they understood that sometimes talking about things didn't make it better—it just created more shit to bubble to the surface and no one had time for that.

Still, he wanted to smooth the faint lines from her forehead and chase away her nightmares.

Too bad she'd never let him.

Tomorrow he had a meeting with the political journalist from the *Tulsa World* daily. They were supposed to meet at an abandoned schoolhouse. He figured the best way to mitigate the risk was to meet someplace with the least amount of prying eyeballs around.

In the quiet dark, it was hard to run from the fear that he might not find the evidence he needed to exonerate himself. The fear that he might actually end up behind bars for a crime he hadn't committed didn't help his insomnia.

He'd made a lot of mistakes in his life—done things he was ashamed of—but never had he ever considered harming a civilian.

More than just Ken McQuarry died that day.

He had their names etched on his brain.

Rosie Grogan.

Butch Halford.

Ronnie Pitt.

Layla Osmundsen.

He wasn't the one who'd planted the bomb but he was complicit in their deaths because he hadn't been doing his job. Remembering their names was his penance. Maybe if he'd been sober, he would've seen the bombs, could've gotten everyone to safety… Hell, he might've been able to defuse the bombs before they'd gone off.

Again with the hindsight.

He needed help kicking his habit, but there wasn't time for that now. To think that a doc had prescribed the drugs for his back pain all legal-like and now he was a friggin' junkie was a dark irony that didn't escape him.

Most days he functioned fine. But there were other days when he was falling down stupid, out of his head, lost in the black hole of addiction.

Get your head on straight. There was no time for his issues. Not right now.

He forced his eyes closed. Morning would come soon enough and if he didn't catch some shut-eye, he'd need toothpicks to hold up his lids.

His last thought as he drifted to sleep was the hope that for the first time in his life, luck was on his side.

Chapter 7

"A three-hour drive?" Scarlett exclaimed when Xander revealed their travel plans for the day. "Why?"

"Because the reporter wasn't willing to risk being seen with me and the location is abandoned so it's unlikely anyone will see us coming or going."

"Sounds like a trap," she grumbled, tucking her gun into her hip holster and pulling her hair up into a tight ponytail. "And you trust this reporter?"

"I don't trust anyone," Xander answered, holstering his own weapon. "But I need answers and this woman seems to be willing to give them to me, so I'm going where she tells me to."

"But why is this reporter willing to give you information?"

"Because I'm paying her a lot of money."

Scarlett was impressed. "Seriously? I thought that only happened in the movies."

"Turns out greed is a very real motivator and reporters don't make jack shit these days so…it's almost a public service. I'm helping to keep journalism alive."

"That's a stretch," she quipped with a dry smile. "But it works out in your favor that you managed to find a reporter whose integrity was for sale."

"You'd be surprised how easy those are to find." Xander winked.

Xander's reason made a certain level of sense, but a three-hour drive to some abandoned place seemed like a bad idea. They were between a rock and a hard place given it would've been personally safer to meet in a public place, but the very thing that made it safe also made it risky.

Scarlett smothered the urge to growl with frustration. She hated feeling vulnerable and went out of her way to ensure that she had the best handle on any given situation, but that wasn't going to happen with this circumstance. *Better get used to it.*

"Fine. I need coffee," Scarlett grumbled, sliding into her jacket, thumbing her nose at the sludge offered in the room. "Whatever *that* is…is not coffee and I'm going to need the real deal if we're going on a road trip to BFE."

Xander crooked a grin that sent tiny sparks straight to her empty belly. "Think of it this way. You get to see parts of Oklahoma you've never seen before."

"Pardon me while I rein in my excitement."

He laughed. The sound coaxed a grudging smile on her part. That was the thing about Xander; he had this way about him that made people forget why they were pissed at him.

It was that skill that had probably kept him alive all this time.

They climbed into the car, stopped by a roadside stop-and-rob and then hit the road. Three hours in a car with Xander sounded like psychological torture but she'd endured worse.

But when he cranked the country music, she had to reevaluate that assumption.

After twenty minutes of country crooning, she'd had enough and purposefully clicked off the radio. "Look, we should use this time to go over the case," she said, ready to do something productive.

"I have a better idea, let's just enjoy the ride," Xander said.

Scarlett exhaled with mild annoyance. "This isn't a Sunday outing. I don't know why I hear the ticking clock more loudly than you, but it's all I can hear. We need to go over the case until we know it by heart."

"What makes you think I don't already?" he said quietly.

Scarlett fell silent, digesting his retort. "I'm sorry. I know you've probably gone over the facts in this case until you're cross-eyed but I can't just sit in the car, listening to tunes like we're out for a picnic more than your ass is on the line."

"I didn't ask you to come with me," he reminded Scarlett. He wasn't being a dick about it, just stating facts. "Maybe I need a break to just coast for a minute."

She opened her mouth to argue but thought better of it. She couldn't imagine what he'd been going through since the moment he found out someone was gunning for him.

Being former military, it wasn't hard to slip into

that mode where no one outside of your unit was beyond suspicion, but that level of paranoia took a toll on the psyche.

Keeping your head on a swivel at all times did something to you as a human being, which was why most of Red Wolf was comprised of people who found civilian life difficult.

Drawing a deep breath, Scarlett rubbed her palms down her jeans and said, "Okay, we'll do this your way, for now, on one condition—" she cut Xander a sharp look "—no more country music. It's classic rock or silence."

He chuckled. "You drive a hard bargain."

"Take it or leave it."

"I'll take it."

Xander punched in a rock station and grinned as Scarlett relaxed and nodded in approval as classic rock filled the car.

An hour went by and Scarlett turned the music down.

Xander sent a playful glance her way. "Ready to give country another shot?"

"Hell, no."

"Okay, well, silence will drive me batty."

Scarlett suddenly realized it bothered her that she knew what Xander sounded like when he climaxed but she didn't know much more about him aside from what she'd read in his personnel file.

And he knew more about her than she ever shared with anyone and it wasn't fair.

It wasn't like she went out of her way to know her team on a personal level, which is why sleeping with one of her team members had been a bad idea, but what was done was done.

And she was a little old-fashioned about some things.

"I need to know more about you, Xander."

"More? Like what? You've read my file. Not much more to tell."

"Bullshit. You and I both know that's not an accurate portrait of a person. If I were to go off your psych eval, I would say you're a narcissistic asshole but I know that's not true."

"I'm telling you, that doc had it in for me," Xander said. "Crack one off-color joke and it's 'no soup for you.'"

Scarlett smothered a laugh at his *Seinfeld* joke. "Okay, so tell me about yourself."

"Would you like to know what's on my dating profile?" he teased.

Scarlett blushed and shook her head. "God, no," she answered quickly, but then a part of her wanted to ask how in the hell he managed to date in their particular line of work. Each time she attempted a dating profile, she ended up sounding like the most generic person in the world because she couldn't afford to put real details out there on the web. "I mean, tell me how you ended up going the military route."

Xander frowned, clearly not his favorite bedtime story. She half expected him to decline and change the subject or worse, return the radio to country but he surprised her with an answer.

"Kinda like your story. Dad was an abusive dick. Didn't have the means to go to college, not that I would've been able to handle more school, but the army was my ticket out of hell. I took it without looking back."

"Is your dad still alive?"

"No. He died when I was overseas. Felt weird to get the message. I mean, I'd prayed for the man's death more times than I could count when I was growing up but when it actually happened, I was numb. Kinda disappointing, really. That was the biggest reveal. I thought I'd feel more. Relief, maybe? Or joy, even? But nope, I felt nothing. My LT gave me the message and ten minutes later I was back on the job."

Scarlett understood the numbness Xander had felt. She'd felt the same when her own father had died.

She'd long come to the conclusion that people who were damaged had two choices: wither and die, or deal with it.

Her way of dealing with the abuse at her father's hands was to walk away and never mention the man's name ever again.

"Funny how the mind works," she murmured. "I didn't feel anything either when my old man kicked it."

Xander nodded, understanding. "I think I felt nothing because he'd become nothing to me. He was no longer my father. The military became my family. My brothers and sisters in arms... They were the ones who had my back. Unlike that asshole who'd done nothing but beat me black-and-blue until the day I was too big and he realized I'd tear him up if he laid another hand on me."

Scarlett would like to say that their stories were the exception but there were plenty of military people with similar backstories. If military life wasn't ingrained in a person from childhood, signing a blank check to the government took some balls or some other driving force, and sometimes that driving force was desperation.

She would've done anything to escape her father. It just so happened, a recruiter caught her ear senior year at career day and she'd been in a frame of mind to listen.

It'd been the best damn decision she could've made. Otherwise, she might've ended up a statistic.

"I hope he's roasting in hell," Scarlett said with a shrug. "My only regret was not being there to watch the light fade from his eyes." Xander nodded without judgment. It felt good to admit her feelings, even if they were savage. "If there's any justice, he's in hell getting his pecker lopped off over and over and over in an endless loop of pain and humiliation."

She waited for the internal cringe at sharing more of her true feelings but nothing happened. If anything, she felt relieved.

Scarlett never talked about the sexual abuse by her father, but its lingering effects had ruined plenty of potential relationships. At the end of the day, it'd seemed better to remain single.

Less questions, less drama.

But it sure got lonely and when loneliness struck, it was difficult to rein in those feelings of need.

Especially when you end up slugging back tequila shots with a man you've been smothering an attraction for since the day you first crossed paths.

"I want you to know that I'm sorry for the way I acted the morning after that night," she said, venturing with hesitation but still needing to say something. "I was really rude to you and I'm sorry."

"You've got no reason to apologize. We're both adults. My feelings weren't hurt."

She glanced at Xander. "Yeah?"

"Yeah, I mean, I get it. You're my boss. We can't be hooking up like regular people. You needed an itch scratched and I was there."

Well, it wasn't quite that cut-and-dried. It wasn't as if she would've gone home with CJ or Zak or even Laird, but it was probably in everyone's best interests if she just agreed. "I'm relieved you understand."

He shrugged. "Sure. Now, I won't pretend to understand why we can't do it again—you're not my boss right now—but I'm respecting your position and I'm not going to push it."

She wasn't one to be wishy-washy but a part of her was wavering in her resolve. Xander made a certain amount of sense. Right now, they were in suspended animation. She wasn't his boss and he wasn't her team member.

Technically, she wasn't supposed to be with him so what was to stop them from taking advantage of the situation to their benefit? It was only temporary and Lord knew they could both use a little stress relief, as Xander had pointed out, but there was a tiny part of her that worried her feelings went a little deeper than physical need. She craved Xander's touch on a level that went beyond simple lust. Hell, the idea of just lying together, arm in arm, was like warm sunshine on her face.

Which was exactly why they needed to avoid each other in that capacity.

Except… She shook her head, confused at the direction of her own thoughts. It wasn't like her to go backwards on a decision but the memory of Xander was too strong to fight.

Maybe if she stopped fighting, she could spend that energy elsewhere…like doubling down on finding who the hell had framed Xander in the first place.

Yeah, that made sense. The band that'd felt wrapped around her chest snapped and she drew a deep breath. As much as she hated to admit it, Xander was right. Seemed kind of hypocritical to say she wouldn't sleep with Xander again because she was his boss when she was willing to break multiple laws to prove he was innocent.

So…sleeping with Xander was back on the table.

But she wasn't ready to say it out loud. Not yet. The last thing she wanted to see right now was Xander's gleeful smirk because Lord only knew he'd probably anticipated her about-face.

Instead, she changed the subject. "What do you know about this reporter?"

In all the time he'd been working with Scarlett, there were still things about her that were a mystery. The reveal about her childhood made him sad, but he wasn't surprised. Life had a tendency to harden people and Scarlett was made of granite.

Still, it bothered him to know that as a child she'd suffered at the hands of someone who was supposed to love her, just like he had. They were like two lost kindred souls, battered and bruised yet determined not to give in. Maybe that was the thing about her that he admired the most.

If he were being honest, he'd had a thing for his TL since day one. But he'd known messing around with a superior was against protocol, so he'd pushed those feelings way down and his method had been working until that night.

His back twinged, reminding him that he needed to take another dose but he didn't dare take one in front of Scarlett. If she saw him popping a pill she would ask questions he wasn't ready to answer. Knuckling down, he ignored the dull roar of pain and focused on answering her question.

"I don't know anything about this reporter. All I know is that she's been writing for the *Tulsa World* in the political section for at least three years and she seems smart. She also agreed to take the money in exchange for information, so there is that."

Scarlett frowned. "Does she know who you are? Does she know you're a federal fugitive?"

"I didn't actually mention that part."

"If she's as smart as you think she is, she will have already figured that out."

"Please. This ain't my first rodeo. I gave her a false name. I told her I was looking into the death of Mc-Quarry, hinting that I knew about a bigger conspiracy and of course, she ate it up. I don't know of any reporter who doesn't salivate at the mere hint of a conspiracy theory."

"And she bought that?"

"Of course, I also told her I was doing research for a tell-all book and she immediately started talking about the book she wanted to write, too. I swear, are all reporters frustrated novelists?"

"I don't hang with journalists so I couldn't say one way or another. I think it's safe to say you're taking a risk. If she's as broke as you say she is, if she finds out about the bounty on your head, she might double-cross you, screwing us both."

"There's a bounty?" Xander seemed impressed. "Yeah? How much? Maybe I'll turn myself in."

Scarlett laughed. "Ten-thousand dollars."

Xander balked. "Are you kidding me? I'm worth way more than that."

Amused, Scarlett agreed but added, "By my way of thinking, they can't put a huge bounty on your head without raising questions. So if you're right and you are being framed, whoever's pulling the strings is going to do whatever they have to to keep this quiet and that includes flying under the radar."

Xander saw Scarlett's logic but knowing he'd been stuck with a bargain basement sticker wasn't a nice feeling. "I'm still insulted."

Scarlett rolled her eyes at his ego. "Get over yourself. It's not about the money. Do you have a backup plan in case this reporter double-crosses you? What if we get there and the place is surrounded with cops and FBI?"

"Ye of little faith. Do you really think I would walk into an ambush? *Please.* I'm the one who suggested the location."

"You said she picked the place," Scarlett said with a scowl.

"She did, but I may have made a suggestion as to why it was a good idea that may have tipped the scales."

"And the reason you picked this place?"

"It's a good defensible space, plus there is excellent line of sight from the south side, which is where we're meeting."

Was that admiration in her eyes? God, he hoped he

wasn't wrong about this meeting. A part of him worried that the reporter was sharper than he figured. His saving grace was that his mug likely hadn't been released just yet to the general public so only law enforcement and government agencies would have his information.

Hopefully, luck was on his side—that would be a welcome change.

"So what conspiracy did you dangle in front of this reporter?" Scarlett asked, curious.

"I was really just being vague and took a chance on what most politicians are hiding—sexual misconduct. I must've said the right thing because judging by the change in her tone, I'm pretty sure her eyes lit up like a Christmas day parade at the juicy prospect. To be honest, I'm kinda curious as to what information she's bringing."

"Sexual misconduct," Scarlett chuckled, equally amused. "At this point, I think people expect politicians to have skeletons and half the fun is wondering when those bones are going to rattle and give them away."

"True enough." He really didn't care about McQuarry's sexual misdeeds; he just wanted information that might give him a direction. Someone had wanted McQuarry dead and they'd been willing to go to great lengths to see it happen. Digging into McQuarry's secrets was the best way Xander could think of to find who might benefit the most from McQuarry's death.

Finally, the abandoned school came into view and it was creepy as shit.

He caught Scarlett's look and nodded, silently agreeing that this was the kind of place where souls went to die. If he were the sort who believed in ghosts, Dearborn Reformatory could serve as the poster child for a place to avoid if you didn't want to die a grisly death.

"This place gives me the creeps," Scarlett announced after a good solid perusal. "What was this?"

"Believe it or not, a school for Native American kids. Specifically, Cheyenne and Arapaho because back in the 1900s it was considered bad form for Indian kids to speak their native language. The kids were sent here for assimilation into society, even going so far as punishing them for trying to hold on to any part of their culture."

"That's barbaric," Scarlett murmured, taking in the desolation of the abandoned place. "No wonder this place gives off a bad vibe."

"Yeah, not exactly the nicest place to send kids. They must've been terrified," Xander agreed but a car was coming toward them, cutting short their history lesson.

Instantly on alert, Scarlett faded into the background to provide cover should things go south as well as protect her identity and involvement.

A short woman with a spiky blond haircut exited the dirt-covered sedan and began to make her way toward the entrance to the school, tentatively calling out, "Mr. Jones? Are you here?"

Xander could practically feel Scarlett's derision at his obviously fake name but he'd been pressed for time and couldn't get creative.

She stepped over the threshold of the building and finally saw Xander. "Oh! There you are. I was starting to think you might've changed your mind."

"Not me. I'm here for the juicy details."

The woman tittered, glancing around to ask tentatively, "Did you bring the money?"

Xander fished out the cash-stuffed envelope and handed it to her. She paused, tempted to count the money but then must've decided Xander looked trustworthy enough and stuffed the money into her purse. "I've never done anything like this, just so you know. I'm a reporter with integrity. I've never in my life given out information like this. I believe in journalistic integrity. It's very important to me."

The fact that she was repeating herself was proof enough that she wasn't experienced but that worked in Xander's favor. If she wasn't in a habit of selling information, then it was likely her intel, to the best of her knowledge, would be legit.

Xander nodded as if he cared and then said, "Tell me about McQuarry's dark secrets."

"It feels wrong to speak ill of the dead, especially in this place. Do you believe in ghosts, Mr. Jones?"

"Uh, no," Xander answered, trying to steer the conversation back to McQuarry. "What was in his closet?"

The woman glanced around as if afraid the senator's ghost was going to pop out from behind the wreck and ruin of the former school and steal her soul, but she answered in a hushed tone, "I have it on pretty good authority that Senator McQuarry was having an affair with a young intern."

On the surface, the intel was *meh*. What politician didn't dip their wick in the company inkwell? But seeing as McQuarry was running on a family values platform, that could prove to be useful information. "Got a name?"

"Again, this isn't substantiated but the rumor was

that Lana Holbert was putting in more than just after-hours support for the senator. McQuarry always made provisions for her travel and she was always in his company."

"But as his intern…wasn't that part of her job?"

"Trust me—she was doing more than file paperwork. I have a witness who swears he caught her under McQuarry's desk late one night when everyone else had left the building. I'll give you two guesses as to what Miss Holbert was doing under that desk and the first guess doesn't count."

Xander could put two and two together. "Okay, assuming it's true that McQuarry and his intern were doing the nasty after hours… So what? That's not enough to want a man dead. Especially in the way that McQuarry went down. I mean, the man was blown to bits."

The woman shuddered. "Yeah, it was awful. His family must be devastated. No matter the man's faults, someone still loved him. He was a family man—married to the same woman for twenty-five years with three kids—I'm sure they're grieving."

Xander nodded. Jealous wife, maybe? But then what would that have to do with him?

Then it occurred to him, "If Holbert was always around McQuarry, why wasn't she killed in the bombing?"

"According to reports, she was sick that day. Caught that terrible flu that'd been going around. Who knew the flu would save her life?"

Yeah, sure. Or maybe she'd been tipped off that something was going down and she ought to make herself scarce. He made a mental note to track down

Lana Holbert for some questions of his own. "You got anything else for me?" he asked.

"I don't know if you know much about McQuarry but he was a real piece of work. He was all smiles, hug-the-babies and shake hands when he was on stage but behind closed doors…he was a pervert."

"First-hand knowledge?"

"Yeah, he tried to grab my ass during an interview. I got out of there as fast as I could. I couldn't believe he would try something so blatant. I mean, he's a freaking senator with a reputation to protect, but he didn't seem to care. Actually, he seemed pretty insulated against consequence, which I found even more distasteful. So I left and never went back."

Xander chewed on that information. A senator with a tendency to play grab-ass wasn't uncommon, either. Frustration welled beneath his breastbone at the anemic leads this meeting had given up. "Anything else?" he asked, almost desperately. "Anything at all?"

The woman pursed her lips in thought, then said, "Well, I don't know if it's anything major but Mc-Quarry was said to be closing a deal to bring a manufacturing plant to Oklahoma, trying to bring industry back when it left for Mexico for less stringent regulations. But now that McQuarry is gone, I doubt it's going to happen. The governor just appointed Carl Sheffton as his replacement until a special election can happen, and Sheffton and Senator Williams have both been very vocal in their opposition against the project."

"Why so? Bringing jobs to a depressed economy is a good thing," Xander said.

"Sheffton alleges that the manufacturer eyeballed for the deal is known for environmental infractions.

I'm talking toxic-waste-level exposure. Sheffton said inviting Wakefield Industrial into any Oklahoma city would be like feeding our kids cancer by the spoonful."

"That would definitely not be a selling point," Xander agreed, thinking. "How close was McQuarry to closing this deal?"

"I wasn't privy to the details but sources say he was pretty close and stood to make a substantial sum of money from the deal."

"A kickback?"

"Without using those exact words, yeah."

"If the governor appointed Sheffton, he must not be on board with the Wakefield deal, either."

The woman shrugged, unsure. "Honestly, I don't even know if the governor knew about the Wakefield deal, but all Sheffton had to do was make himself look like the best candidate in the interim, therefore freeing up the governor to deal with other things. Once Sheffton hit the office, it was short work for Sheffton and Williams to shut down the deal."

"And how exactly would he have managed that if the deal was close to closing?"

"McQuarry had offered certain tax credits if Wakefield chose an Oklahoma location, but my guess is that Sheffton and Williams withdrew those tax credits, which would've been a major incentive to set up shop here rather than Mexico."

"Let's get real. Politicians don't care about people. What's the real reason Sheffton and Williams wanted to axe the deal?"

The woman smiled, impressed. "The real reason? The oldest motivation in the book—money. Neither Sheffton nor Williams was cut into the deal, and they weren't about to let McQuarry rake in the dough while they got nothing."

Now they were getting somewhere.

Greed was the most powerful motivator—powerful enough to create killers out of suit-wearing politicians.

Chapter 8

It was hard enough to keep quiet in the shadows while Xander did his thing but now that they had some serious leads, the three-hour drive back to their crap motel was torture.

"As soon as we get back to the motel, I need to run a few names through the database and see what pops up. That Wakefield deal was shady as hell. Why is it that politicians always end up with dirty fingers?"

"Because they're always poking them where they don't belong," Xander answered. "Yeah, I agree. That's a solid lead. The saying 'money is the root of all evil' didn't get the reputation for nothing. We're probably talking millions in kickbacks on the line."

"You know, I've heard about Wakefield and what that reporter said was true. Wakefield was busted twenty years ago on their environmental waste storage, racked up a huge fine and then picked up and left for Mexico where the hazardous waste rules were less tough."

"But why return to the States? Even with a hefty tax credit, it couldn't possibly have measured up against what they were getting in Mexico."

"It could be that the violence in certain parts of Mexico has gotten out of hand?" Scarlett speculated. "When Hershey moved their plant to Monterrey, Mexico, they had to hire a private security detail for on-site protection from the drug lords that have claimed that area. I know this because Red Wolf had put in a bid for the assignment. That kind of protection gets expensive."

Xander was surprised. "Yeah? A detail in Mexico could've been nice. I love Cabo."

"It wouldn't have been a picnic. It's a legitimate war zone down there. The cartels are equipped with semi-automatics and there's more of them than there are of law enforcement. Plus, a lot of the cops are on the take so you can't really trust them, either. Honestly, there's no beach in the world that would've made that detail any fun. I'm glad we got outbid."

Xander nodded, thinking. "If it's as bad as you say it is, a return to the States could warrant a second look."

Scarlett agreed. "And if there's a politician willing to grease the wheels for a little extra green...could really sweeten the prospect."

Xander grinned, pleased. "That's a solid lead. Can you run Wakefield Industries through the Red Wolf database without tripping any alarms?"

"Yeah, it shouldn't be a problem."

Xander nodded, visibly appreciative of Scarlett's

help. He would've had a bitch of a time getting the same information that Scarlett could get with a few keystrokes.

But she would have Zak run Sheffton and Williams through the database to see what popped up. Red Wolf had one of the most extensive background-check programs, borderline-illegal in the intel it could glean from a few queries.

"I still think we should look into the intern angle. I know it seems small in comparison to the Wakefield deal but I don't feel comfortable leaving any stone unturned," Scarlett said, pleased when Xander readily agreed.

"Greed is a solid motivator but I wouldn't rule out the possibility of a jealous wife. Although, blowing a man up for messing around, even if she felt humiliated, seems a little harsh."

Scarlett shrugged. "Women can be vicious."

"No argument there."

She laughed, sensing a story. Feeling far more at ease now that they had a direction to head into, she asked, "Were you ever on the receiving end of a jealous woman?"

"What man hasn't?" he quipped, shrugging as he added, "Let's just say I seem to pick the ones all wrong for me."

"Oh, so you're a cheater?"

"I didn't say that. I just have a bad habit of attracting the crazy ones and they tend to overreact when I flirt a bit." He graced her with a quizzical look. "So how about you? What are you like as a girlfriend? The crazy kind, I bet."

"I don't let anyone in long enough to make me

crazy," she answered coolly. That was the truth. If Xander thought he was bad at relationships, he didn't have anything on her. Her career choice had led to some ill-fated partnerships, which had then led to the epiphany that she wasn't cut out for the his-and-her matching towel set. "Red Wolf is my life. I don't need anything else."

If that came out sounding as hollow as it felt, she wasn't sure but Xander seemed to understand. "Yeah, people like us, we're just made for the job. Civilians couldn't possibly understand the rush, the adrenaline high that comes from what we do. It's addictive."

"No argument there," she said, grinning. "Remember that detail in Morocco with the prime minister's son? Holy crap, I thought we were going to eat a bullet on that one."

"Damn straight. I thought so, too. That kid needed a muzzle to shut his trap. By the end of the detail, I was half tempted to hand the kid over to the nearest terrorist group just to be done with him. That kid sure as hell wasn't worth dying for."

Scarlett laughed, remembering when Xander shoved the lanky young man against the wall, his fists curled into the silk of his shirt after the kid had mouthed off one too many times. "I confess I was kinda hoping you were going to pop him in the mouth. It would've cost us the job but it would've been worth it."

Xander shared her laughter, his gaze dancing at the memory. "You have no idea how close I was, but Zak was the cool head and pulled me back. The kid didn't realize how lucky he was. I was about to rearrange his teeth for what he'd said."

"He was a stupid spoiled brat," Scarlett recalled,

adding wistfully, "But his daddy paid well and we all got bonuses for keeping his spoiled ass safe until the threat was neutralized."

Yeah, and by *neutralized*, she meant a bullet put squarely between the eyes of the man behind the terrorist cell threatening to kidnap the kid for ransom.

Afterward, a few days spent on Legzira Beach hadn't sucked. Now that she recalled, she and Xander nearly shared a moment then, too, but she'd pulled back just in time—possibly before he'd even noticed the intent in her eyes.

Thank God, she hadn't kissed him.

"Good times," Xander said, nodding.

"Yeah," she murmured, casting her gaze out the window. Maybe that night at the bar had been destined to happen at some point or another. The attraction between them had always been like a ticking time bomb, just waiting for the right opportunity to blow.

And now that they were on their own, playing by a new set of rules…did that mean she was willing to return to his bed?

Scarlett drummed the window lightly in time to the thoughts in her head.

She already knew the answer—possibly had known all along.

It was just time to stop fighting it.

Xander was eager to put what they'd learned into play but by the time they'd returned to their motel, it was too late to make calls and they were both starving. They couldn't risk a restaurant so it was another dinner of burgers and fries.

"With a steady diet of fast food, I'm getting a jump

on my future Dad bod," he joked, rubbing his stomach. "Nothing says you're getting older than discovering your metabolism has slowed to turtle speed."

Scarlett scoffed at his complaint. "Men have it easy. All you have to do to drop a few pounds is stop eating carbs and drinking beer for a few days and you'll be back to fighting weight. Women are biologically engineered to gain weight for the good of the species."

Xander grinned. "Thanks for taking one for the team."

"Yeah, you're welcome," she retorted, finishing her fries. "Well, I don't plan on having kids so if my ovaries could stop sending the estrogen overload straight to my hips, that'd be great."

"I don't see anything wrong with your hips," Xander said, holding her gaze, daring her to shut him down. "If I recall…your hips were perfect for gripping with two hands…"

She flushed and he knew they were both remembering that night. Hot damn, the memories were scorchers.

But he throttled himself down. As much as he wanted a repeat of that night, he would respect her boundaries.

Scarlett deliberately unbuckled her holster belt and placed it on the table, her nimble fingers moving to her belt and zipper. The spit dried in his mouth as she shimmied out of her jeans. He managed to quip, "I don't want to get the wrong impression but…" before she stripped off her shirt and tossed her bra. "Okay, now I'm confused but in a good way."

Scarlett smiled and pushed him to the bed, straddling him. "Let's just say you make a persuasive argument," she said, right before sealing her mouth to his.

That was all the encouragement he needed. He slid his hands up her bare back to grip the back of her neck, moving to caress her face and it was like putting gasoline on an ember. Within seconds, he was struggling to get out of his clothes but right at the worst possible moment, his back spasmed, punching the air from his lungs and all he could do was stiffen and gasp. He hadn't had a chance to take a painkiller with Scarlett around and the piper was coming for his due.

"Xander?" Scarlett climbed off him, concerned, but he couldn't move, his muscles were contracting in a cataclysmic symphony of complete agony. "What's wrong?" she asked, the urgency in her voice climbing.

He managed to gasp, "Over there, in my jacket pocket…"

She scrambled off the bed and rifled through his pocket to find his pill bottle. Her gaze narrowed at the narcotic but shook out two pills and returned to Xander with water, helping him get the medicine down his throat.

It would take about fifteen minutes for his body to metabolize the meds but he was sweating from the pain.

Scarlett quietly put her shirt back on and leaned back against the headboard, watching him. He could practically feel the questions building in her sharp mind but he couldn't focus on much more than the pain racking his body.

To her credit, she waited until the meds kicked in before her interrogation began.

"There's nothing in your file that says you're on narcotic pain meds," she said.

"I didn't get them from a Red Wolf physician," Xander said gruffly as he slowly rolled to a seated position, the pain finally subsiding to a dull roar. "For that precise reason."

"You know that's a violation of protocol," she said.

"Of course I know that."

"Which begs the question, why would you do it if you knew it went against the rules."

He sighed, not ready to have this conversation. Scarlett absolutely deserved the truth but he didn't have the balls to go the full Monty just yet. In the interest of self-preservation, he went with a variation of the truth. "Look, don't make a mountain out of this. Here's the deal, I jacked up my back about six weeks ago doing something stupid at home and I knew I wouldn't qualify for any benefits through Red Wolf, so I just went to my private doc for some pain meds to get me through. I'm almost out of my prescription and once it's gone, I won't refill it. I'd already decided on that but I'm in the process of weaning myself off the shit right now and that means dealing with the occasional temper tantrum from my back."

Some of the suspicion faded from her gaze. His explanation made sense, even if some of it was embellished.

True, he'd messed up his back off-hours and knew he couldn't turn in the claim to Red Wolf. He never figured the meds would turn him into a junkie. Hell, he'd truly thought that a few weeks on the stuff would help heal his back and then he'd be done.

But that wasn't the case.

And his injury wasn't six weeks ago... More like six months ago. A person didn't turn into a full-blown addict without sufficient time to settle in properly to the new reality.

He rose stiffly to grab some more water. "Look, I don't want you to worry that I can't handle myself. I'm almost back to my regular messed-up self. I can promise you that."

More lies.

For damn's sake, he needed to just shut up.

When backed against the wall, use humor to defuse the situation—that was his MO.

"Give me a few minutes to redeem myself and we can resume what we were doing," he said, casting a hopeful look her way but he could tell that ship had sailed, at least for tonight. "Or maybe a rain check on that booty?"

By way of answer, Scarlett swung her legs over the side of the bed and popped up with the curt announcement, "I need to shower," leaving Xander hunched over like an old man, feeling like a total shit for not having the courage to be truly honest.

Lying was a crappy way of showing his appreciation for her help, but he knew how that conversation would go and he couldn't afford the luxury of honesty right now.

He needed Scarlett on his side or else he was truly screwed.

When this was all said and done, he'd level with her and let the chips fall where they may.

Until then…he had to stay the course.

And be much more diligent about hiding his dirty little secret.

Chapter 9

Last night weighed heavily on Scarlett's thoughts, but she didn't have time to dwell much longer as the day had already started with a troubling phone call on her burner.

"We got an issue," her buddy with the FBI, Special Agent Conrad Griggs, said. "I'm giving you a heads-up that pressure is coming down hard to bring your man in. I don't know whose cornflakes he pissed in but he's made the wrong people take notice. My boss just ordered me to make bringing Scott in a top priority."

"Damn it," she muttered, shaking her head. "Why?"

"I don't know but I've never seen Platt so agitated about a case that's basically below his pay grade. He doesn't give two shits about most arrest warrants but he's ready to throw every resource needed to put Scott's head on a platter and deliver it with mustard sauce."

"Do you know anything about Wakefield Industries?" she asked.

"Doesn't ring a bell. What is it?"

"A company that'd been ready to strike a deal with McQuarry right before he died. Think you can poke around for me?"

"I don't know. There's a fair amount of heat on this case, which means that there's more to it than anyone is willing to talk about."

"Yeah, my thoughts, too. I know it's asking a lot but do what you can to stall your team. We've got some leads we're running down but we need more time."

"Time is the exact thing you don't have. I don't know, maybe the best thing would be to convince Scott to come in on his own. We could do some digging behind the scenes once he's in custody."

That idea gave her a chill. Maybe Xander's paranoia was contagious but she firmly believed that Xander wouldn't make it out of lock-up alive.

"Not an option," she answered, shaking her head. "Look, there's something dirty going on and that affects us all, not just Xander. If they could frame a highly decorated vet, what's to stop them from framing you or me? None of us are safe when there's an internal threat—you know that."

A beat of silence passed between them until Conrad responded with a heavy sigh. "Yeah, you're right but we could both end up on the wrong side of this fight depending on how high up the threat is."

"I'm well aware of the danger," she said. "Can you do this for me?"

She was asking a lot but she didn't have much of a choice.

"Yeah, I'll do what I can," he finally agreed, and she exhaled in relief. Having Conrad on their side was a big advantage. She only hoped it didn't get him fired. "I'll be in touch."

Conrad clicked off and Scarlett immediately called Zak. "FBI is starting to gear up. I've got someone on the inside running interference but I need you to dig into the following names: Carlton L. Sheffton, Gary S. Williams and Lana J. Holbert."

"Sure thing," Zak said. "You got some leads?"

"Yeah, but we've got some more digging to do. In the meantime, I need background intel on these people ASAP."

"You got it, TL."

She clicked off just as Xander exited the bathroom, towel wrapped around his midsection as he dried his hair. "Anything worth sharing?" he asked.

"Yeah, we're screwed if we don't kick it in gear. FBI wants you bad. All resources are being directed toward bringing you in."

"Damn, look how I rate," he joked but she didn't find it funny. People were walking a razor tightrope for Xander and he'd better start realizing it.

"Humor is neither appropriate nor appreciated," she said, rising to strap on her weapon. "You seem to forget that the world doesn't revolve around you."

"Hey, hey, settle down, sheathe those claws. I didn't mean to be dismissive. I was just trying to lighten the mood. Bad idea on my part. I'm sorry."

She rolled her head on her shoulders, her neck cracking in several places. Mollified by his apology, she said, "Our timeline just got shorter. We need to hurry if we're going to find answers before the FBI finds you."

Xander nodded in agreement. "We should talk to McQuarry's widow and his mistress and see if their stories match up."

"Good idea." She cut him a dismissive glance. "While you get dressed, I'm going to get some coffee."

She didn't wait for his response and left the room. She was currently operating in bitch mode, but she couldn't shake the feeling that Xander hadn't been completely honest with her last night. Her intuition was something she never questioned and it'd kept her alive when circumstances had tried to snuff her out.

But why would Xander lie?

The nagging sense that Xander was hiding something kept eating at her but with the FBI breathing down their necks, she didn't have the time to pull the truth out of him.

Not now at least.

Later, she'd find out what he was hiding and then decide the appropriate course of action.

Feeling generous, she returned with two coffees, pleased to find Xander had already set up meetings with both women.

"You have some strange voodoo that enables you to get what you're after," she said. "How'd you get the women to agree to meetings?"

"I told them the truth…"

"The truth?"

"Yeah, that I was investigating McQuarry's death."

"From what angle?"

"I was vague on that point but they took the bait without much more needed."

"Interesting. All right, what time?"

"In an hour with the widow, lunch time with the mistress."

She nodded with approval. "Good. Let's make it happen. Time is ticking."

Grabbing her coat, she swung it around her shoulders but was surprised when Xander pulled her close by her lapels.

"What are you doing?" she asked, wary.

"Just reminding you what's between us," he answered, brushing his lips against hers, igniting heat with the slow slide of his mouth. She didn't need reminding. Her mouth opened and his tongue accepted the invitation, dancing with hers. A dangerous fire burned between them but they didn't have the time to play. It took extreme force of will to break the kiss but she did. Xander released her and she left everything unsaid, choosing to spin on her heel and walk out the door.

Physical attraction didn't erase the feelings of doubt and it sure as hell didn't prove Xander's innocence.

And by God, he'd better be innocent or she'd put him down herself.

Something with Scarlett was off, but she was too focused to let personal feelings interfere with the investigation.

He admired her willpower. Scarlett would never find herself addicted to pills. Scarlett would probably chew her own arm off before she succumbed to something as basic as pill addiction.

Yeah, that line of thinking was productive. Not.

Xander shrugged off his own thoughts and put his head in the game where it belonged. "The widow agreed to meet at her place, which is in some gated community filled with the ultra-rich."

"Not surprising," Scarlett said with derision. "Have you ever known a bigwig politician to live modestly?"

"Nope."

"Exactly."

They climbed into the car and headed for the widow's mansion in the tony area of Tulsa, arriving with ten minutes to spare.

The colonial mansion, built in the 1800s by a founding father, had been restored and upgraded with stately elegance, flanked by exquisitely manicured lawns and foliage that probably cost a fortune to maintain. No wonder McQuarry needed that kickback. This place seemed a bit above his pay grade, even for a lawyer turned state senator.

"Nice digs," Xander murmured and Scarlett agreed. "Must cost a pretty penny to keep the lights on."

Scarlett knocked politely and within moments, the door opened. A stereotypically attractive older blonde woman with stylish attire and a smart bobbed haircut answered with a strained smile.

"You must be Detective Jones," she said, extending her hand. "Pleasure to meet you."

Scarlett slid her gaze over to Xander but remained quiet, following his lead. "Yes, thank you, Mrs. McQuarry, for meeting with me and my associate during this difficult time."

She nodded and ushered them into the beautifully furnished home to a quiet sitting room filled with books and assorted antiques that complemented the home's colonial style.

It was definitely camera-ready for any home-and-garden-type magazine.

"You have a lovely home," he said, playing the part of the gentleman. If Scarlett was choking on her tongue, she showed no sign of it. Another point for her power of will. Xander knew she was probably resisting the urge to roll her eyes. Xander purposefully sat near the widow while Scarlett took a position where she could watch the exits. Force of habit. Always know your points of entry.

"Have there been any leads into who did this to my sweet Kenny?" she asked, her voice quavering a little. "He was such a good, God-fearing man. I can't imagine who would want to do this to him."

"And the other innocent victims," Scarlett added quietly.

"And yes, of course, the other victims as well," Mrs. McQuarry said with a delicate sniff as she dabbed her eyes with a handkerchief. "It's all so awful."

"So tell me what happened from your point of view that day," Xander said.

Mrs. McQuarry drew herself up, gathering strength to recall. "Kenny was scheduled to speak, kicking off his campaign re-election trail. Of course, we decided he should start with Tulsa because that's where our dedicated base begins but I never would've imagined that someone would do something so horrific on what was supposed to be a wonderful day."

"Did your husband have any enemies?" Scarlett asked.

"No, he was beloved by everyone."

"Even Senator Williams?" Xander asked.

At the mention of Williams, Mrs. McQuarry stiffened slightly, her fingers curling into her handkerchief. "They were colleagues and peers. With men of their position, they were bound to disagree at times but never enough to warrant murder."

"Even if there was a lot of money on the line?" Xander watched Mrs. McQuarry's reaction closely.

"What do you mean?"

Was that real confusion or feigned? It was true not all men included their wives in financial decisions but Mrs McQuarry seemed sharp enough to be involved with her husband's political career, so why stop there? Xander decided to gently clarify. "We recently discovered your husband was very close to closing a lucrative deal with Wakefield Industries but Williams and Sheffton weren't in favor."

"Everyone knew about the Wakefield deal. It was going to revitalize industry in Oklahoma. For goodness' sake, it was going to be a blessing!"

"There were some who believed Wakefield would've been a nightmare with their rampant environmental hazards. Not everyone was on board with bringing Wakefield to the state."

"Small-minded people, perhaps." She lifted her chin, her gaze glittering. "My Kenny always wanted what was best for his constituents."

"But was Senator McQuarry truly brokering that deal for the people or his pocketbook?" Scarlett asked pointedly.

"How dare you!" Mrs. McQuarry gasped, outraged at Scarlett's question, her face flashing a spectacular shade of red. "And who are you again?"

Xander sidestepped her question. "I apologize for my colleague's abrupt nature but were you aware that

Senator McQuarry stood to gain a substantial amount of money from the deal if they closed?"

Mrs. McQuarry opened her mouth, presumably to fire off another angry retort but she stopped short. Maybe it was something in his expression that warned her lying wasn't in her best interest or maybe she was simply tired of playing the part of the devoted wife because her expression cooled as she settled against the sofa to answer. "Kenny worked hard for his constituents. It seems only fair to be compensated."

"So you were aware."

"Of course. Kenny and I had no secrets."

Xander shared a look with Scarlett before going for the next skeleton in McQuarry's closet. "So you were aware of the affair he was having with Lana Holbert?"

Mrs. McQuarry drew a measured breath before sliding a shrewd look toward Xander. "Are you married, Detective Jones?"

"No."

"Then you can't possibly understand the intricacies of a lifetime with the same person, sharing hopes and dreams, children, career goals…"

"No, you're right. I can't."

"Then I can't possibly explain to you how sometimes when you're in a partnership, you have to make certain sacrifices to ensure the success of that union."

"So you knew about Lana," Scarlett supplied.

"Again, like I said, Kenny and I didn't have secrets," Mrs. McQuarry answered with a layer of frost. "Of course I knew."

"And you were okay with him sleeping with another woman?" Scarlett asked, incredulous.

"Is there a point to the direction of these questions? I

fail to see how Kenny's extracurricular activities could have any bearing on his horrible death."

"That's the thing. We don't know that it doesn't. If we left any stone unturned, it could be the one with all the answers. I'm sorry if our questions seem intrusive. We don't mean to be disrespectful."

Xander's apology seemed to help, but so far Mrs. McQuarry was turning out to be a dead end.

"Is there anything else you can tell us that might help us in our investigation?" he asked.

Mrs. McQuarry looked down at the handkerchief in her hand and shook her head. "No, like I said, Kenny was beloved by nearly everyone he met. He was charismatic like a Kennedy. Everyone said so."

And politics aside, Kennedy had been a rampant philanderer.

Maybe there was more than just one mistress out there?

Xander rose and Scarlett followed. "Thank you for your time, Mrs. McQuarry. We appreciate your willingness to revisit a painful topic for the sake of justice."

"I loved my Kenny," she said. "He was a good man."

Xander nodded but didn't comment. He'd never understand the dynamic between husbands and wives in politics. But he wasn't one to lie and kiss ass so a life in the political arena had never been in the cards for him.

Thank God.

Mrs. McQuarry saw them out and as soon as they were out of earshot, Scarlett said what he'd been thinking.

"How much do you want to bet that as much as the wife thought good ol' Kenny was on the up and up, he still had secrets she didn't know about?"

Xander nodded. "And sometimes mistresses know more than the wives could ever know."

"Here's hoping Lana Holbert has more to say about the good senator," Scarlett said. "Or else, we might've just wasted precious time following a dead end."

Chapter 10

Paul Platt poured himself another generous scotch before allowing his girth to drop onto the leather sofa. *Helluva day.* If Griggs didn't find Scott soon, his head was on a platter. How in the hell did a simple operation turn into such a nightmare?

Scott was turning out to be a major pain in his ass but he didn't have much of a choice—the wheels were already turning.

The alcohol had only just started to settle his nerves when his cell buzzed. He grunted with the effort it took to sit up and grab his phone. Whatever benefit the scotch had provided evaporated as soon as he saw the caller ID.

He wanted to ignore the call but he couldn't.

With dread, he accepted the caller.

"Is Scott in custody?"

"Not yet."

"Why the hell not?"

"Because he's a slippery bastard with more re-sources than previously thought," he answered dryly, the alcohol loosening his tongue. "Look, I've got my best man on it. He'll be in custody within days."

"Need I remind you what you stand to lose if Scott isn't brought in?"

Platt swallowed, knowing full well how tightly his balls were in a vise. "I'm aware."

"Then get off your fat ass and make it happen."

Platt had worked his entire life building a career in the FBI and to have everything he held dear being held hostage over a mistake he couldn't take back, he had no choice but to see it through.

"I'm working on it."

"Work harder."

"Yes, sir." He downed the scotch. "Anything else?"

"Watch your tone."

Platt smiled without humor. "Apologies." *I'm not accustomed to being treated like a bitch.* "It's been a long day."

"I don't give a shit about your day, Platt. I want re-sults."

Of course you do. Nice to have someone else do your dirty work. "You'll have them. Scott is as good as caught."

"Dead works, too."

Platt ground his teeth, eyeing the scotch bottle, knowing he was going to kill it tonight. "If it comes to that…"

"No doubt he'll resist. Take him down if he does."

Platt rubbed his mouth with his free hand, wishing

he could wipe away his sins along with the feeling that he was selling his soul for pennies. "Look, I'm doing the best that I can. What do you expect me to do? Work a damn miracle?"

"Platt, you know the reason why you'll never rise higher than your position right now? Because you're weak. You don't have the stones to do what needs to be done—and that means being willing to get your hands dirty."

The asshole was crazy—Platt's hands were as dirty as they came.

The hypocrisy made Platt want to puke but what could he do but nod and accept whatever was being shoved down this throat? He rose and poured another glass, this time leaning against the bar as he downed the double shot. "Yeah, I guess you're right," he said, his agreement secretly laced with sarcasm. "Clearly, I'm not as smart as you, right? I didn't have the sense to cover my tracks better. Unlike you. Oh, wait, that's not the case, either, because if it were true, you wouldn't need me to clean up your mess."

Ahh hell, he'd probably just screwed the pooch but they were in this together now. If Platt went down, he'd make sure to take down every asshole with fingers in the pie.

"But then nobody's perfect, right?"

Platt finished with a smirk when he was met with silence on the other end, until the caller spat, "Just find Scott," and hung up.

Platt clicked off and tossed his phone to the counter, thinking idly that hanging up on someone just didn't offer the same level of satisfaction on a cell phone as it used to with an actual phone.

Those were the days.

The days before video surveillance tracked Americans' every move.

The days before private activities became searchable with the right program.

The days before cell phones were ever invented.

Pushing the glass away, he grabbed the bottle and headed for the bedroom. At this point, pouring by the glass was just a waste of time. He was going to get drunk off his ass and try to forget how screwed he truly was.

In comparison to the McQuarry mansion, Lana Holbert's place was modest and tidy with only hints here and there that she had access to money.

Another blonde—seemed McQuarry had a type—and suspiciously similar to what his wife may have looked like when she was younger, Lana was only too happy to talk to someone about her former lover.

Only, she wasn't as broken up about his death.

"Finally, someone is ready to listen to my side," Lana said, flopping into the oversized chaise, tucking her feet beneath her. "No one ever wants to talk to the one who has all the answers, the real deal about what's going on."

Scarlett smiled, amused by the young woman's chutzpah. "Yeah? So tell us, what was really happening behind the scenes? Do you know of anyone who wanted to hurt Senator McQuarry?"

"Uh, duh, probably his bitchy wife."

Oh, that's an interesting turn. "We spoke with Mrs. McQuarry and she seemed heartbroken over his death."

"What else is she supposed to say? That she hated

the bastard and that she wanted to stick a fiery hot poker up his ass?"

"She knew about you and she seemed fine with the arrangement," Scarlett said, curious. "Or was that an act?"

"That woman should've been an actress for all the lying and scheming she can do with a smile on her face."

Xander narrowed his gaze. "Okay, so give us the real deal. Do you think she had motive to have Mc-Quarry killed?"

"Motive, sure. Opportunity? I don't know. Look, Ken was fun in the sack and he loved buying me presents." She lifted her wrist to show off a pretty diamond bracelet. "But I wasn't the only one he was messing around with behind his wife's back."

"And that didn't bother you?" Scarlett asked.

Lana scoffed. "Why would it? He wasn't my husband. Besides, I'm not stupid. There's no future for the *other* woman in politics. Clara McQuarry would always be the queen and she knew it. I wasn't about to change that. It was enough for me that he treated me well and paid my bills. Unlike some, I wasn't greedy."

"What do you mean?"

Lana turned coy, playing with her bracelet. "I guess it doesn't matter now that he's dead but…Ken liked to play."

"Clearly," Scarlett said, gesturing to Lana but that's not what Lana was referring to. "Play how?"

"Let's just say that Ken didn't like to restrict himself to one platter on the table. He liked tacos but he liked sausage, too."

Scarlett narrowed her gaze, catching the woman's innuendo. "Senator McQuarry was bisexual?"

Lana nodded. "And no matter how many times I warned him to be careful, sometimes he wasn't very discerning with his play partners."

Xander shook his head. "Okay, so he liked to play fast and loose. Who could he possibly have hooked up with that had access to explosives and would've used that knowledge to kill him? Seems a bit much."

"Look, all I know is that Ken was seeing someone with a lot to lose if it were found out. Ken thought it was exciting, the thrill of having a dangerous secret."

Scarlett looked to Xander with derision. "Why is it the ones who run their campaigns on the power of family values always have the dirtiest secrets?"

Xander nodded, then returned to Lana. "Okay, got a name?"

"Hell, no. And even if I did, I wouldn't share that information. Ken is dead. I sure as hell don't want to end up the same way."

"Do you think Mrs. McQuarry knew about her husband's male lover?" Xander asked.

Lana sighed as she considered the question. "I don't know. Maybe. She had secrets of her own. Maybe she didn't want to know."

"Protecting a dirty secret takes a certain level of commitment. Depending on the secret, some people might do anything to keep it private," Scarlett said.

Lana nodded, adding, "It's all so lame. People should be free to love who they want. Love is love, right?"

Scarlett refrained from quipping something sarcastic and asked, "Can you tell us if his lover was some-one in politics?"

Lana pursed her lips, considering her answer. Fi-nally, she said, "All I know is that he was important and Ken was crazy about him. I mean, I really think he might've loved him. Sad, huh?"

It was sad that McQuarry was a damn liar and a fraud. Was anyone in politics a decent human being anymore? Maybe there never were any but Scarlett was beginning to question if there were any good people in the world, *period*.

Her gaze slid to Xander and that nagging at the back of her mind increased. She wanted to believe Xan-der was innocent but if he wasn't and he was simply dragging her along on a wild-goose chase in some at-tempt to appear innocent, she didn't think she could take the betrayal.

As much as she wanted to say she didn't, she cared about Xander. She wanted him to be innocent—needed him to be telling the truth.

"What do you know about the Wakefield deal?" Scarlett asked.

"I know that Ken dying screwed us all out of a shit-ton of money," Lana answered with a pout. "Ken prom-ised me a nice sum and I was looking forward to finally getting my dream car. Now I'm stuck with my old one."

Ahh, the lamentations of a gold digger. Poor girl. Boo-hoo. "Guess you'll have to earn it the old-fashioned way," Scarlett said without sympathy.

But Lana was quick on her feet and shot back, "And I was. Go ahead and judge me, but women have been selling themselves since the beginning of time. At least I sold myself for a higher price than most."

Xander sent Scarlett a look that said to drop that angle and move forward. "No one is judging you," he assured the woman. "We're just trying to find answers."

"Speak for yourself. She's judging me pretty hard. I can see it in her eyes," Lana said. "Don't think I haven't seen that look on plenty of women's faces. I saw it every day on that snooty bitch Clara's face, as if she hadn't sold herself years ago for all that she's accumulated. She sacrificed her dignity when she agreed to look the other way while her husband screwed everything but the light socket in exchange for her lifestyle. Have you seen how much that woman spends on shoes alone? It's no wonder Ken was so hot for that Wakefield deal. His wife was spending his money faster than he could make it."

So the wife and the mistress had both been fighting for pieces of the same pie; typical story, but that didn't make them capable of murder.

Especially not in the way McQuarry died. Pissed off women didn't generally plant bombs—they preferred methods that were more personal, such as poison or shooting the man at point-blank range. They wanted to see the horror and fear in the man's eyes before he died.

No, a bomb was more a man's style.

Impersonal, quick and final.

If they were looking at someone offing McQuarry because of a lover's spat, they needed to find out who McQuarry's secret lover was.

But even so, Scarlett couldn't believe a lover's spat would be so epic that it warranted such a grand exit.

"Where were you the day of the bombing" Scarlett asked.

"Sick as a dog," Lana answered with a grimace. "Seriously, I got that stupid flu and was stuck in bed all day. So gross. I felt like I'd been hit by the vomit train."

Scarlett exchanged a look with Xander, confirming what they both were feeling. Lana wasn't likely their killer.

No, again, Scarlett believed the true motive remained greed. People were willing to kill for great sums of money.

Which led her back to Wakefield.

Scarlett rose. "Thank you for your time, Miss Holbert."

"I hope you find who killed Ken," she said, rising to stand with her arms crossed. "I mean, he had his faults but he was a good guy, you know?"

Scarlett offered a brief smile—she would never understand the inner workings of women who defended shitty men—and let herself out.

Scarlett's silence was worrisome. Xander knew when Scarlett was chewing on something and he had a good idea what she was chewing on was him.

If he weren't such a coward, he'd have come at her point-blank and insisted that they talk about his situation—he'd have come clean and they'd have dealt with the facts like adults—but each time he thought of admitting just how he'd messed up his life, he redirected.

Which was exactly his plan now.

"It's highly unlikely that either of McQuarry's women had the resources to pull off the Tulsa bombing," he said.

"Yeah, my thoughts, too." Scarlett climbed into the car and buckled up. "But we still need to find out what high-ranking official McQuarry was sleeping with. It's far-fetched, but there might be something there."

Xander sighed with frustration. Their leads were becoming anemic and the day was just about over. He didn't like to make too big of a deal but he felt the ticking clock as sharply as Scarlett did.

"Any word from Red Wolf?" he asked, hoping Zak had managed to scrounge up some leads but Scarlett's headshake wasn't the answer he was hoping for. "How about that FBI friend of yours?"

"No, but I don't expect a call from him until after hours when he's out of the office. He's got to watch his back, too."

"So who is this guy?" he asked, curious for more than just professional reasons. Fishing, he guessed, "Old boyfriend?"

She surprised him with, "Something like that," and Xander needed to know more. Was it jealousy he felt? Maybe. His emotions were so jumbled up these days he didn't know what was real anymore. It was probably an effect of the drugs, damn them. He was surprised his dick still worked. Maybe if that'd stopped working, he would've moved heaven and earth to kick the habit. Alas, his Johnson worked just fine.

"What do you mean? Were you dating?"

Scarlett paused, irritated at his questions. "What does it matter? He's willing to help and we can use all the help we can find."

Yeah, true, but he still wanted to know details—even if he was being a nosy bastard. "How do you know you can trust him?"

"Because I can. Conrad and I go way back. We sort of dated but I knew it wasn't going to pan out and

I cut him loose. I'm just not the kind of woman who dreams of the domestic scene and that was more than Conrad could deal with. It was really a mercy on my part to end it."

"Ahh, so he had a crush on you and you crushed his dreams—and you think you can trust him? What if he's been waiting all this time to stab you in the back?"

"You are paranoid," she said, sighing. "I'm starting to think that psych eval wasn't that wrong. Listen, relax. I can trust Connie and if you trust me, you'll believe that I wouldn't put either of us in harm's way."

"*Connie*?" he mocked. "That's a girl's name."

Scarlett graced him with a narrowed stare. "You're being a dick. Connie is his nickname. Only those close to him call him that."

"And you're that kind of close."

"What is your problem, Xander? He's helping us, just be grateful."

He was being a dick but he couldn't quite stop. Maybe it was the stress of the situation or the fact that he didn't like the idea of Scarlett getting naked with someone else but he was getting grouchier by the minute.

"I need food. Real food. Not that processed shit we've been shoveling down our gullets."

"What do you suggest? We can't exactly walk into a nice restaurant and order a fat, juicy steak and our motel doesn't serve up room service."

"I'll pick a steakhouse, place the order and then you can pick it up to go. You're not on the run. There's no reason why anyone would be looking for you."

Scarlett nodded, accepting his solution. "Good

point. I could go for some real food, too. A medium-rare steak would go down nicely."

Food always helped defuse tension. "I'll make the call."

An hour later, they were heading back to their motel with two steak dinners.

Just as they were ready to dig in, Scarlett's burner phone went off. It was Zak checking in.

The conversation was short and to the point and when it was over, she shared her intel.

"Zak found some interesting things about Wakefield," she said, tucking into her steak, talking between bites. "The environmental fines and sanctions are public record but there are a few things that aren't."

"Yeah? Like what?"

"Like the fact that someone you might recognize holds a majority share of Wakefield Industries." She waited a beat before sharing, "Mark Bettis."

Xander chewed on that for a minute. "The secretary of defense?"

"The very same."

"How'd Zak come up with that information?"

"Bettis flies under the radar by routing his business affairs through various shell companies, legal but barely so. Now, on the surface, I'd say there's no law against Bettis owning shares in a company but it does beg the question why he chooses to do so under the cover of smoke and mirrors. The simplest answer is that he has something to hide, right?"

"Yeah, if you subscribe to the if-it-walks-like-a-duck theory," Xander said. "But just playing devil's advocate, why would Bettis risk his career by having a no-name senator blown up? I mean, seems kinda overkill, even if he had a beef with McQuarry."

Scarlett nodded. "True. But what if Bettis was the high-ranking official Holbert was talking about?"

Xander wasn't sure if he could buy that. "I don't know. That's pretty far-fetched. If that were true, there'd be no way Bettis could keep an affair like that quiet. As much as I'd love to chase that lead…it seems too out there to be real."

Scarlett wiped her mouth and swigged her beer, allowing for a noncommittal, "Maybe," but added, "We can't afford to leave anything to chance. I say we dig into Bettis and see what shakes out."

Seemed risky, given Bettis's position. "Poking into the affairs of the secretary of defense is like walking with a tambourine into the cave where a known grizzly bear is hibernating. I'm not sure that's smart."

Scarlett rose to toss her trash. "Don't be a pussy, Xander. All operations come with risk. I've never seen you so reluctant to jump into the fray. This is your life on the line. Frankly, I've seen you more gung ho for operations with lesser chances for success and you didn't even have a personal stake in the outcome."

He couldn't argue that point. Maybe he was feeling the pressure of knowing that it wasn't just his life hanging in the balance. He didn't want to screw with Scarlett's life but he supposed that ship had already sailed.

"Yeah, well, the stakes are higher," he said, leaning back in his chair, covertly watching Scarlett as she changed efficiently from her street clothes to casual. They'd all seen each other naked at one point or another. Sometimes out in the field, there was little time for something as trivial as modesty. But unlike the rest of the team, Scarlett and Xander had that one night to-gether that essentially changed everything, even if they tried to pretend that it hadn't.

Now that his physical hunger was sated, a different kind of hunger rattled his bones. Scarlett was under his skin in the worst way.

But Scarlett looked as approachable as a wet cat. He knew his TL well. She was still thinking about those pills and why he'd kept it a secret. His explana-tion might've held water at first but she was too smart to be fooled for long.

The question was…how long did he have before his time was up?

Chapter 11

The following morning, Scarlett rose early and went for a run to clear her head. Ignoring her physical needs created a restlessness that only responded to punishing workouts.

Given the fact that she was ripped from head to toe probably gave one pretty good insight as to how frustrating her sex life had become.

It took an extreme force of will to shove away her attraction to Xander and keep her head focused on the straight and narrow. Physical attraction, sexual lust—all that could be controlled with the right tools, but there was something about Xander that messed with her internal process.

It wasn't the first time she'd had to crush an inappropriate attraction but with Xander, it was the first time she'd had to exert so much energy to prevent herself from giving into her baser desires.

Time to focus on the facts, not on how she wanted to devour that difficult man from his stubborn head to his calloused toes.

As she ran, Scarlett processed the information they'd gleaned so far.

On the surface, the two women that McQuarry had been associated with had turned out to be dead ends. Clara McQuarry was the stereotypical political housewife who'd long ago sold her own personal happiness in favor of wealth and prestige, while the little gold digger had only been in the relationship for whatever she could get while the getting was good.

While no one was innocent in this scenario, it galled her that it was men always thinking with their dicks that caused the most turmoil in the world.

But they still hadn't figured out who the high-ranking official was that McQuarry had been banging on the super sly. Damn family values platforms were such a crock of shit. The ones who shouted the loudest about traditional values were usually the ones screwing the underage babysitter, visiting hookers or sucking a dick in a back alley.

Oh, sure, they cried great big crocodile tears when they were inevitably caught but no one bought that act anymore. It looked good on camera, though. *Repent, ye sinner!*

Scarlett swallowed a sudden lump in her throat and wiped at the sting in her eyes.

Why did her father's voice suddenly jump from her memory?

Ahh, because he'd been a sanctimonious prick just like McQuarry. Spouting off scripture, condemning the actions of others for their ungodliness and yet behind closed doors, he'd been the monster of her nightmares.

Scarlett pushed herself harder, sweat pouring down her back in spite of the chill in the morning air.

It'd taken a long time to push the memories away but there was something about this case that'd pulled everything right back to center.

Maybe it was the salacious hypocrisy that had gotten to her the most.

Or maybe it was the fear that no matter how far she ran from the memories of what that man had done to her, she'd never escape the urge to flinch whenever a man tried to get close.

Poor Connie had gotten the worst of her. She had no idea why he still cared, but she was grateful that he was a better man than she'd been a girlfriend.

In spite of Xander's suspicion, she trusted Connie with her life.

The bigger question, the one she was still wrestling with, was did she trust Xander?

He was lying to her about something. She could feel it.

Could it be the pills? But why would he lie about an injury? The prescription was legit and he was nearly out of his pills so that issue was actually a non-issue, but Xander had definitely been twitchy when explaining.

Was he guilty of killing McQuarry? Did Xander have a private beef with McQuarry that he'd decided to settle that day in Tulsa?

Scarlett skidded to a stop, bending to dry heave for a minute. Exhausted and breathing hard, she straightened and wiped at her face with her sleeve. She could speculate all she wanted but until she came at Xander for the straight answer, she'd drive herself crazy with the millions of scenarios that could potentially be accurate.

They didn't have time for bullshit.

And she couldn't risk the mental breakdown.

So it came down to this—pin Xander down and demand the truth, or walk and let him deal with this mess on his own.

Scarlett had always operated more efficiently with a plan, even if the plan scared her.

She needed answers and she was going to get them, one way or another.

Spinning on her heel, she started the long trek back to the motel where hopefully Xander had drinkable coffee ready. Otherwise, she'd have to come at this situation in full-on bitch mode.

For his sake, Scarlett prayed Xander would do the smart thing.

Scarlett returned from her run, sweaty and looking like breakfast, but he could see from her expression that whatever she'd been hoping to exorcise was still riding shotgun in her mind.

Quietly, he slid the coffee he'd purchased toward her along with her preferred protein bar. She graced him with a brief smile and quickly stripped as she bit into the bar and washed it down with the coffee.

She used her shirt to wipe away the sweat and then said, "We need to talk" as she pulled a clean shirt over her head.

He'd known this conversation was coming but he still dreaded it. "Yeah? About?" he asked, pretending ignorance. "Ready to cash in that rain check?"

Scarlett ignored his play and said point-blank, "I know you're lying to me about something. Come clean so we can move forward. We don't have time for games."

"What makes you think I'm lying?" he countered, not quite ready to show his hand. "Maybe you're just being paranoid."

Wrong move. "Don't try to get in my head, Scott. My instincts have kept me and my team—which includes you, asshole—alive, so don't try to make me question what my gut is telling me. Fess up or I'm walking."

Damn, so much for dancing around the truth. Hell, Scarlett deserved the truth. But could he trust her with it? Scarlett was a hard-core rule-follower and if she knew…how could he trust that she wouldn't just bail anyway?

"You're weighing the pros and cons of spilling the beans," she guessed accurately—sometimes the woman was scary—and Xander could only shake his head at the rock and the hard place he was wedged against. "Out with it, Scott. I'm done with the games."

"I'm not playing games," he assured her. "I respect you too much to play games."

"So tell me the truth."

"I've told you everything."

"Bullshit."

Sweat threatened to break along his hairline. He covered it by rubbing his hand through his hair, stalling. "This is a waste of time. I can't have you chasing after me with some paranoid crap every time you get a hunch. If I seem a little twitchy, it's because, oh, maybe, my whole life has been turned upside down and I'm trying to figure out how to save my ass before it's too late. That might account for the fact that I seem distracted, or disingenuous, or whatever else you have cooked up in your head. I've said it plenty of times and it still holds true—you don't have to stay. There's the door."

He was playing a damn risky game and he hated being dishonest with Scarlett but he didn't have a choice. If Scarlett knew that he had a pill addiction that had caused him to black out the day of the bombing, she wouldn't trust anything he had to say from that moment forward.

He'd already made a solemn vow to kick the habit as soon as he figured out who was trying to frame him for McQuarry's death but until then, he had to shove that problem to the back of the line.

Scarlett would just have to deal with his answer or leave.

The tension between them thickened. Xander didn't know if Scarlett would stay but he hoped to God she did. He needed her—and not just because she was a hell of an asset to have on his side—she helped keep the demons at bay.

Guilt was an insidious force to reckon with and some days he felt the grip on his neck so tightly he couldn't breathe.

The people who'd died... He might as well have planted that bomb because he'd screwed up. Taken for granted what had seemed like an easy detail and had overdosed himself by being careless.

If he could relive that day and make different choices, he would. But that wasn't an option so he was left with the actionable decisions available.

And that meant putting his nose back to the grindstone and finding the person who was truly responsible.

"So that's it? Stay or go?" Scarlett shot back, her gaze hot.

"Making it pretty simple for you."

"Yeah, right. Simple," she growled and if looks could kill, Xander would have been spurting from his jugular. After a long moment, she exhaled with frustration but she wasn't gathering her things to leave, so that was a good sign. "If I find out you're lying to me, I'll not only kick your ass but things between me and you will never be the same. You get me?"

Yeah, he got her. The message was loud and clear. Even if he found who had framed him, he was basically committing to the realization that his relationship with Scarlett would be irrevocably screwed.

But what choice did he have?

He shrugged with forced nonchalance. "Well, until then, let's just focus on the case," he suggested, rising to toss his cup. His hands were shaking. It was time for another pain pill but with Scarlett there watching him, he couldn't exactly pop his meds without raising more suspicion.

However, luck was on his side because Scarlett announced she was going to shower and disappeared into the bathroom.

Xander waited a beat until he heard the water going and then he quickly swallowed two pills from his ever-shrinking stash. He'd have to do something really risky—find a dealer to purchase more.

Back home, he had his regular guy and they had an arrangement. He left the money in an envelope with a certain convenience store clerk and when he returned, the clerk had a package for him. It was all very cut-and-dried but expensive as all get-out. When you're stuck purchasing meds on a per-pill basis…it got real pricey.

But he couldn't get a refill on the meds through the regular channels. The doc had already suspected a problem and had cut him off when he'd blown through his usual prescription within the first two weeks of getting it refilled.

So, yeah, getting a prescription the legal way…not an option.

At first, he'd thought it was a positive thing—if he couldn't get the meds, he couldn't keep taking them— but then he'd found someone who sold them on the black market and, well, there went his decision to quit cold turkey.

He was the first to admit he'd played fast and loose with his meds. He supposed he still suffered the belief that he was invincible but that blackout had been a wake-up call in more ways than one.

If he thought Scarlett would understand, he'd gladly spill that truth but he knew in his gut that Scarlett would lose all respect for him and he couldn't risk that right now.

Maybe not ever.

If he could kick this habit on his own, she never needed to know.

Chapter 12

Zak Ramsey and CJ Lawry were waiting in the debriefing room when Scarlett's friend, Special Agent Conrad Griggs, walked in. Too keep up appearances, Laird Holstein was on another assignment for the time being, which had gone over like a turd in a punch bowl with Laird but he'd gone along with it for the sake of mission Double Down.

Scarlett had told them that Griggs was cool and on their side but it felt weird to have an FBI agent working behind the scenes with them.

Still, Zak trusted his TL so he went with it.

After brief introductions, Conrad said, "It's a pleasure to finally meet the infamous Red Wolf team that Scarlett is so proud to lead. I've always admired the work you do and, if I'm being honest, a little bit envious of all the friggin' cool shit you guys get to do."

"We have the best guns, too," CJ quipped without a hint of modesty.

Conrad, being a good sport, agreed. "Hands down, you win the cool award. Now I know why Scarlett never even considered joining the Bureau once Red Wolf started calling. Hell, are you guys hiring?" he joked.

Zak chuckled politely, knowing the agent was just making conversation. Scarlett was an excellent judge of character and judging by his first impression of Griggs, her track record still stood.

"We appreciate your help in this. I know it's asking a lot," Zak said.

Conrad drew a deep breath, moving into no-bullshit mode. "Look, I'm going to be straight with you. Scarlett has made a name for herself here with Red Wolf and I couldn't be more proud but I gotta say, this whole situation with your buddy makes me nervous. I've never known Scarlett to act impulsively or rashly and running off with a federal fugitive isn't something I'd ever say she'd do. Understand where I'm coming from?"

Zak nodded. "You're worried that Scarlett is acting out of character and this might blow up in her face," he said.

"Exactly. So what can you tell me about your boy that will make me breathe a little easier?"

CJ and Zak exchanged glances before Zak spoke up. "All I can say is, if Scarlett believes that Xander is innocent, we believe it, too. In our line of work, there's no room for second-guessing. We have to trust our TL with our lives and we do. She's earned that respect because she's smart, capable and her gut instinct is almost scary. Just as she trusts you, we trust you. Same goes for Xander."

"But what if she's wrong?" Conrad asked, still wary. "I don't want to see my friend get burned over this."

"She won't." Zak's faith was unwavering. "Xander is innocent."

When Conrad saw that there was little room for doubt, his fears seemed to lessen. He nodded, accepting Zak's answer before launching into the true reason for the face-to-face. "The information I have is sensitive and I didn't trust the phones, even a burner, so I wanted to come personally."

"Yeah, the FBI has everyone on speaker phone in some room," CJ quipped with a shit-eating grin, then quickly sobered to add, "No, seriously, that's not just an urban legend, right?"

Conrad smiled but revealed nothing. They all knew the score. The FBI had stopped pretending it wasn't true and the American people, for the most part, had accepted this new reality and made funny memes about it.

"Have you heard from Scarlett?" Conrad asked.

Zak answered, "Briefly. She gave us some leads to run down but nothing really tripped an alarm."

"What names?"

"Carl Sheffton, Gary Williams and Lana Holbert."

"Sheffton and Williams are senators. Sheffton was only recently installed at the governor's discretion after McQuarry died. I don't recognize Holbert."

"Holbert was the mistress," Zak said. "Young, pretty and ambitious—the usual sort you can find hanging around morally weak politicians."

"I've yet to meet a politician who *wasn't* morally

weak but people always seem to mix up morals with politics. I guess you don't need to be a faithful husband to pass good policy."

Zak agreed. "So Holbert was a dead end. She's nothing but a skirt looking to cash in while she could and after digging into her financials, she seemed to do pretty well by McQuarry."

"How well?"

Zak looked to CJ. "About how much would you say?"

CJ shrugged. "About fifty thousand, give or take a few thousand and that's not including the gifts and trips."

Conrad chuckled ruefully. "Ever get the feeling we're in the wrong business?"

"I'd say you can't put a price on dignity but I think I could sell mine for a few million," CJ said with a grin.

Conrad shifted in his chair, thinking out loud. "All right, so Holbert was a dead end. What about Sheffton and Williams?"

"Williams and McQuarry were Oklahoma senators in the middle of their terms. They were conservative but Williams seems sympathetic to some environmental concerns as he immediately put the brakes on the Wakefield deal that McQuarry had been pushing," Zak said, sending a file toward Conrad. "If I were just looking to motive, I'd say Williams had the most to gain by McQuarry's death."

"Sheffton backed Williams's decision to kill the Wakefield deal, so at the very least Sheffton deserves a second look," CJ added, to which Zak nodded.

"And you told Scarlett this?"

"I haven't yet," Zak said. "I was planning to call her tonight."

Conrad took a moment to thumb through the file, then sighed with an expression that promised bad news. "I've run out of time. I can't stall much longer. Platt is riding my ass like I'm a thoroughbred and he's pushing for the Winner's Circle at the Kentucky Derby. There's not much more I can do to keep the FBI from running down your man."

"Why's he so hot for this case?"

"Prestige? I don't know. Seems personal, honestly, but I have no idea the pressure that's being put on Platt from above," Conrad said. "He has been acting off, though."

"How so?" Zak asked.

"Hard to explain. Platt's never been a people person but lately he's been worse than ever. Like he went from overall general asshole to Grade-A, top-tier asshole."

"Does he know Xander? Xander seems to have that effect on people," Zak said.

Conrad shook his head. "Not that I'm aware. My honest assessment is that Platt is getting squeezed by his boss and you know that saying, shit rolls downhill. Everyone wants this case to go away. Your man is good for the crime and no one seems interested in finding a different fit."

"Even if he's innocent?" CJ asked, bristling. "Whatever happened to due process? Xander Scott is an American hero. Shouldn't that count for something?"

"It should," Conrad agreed. "But it doesn't. Not in this case. I've never seen Platt so hungry for someone's head."

CJ said, "We know why we're doing this, but why

are *you* going out on a limb for a guy you've never met?"

Conrad answered honestly. "I'm not doing this for Scott. I'm doing this for Scarlett. I have no idea if your man is guilty or innocent and I'm not sure I care, but Scarlett seems to believe in the guy and I believe in Scarlett so I'll do what I can."

"Fair enough." Zak accepted Conrad's blunt answer. He appreciated his forthright manner and could see why Scarlett trusted him. "We'll take whatever help we can get."

Conrad rose and shook hands with both men. "Good luck," he said, shaking his head. "Your man is going to need it."

Zak had a feeling so would Scarlett.

The sexual tension between Scarlett and Xander was enough to choke an elephant but she couldn't bring herself to act on any impulse when there were too many questions swirling in her head.

Today, they were heading out to talk with Senator Williams to see why he put the kibosh on the Wakefield deal and to feel out if there were any sketchy vibes that warranted further investigation.

But Xander was on edge. She could feel the negative energy coming off him in waves, so much so that she made him pull over before they got to Williams's office.

"We can't walk in there with you acting like a pissed-off criminal. What's wrong with you?"

"Nothing, I'm just stressed out. Our leads have turned up squat so far and I'm running out of time to prove that I didn't kill McQuarry."

"Calm down," Scarlett ordered, sliding easily into TL mode. "Get your shit straight. It doesn't matter the odds. We have our mission and we execute. Got it?"

Xander caught her gaze and held it. The odd tension coming off him was disconcerting. Clearly, he was too close to the situation to think objectively—but she wasn't about to let him do anything stupid. Not when her ass was on the line, too.

"And if Williams turns up a dead end, too?"

"Then we move onto the next lead and we keep doing that until we run out of options."

"Easy for you to say," he growled, squeezing the steering wheel hard enough to make a squeaking noise. He scratched behind his ear with a quick, agitated motion. "Maybe I ought to hang back, let you take point on this one. What if Williams recognizes me?"

"And what will you do while I'm talking to Williams?"

"I don't know, maybe see what I can dredge up on Wakefield."

Scarlett nodded. Maybe Xander was right and he ought to hang back. It was possible Williams might recognize him or have contacts close enough to the FBI that he'd know Xander was on the most wanted list.

But that nagging sense that Xander wasn't being completely honest still chewed on her hide. "Are you sure that's it?" she asked.

"Stop, Scarlett," he demanded, causing her hackles to rise. "I need you to stop picking at me. I've got enough on my plate, and I don't need you looking for more reasons to psychoanalyze me."

The urge to smash her elbow into his nose was strong but she held it back. "Fine. You chase down

Wakefield. You can drop me off at Williams's office and I'll catch a cab back to the motel."

He didn't argue. The tense silence between them didn't let up, not even when he dropped her off and drove away.

She had a bad feeling about whatever Xander was hiding. Before she headed into Williams's office, she called Zak.

"Just the person I was about to call," Zak said as he picked up. "I have bad news."

She ignored that for a minute. "I need you to chase something down for me," she said. "I need you to find out if Xander is a patient of a Dr. Yarrow at Crossroads Medical Services."

"Why?" Zak's confusion wasn't surprising. "What's that got to do with the case?"

"Just do it. I need to know when he last saw the doctor and what he was prescribed and why. Screw doctor-patient confidentiality…find a way to get him to talk."

"Okay," Zak said, unsure but willing to do as he was asked. "Are you ready for my news?"

"Yeah, hit me."

"Your friend Conrad was here. He said his boss is hungry for Scott's head and he can't hold back the FBI any longer. They're going to start using the big guns to track Scott down, which means if you're around when they do…you're going to get caught in the snare, too."

"Yeah, Conrad already told me that. Anything else?"

"You're handling the news that you're about to be chased like a rabbit pretty well."

"It is what it is. We knew it was going to happen at some point."

"Got any leads?" Zak asked, hopeful. "I mean, surely someone's got to have something to go on?"

"Our leads have turned out to be flimsy at best. Honestly, I'm starting to sweat. How could there be so little to find?" Scarlett asked, allowing some of her worry to come through her voice. She trusted Zak, which was more than she could say for Xander. Hell, what a fine mess. "Have you found anything on Wakefield?"

"I have a contact name and number," he said. "I'll send it to your phone."

"Good. With some luck, maybe something will pop up. I'm running out of ideas."

"Something will happen. There's no such thing as a perfect crime," Zak assured her. "Someone left behind a clue."

"Yeah, but finding that clue in the time we have left... I don't want to be a pessimist but I'm not feeling too good about our chances."

"Look, you keep doing what you're doing. We'll do what we can on our end. You and I both know that Xander didn't set that bomb. He's being framed. Just hold on to that fact and let your gut guide you."

Scarlett nodded, appreciating Zak's solid advice. Usually, she was the one propping up the team, holding them together when things got dicey, but she was grateful her team was smart enough to pick up the job when she faltered. Zak's faith renewed hers. "You're right. Someone had to leave behind something. I just need to find it."

"That's the TL I know. Remember with the FBI mobilizing, they're going to be flagging credit cards and using all the surveillance available to them—traffic cams, satellite footage, whatever they can get their hands on, especially if they've been given the green light to use any resource."

"Yeah, I know," she said grimly. "Well, we're not using our cards. Xander is using cash. For once his paranoia has been a blessing."

"Well, that doesn't do anything for the camera footage. Be aware of your surroundings, maybe get a disguise."

"I've always wanted to try out blond," she said.

"Now's your chance."

"I'll be in touch." Scarlett clicked off and headed into Williams's office building.

Time to see if she was any good at spewing bullshit.

Get it together.

Xander clenched his fists in frustration when they wouldn't stop shaking. With Scarlett around, he'd tried to limit the pills he was taking but the sudden decrease in dosage was messing with him in a bad way.

At this rate, he wouldn't be able to hide his problem from Scarlett much longer and that made him sweat even harder.

The obvious solution was also the most unsavory—replenish his supply on the DL and hope that Scarlett didn't notice.

Fat chance of that. Scarlett had eagle eyes. She already knew something wasn't right and he felt like a prick for blatantly lying to her.

But he didn't have time to deal with that issue right now. Time to triage the priority list. He needed to find a dealer in the city and take his chances with a scumbag he didn't know.

Yay. Being a drug addict was fun, said no one ever.

But all cities were the same. When you had a problem like this, you learned how to recognize the signs that led to what you were looking for.

His preference was a white-collar-trust-fund brat who sold pharmaceuticals on the side, but he didn't have time to hang around a college campus or trendy bar so he'd have to go for the low-hanging fruit, which meant the seedy part of town.

A quick look at a map on his phone revealed some options within a short enough driving radius.

He slowly cruised the streets, his gaze peeled for the telltale signs of a drug dealer waiting to snag someone looking to score.

Xander felt dirty all over but he didn't have the luxury of dignity, not with the clock ticking and his detox in full swing.

His stomach was already starting to rebel, threatening to unload the coffee he'd downed that morning.

After about fifteen minutes, he saw someone with potential.

Xander parked down a side street and jogged over to the young man slouched against the brownstone stairwell.

The kid had shifty shark eyes, a lanky build and a jaded vibe about him that said he'd seen too much, too soon, which had taught him life was about the hustle.

Yeah, he'd do.

"You lost?" the kid asked, sizing him up as quickly as Xander had sized him. "Or are you a cop?"

"Not a cop. Far from it. You carrying?" he asked.

"Carrying what?"

Xander didn't have time to play this game. "I'm looking for Oxy. You got some?"

"I don't know what you're talking about."

Xander gritted his teeth and pulled a wad of cash. "This jog your memory?"

The slow spread of the kid's smile told him it did. "How much you need, big man?" he asked, coy. "You got more of that kind of wad in your pocket?"

"I got enough to buy if you've got some."

"Yeah, I've got some. Quality stuff, too."

"I want the real deal, not some cooked-up generic that some amateur whipped up in his kitchen."

"Cool your jets. I got you," the kid assured Xander. "But I don't have it here. That kind of product I keep elsewhere. You gotta follow me."

No, that wasn't going to happen. He shook his head. "No, I'll wait here. You get the meds and bring it to me."

"That ain't how it works," the kid said. "Either you want the product or not. No sweat off my balls if you don't get your fix and by the looks of you…shit's about to get real ugly, fast."

Xander pressed his lips, hating that his addiction was showing so easily. He could feel the sweat on his skin and he could imagine how pasty and pale he was starting to look as his body fought against the detox. He grabbed the kid by the shirt and yanked him up. "Look, I don't have time for your thug-life crap. I know you think you're gonna roll me for my wad but that ain't happening. If you think you and your crew can take me on, you're mistaken. I take bigger shits than you on the daily and I'll wipe my ass with your face if you try anything. You feelin' me?" Xander released the kid with a jerk. "Now, go get the damn Oxy and bring it to me."

The kid shook off Xander's touch and straightened his shirt with a scowl. "Calm yourself, bro. I ain't trying no shit. This place crawls with cops. I gotta protect myself."

"Sure you do," Xander responded, jerking his head. "Go."

The kid scuttled off, leaving Xander alone to face the curious stares and hostile vibe from the locals. Every city had their cast of characters and it was getting too easy to pick out the ones up to no good. That probably included him.

He was a damn hypocrite. If Scarlett could see him right now—twitchy, sweating like a pig, ready to throw up—yeah, real attractive.

Xander leaned against the stairwell, staying sharp, even though it was an effort to keep from putting a bullet in his own head just to stop the merry-go-round he'd unwittingly hopped onto.

It's funny how people lied to themselves, saying they had a handle on things when they really didn't, and then something happened, bringing everything into sharp focus, but it was too late to fix the problem.

Yeah, that was drug addiction.

He'd watched plenty of buddies lose their shit to cocaine and heroin but he never really thought about prescription meds becoming a problem.

Wellll hello, problem.

The day of the bombing, his back had been jacked up from the plane ride. Usually they had a day to recover from travel but not that day. It was supposed to be an easy detail so it made sense to get in, do the job, leave.

But he'd barely been able to walk off the plane without crumpling and he'd popped one too many pills too close together. By the time they'd reached the amphitheater, he'd been high as a kite but he'd become a master at hiding how out of it he was.

He remembered breaking off to find a spot to chill for a minute and then he remembered the loud boom, shrapnel slicing into his cheek and a general sense of WTF flooding his panicked brain.

Scrambling to his feet, he met up with his team, told a flat-out lie as to where he'd been and then after the appropriate security protocols and follow up, Red Wolf had packed up and returned to headquarters.

He'd mistakenly thought his guilt had been the only thing he was going to have to deal with.

Nope.

Being framed and set up had been a nice cherry on top of a shit sundae.

Speaking of a shit sundae...

The kid returned, pulling a baggie with the meds from his grimy pocket. Xander did a quick look to check for the pharmaceutical stamp on the pills and then gave the kid the cash. "Thanks," he muttered, stashing the drugs in his jacket pocket, ready to bolt. But before he returned to his car, he said to the kid, "I know you won't take my advice but get out of this lifestyle, man. This road leads to one place and it ain't good."

"Coming from a junkie like you, I'll really take that advice to heart," the kid quipped with a sardonic grin.

When Xander narrowed his gaze, the kid added with a shrug, "Just keepin' it real, dawg."

Xander backed away, shaking his head. What the hell was he doing giving advice? No one should ever listen to advice from him.

All he was good at was blowing shit up, ruining lives and making bad choices.

Chapter 13

Scarlett was a terrible liar so she decided to forgo any deep subterfuge when she walked into Williams's office.

She was going to come at him from the Red Wolf angle because she had a vested interest in discovering what had happened that day with McQuarry.

A sharply dressed secretary led Scarlett into Senator Williams's office. She'd been in many politician's offices and they all seemed to use the same decorator. The room was awash in navy blues and burgundy—basically, strong manly colors, no matter their gender.

Williams, an older man in good shape, gestured from his executive chair. "Please, come in. Pleasure to meet you. I wish it was under different circumstances," he said, extending a hand.

Scarlett indulged in a brief handshake. "Thanks for

meeting with me. I really appreciate the time you're taking out of your busy schedule. I just want to come out and say that Red Wolf is beyond embarrassed that something of this magnitude happened on our watch."

Williams waved off her apology. "No need to take that on. Sometimes you can't account for every detail. Who knew that one of your own was so damaged."

Scarlett chose to let that comment slide. "Can you walk me through some of the backstory between you and McQuarry? I feel that would be helpful in our investigation."

Williams settled into his chair with an expectant expression. "What would you like to know?"

She drew a deep breath and decided to go for it. No time for polite dancing around the issue. "I've recently learned that you weren't on board with the Wakefield deal McQuarry was brokering. I'm curious…why not?"

Williams took a moment to consider his answer, then said, "It's no secret I was against the Wakefield deal. While on the surface bringing more industry into the state is good because it creates jobs and stimulates the economy, it is my belief we need to be smart about who we choose to do business with."

"Of course," she murmured in agreement. "And you didn't feel Wakefield was a good investment?"

"May I be frank?"

"Please do."

"I didn't like the idea of doing business with a company with a long and sordid history of environmental sanctions. There's a reason Wakefield picked up and left the United States for their industrial and manufacturing needs and I'll just leave it at that. My constituents deserve more than a politician who is only looking at the bottom line. Quality of life is a major component in the health and happiness of voters."

"Were you aware that McQuarry was going to profit from closing the Wakefield deal?"

Williams laughed. "Of course I knew. You and I both know that backdoor deals happen all the time with politics. I'm not going to be able to stop that and neither are you, but my opposition to Wakefield had nothing to do with McQuarry benefiting from the deal."

"So you're saying your only concern was for the environmental issues that Wakefield presented if they chose to set up shop in Oklahoma?"

"Of course."

Scarlett wasn't sure she bought that but so far Williams had done a very good job appearing earnest and sincere. However, the mark of a talented politician was being able to seamlessly hide their true colors without batting an eye.

"Is there anyone you can think of who would want to hurt McQuarry?"

"We all have enemies—enemies that we are aware of and enemies that we aren't. I'm sure McQuarry had a few. However, I thought it was a pretty open-and-shut case that your man was the one who set the bomb so I'm not sure where these questions are going."

"That's certainly a theory but there are details that don't add up. I know my team member better than anyone and it's a hard pill to swallow that Xander Scott would've hurt civilians even if he had a beef against McQuarry, which he didn't. He didn't even know McQuarry until that day."

Williams paused, tapping his finger lightly on the desktop. "Well, the evidence speaks for itself from what I hear."

"And what evidence is that, exactly?" Scarlett asked, curious to know who was leaking information to Williams and for what purpose. "Would you care to share your source?"

Williams shook his head. "I don't think that would be wise. But I have it on good authority that Xander Scott's DNA was found on the plastic explosives that blew up the amphitheater. Hard to argue with science."

"You're right about that. Science is hard to refute, however, sometimes we have to look at motive as well. Xander literally had no reason to hurt McQuarry. However, McQuarry was near to closing a deal that would have put millions in his pocket simply for facilitating. You and Sheffton were quick to shut that deal down."

"For reasons I've already disclosed," Williams reminded her.

"Yes, but according to Clara McQuarry, in spite of your assurances, you were pretty angry when you weren't included in the payout."

She was playing with fire. She didn't have time to softball these questions but she tried to seem less accusatory.

"I don't mean to be offensive but my man's life is on the line. If he's guilty, I'll be the first to bring him in. But if he's not and someone else is trying to pin McQuarry's murder on him, I'll do whatever I have to to bring that son-of-a-bitch down."

Williams shifted in his chair, visibly uncomfortable. "I'm not really sure what you're implying."

"I'm not implying anything. I'm asking, is McQuarry's widow lying to me? And if she is, why? Clara McQuarry had no reason to want her husband dead because if her husband was getting that payout, she was, too. However, both you and Sheffton had reason to care if McQuarry was able to close the deal with Wakefield."

Williams's strained chuckle was a warning but she couldn't back down now. "I have to tell you, I don't appreciate your tone and I don't appreciate the implication that I had anything to do with McQuarry's death," he said. "Yes, we were on opposite sides of the Wakefield issue but I didn't want him dead. Wakefield was a bad deal. Plain and simple. It doesn't take a genius to see that wherever Wakefield sets up shop, cancer rates skyrocket. It's my job to look out for my constituents, and that's a job I take seriously. McQuarry's dying was a tragedy, but axing the Wakefield deal was the right thing to do and I won't apologize for it."

Scarlett sensed a certain level of truth from Williams on that score. While it was certainly a good thing that Williams didn't appear to be dirty, it put them back at the drawing board and that made the panic in her chest flutter a little bit more desperately.

"I apologize if I've offended you. I'm just trying to get to the bottom of this. My team member's life depends on it."

Williams seemed to understand. "I don't begrudge you your attempts to clear your man's name, but at the end of the day you have to look at cold hard facts. Xander Scott's DNA was on the explosives. Unless you can find a reason why someone would want to frame him, sometimes if it walks and talks like a duck, it is a duck."

She knew that, but she still wasn't convinced that she was looking at a duck. Or was she? She didn't know. Right now, everything was jumbled in her head.

She'd already lost her objectivity—that was clear when she'd jumped on the plane and hadn't put handcuffs on Xander as soon as she'd seen him. But just as her instincts were telling her that Xander was lying to her about something, they were also saying that Xander was innocent of McQuarry's death.

"Just playing the devil's advocate, let's pretend for a second that Xander's DNA hadn't been found at the crime scene. Who in your estimation had a reason to see McQuarry die? And in such a public venue. Honestly, if somebody had wanted him dead, wouldn't it have been easier and cleaner to just put a bullet in his head while he was sleeping?"

"Certainly. However doing it in a public venue drew attention—made a statement, wouldn't you say?"

"And who would want to make that statement? McQuarry had to have pissed someone off big-time in order to compel someone to make that big of a statement."

Williams nodded. "I can tell you it wasn't me. I'm a lot of things but I'm not a murderer."

"Why did McQuarry's widow think you wanted a piece of the Wakefield pie?" she asked.

Williams sighed. "Clara is a nice lady but she has her own issues. Unlike McQuarry I don't run around on my wife. My wife has been my partner and my rock since the day we married and I wouldn't do anything to jeopardize that. Clara McQuarry made a pass at me and I tried to gently let her down but she didn't take kindly to my rejection. She's been on the warpath against me since then."

Beware the wrath of a scorned woman. "So you're

saying that Clara threw you under the bus because she was miffed at being rejected?"

"Clara can be a petty woman," Williams said. "I'm just thankful my wife never bought into the nonsense she was trying to spread around as fact."

Another dead end. Scarlett resisted the urge to groan with despair. Why was every lead turning out to be crap? So far, all they'd discovered was that McQuarry was a self-serving, philandering asshole with a fluid sense of sexuality.

A fluid sense of sexuality… Scarlett straightened. "So you knew about McQuarry's indiscretions?"

Williams cast a patronizing look her way. "Everyone knew about Ken's wandering eye. He didn't try to hide it very well."

"He and Holbert were pretty open about their affair?"

"Not open, but not secret. Does that make sense?"

Not really, but that's not what she was most interested in. "How about his other lover? His *male* lover. Did anyone know about that relationship?"

Williams didn't want to answer. So it was clearly business as usual when McQuarry was banging the hot female intern but nobody wanted to talk about the man McQuarry was doing after hours, too.

"I know whoever it was, was presumably a high-ranking official. I just need a name."

"That's a tree you don't want to bark up," Williams warned, shaking his head. "Trust me when I say, even if that rumor was true, he didn't kill McQuarry."

Then why was everyone protecting him?

"I just need a name," she repeated, an excited tingle starting in her stomach. "Please."

"I'm sorry. I can't do that. Besides, I'm sure it was all rumors and gossip and there's no point in dragging a good man's name through the mud when he's no longer here to defend himself."

"Were you and McQuarry friends?"

"No, but we weren't enemies, either. Colleagues with a professional understanding. McQuarry was affable, charming and, ultimately, greedy but overall, a good man. Now if there aren't any more questions…." Williams rose politely. "I have another appointment."

The window of opportunity had closed. Williams wasn't going to tell her anything more about McQuarry's secret lover, even though he damn well knew whom it'd been.

Well, shit.

"Thank you for your time," she murmured, letting herself out and quickly hailing a cab.

They needed to find the identity of McQuarry's mystery lover—fast.

Sitting in his parked car, Xander closed his eyes, willing the meds to work fast. The familiar rush of euphoria followed by the drugging lethargy was a sweet hell that he couldn't seem to stop craving.

The shame, the guilt, the anger—those emotions were in there, too—but the drug managed to dull the sharp edges long enough for a moment of relief.

What felt like minutes had actually turned into an hour and when Xander finally roused himself out of the stupor, he realized in a panic he'd been out for too long. He fumbled with his cell and saw three missed calls from Scarlett.

Shit. Starting the car, he eased out of the alley and

hit the street, his heart hammering. He had nothing to go on. He'd spent too much time trying to score to chase down any leads on Wakefield like he'd promised Scarlett.

Sweat beaded his brow as he swore under his breath. At this point, Scarlett was doing all the heavy lifting and Xander felt like a worthless chump.

He reached for his cell but he hit a bump in the road and his cell bounced off the passenger seat and fell onto the floor.

Damn it.

He'd just have to wait to talk to Scarlett when he got back to the motel, but he hated that she'd called three times and he'd been out of his head.

Worry that something had gone wrong ate at him, but he knew Scarlett was a badass and could likely handle any contingency with extreme prejudice.

Hell, the woman could break a man's hand in five places with one quick snap of her wrist... Yeah, she could handle herself.

He pulled into the motel parking lot and went quickly to their room. Scarlett looked up with a narrowed gaze as he entered. "I tried calling you three times," she said flatly.

"Sorry, I was out roaming the streets," he said, which was true. "I left my phone in the car."

"Why would you do that?" she asked, irritated. "Not only is that irresponsible, it doesn't make sense."

"I thought I had my phone in my pocket but I didn't. By the time I figured out that I'd left the phone in the car, I was blocks away. Are you going to grill me for being distracted, TL? Or are we going to talk about your meeting with Williams?"

Scarlett seemed to recognize the logic in his statement and grudgingly continued. "Williams is clean but he knows who McQuarry was sleeping with...and he's not talking."

What started out as a flicker of hope died a quick death. "Why wouldn't he share?"

"I don't know. It could be that he doesn't want to believe that McQuarry was bisexual, or he's protecting the man McQuarry was sleeping with. Either way, he's not budging."

"But you think Williams is clean?"

"Yeah," she answered, her mouth tightening to a grim line. "As much as I wanted to have something else to go on... Williams was another dead end."

"I'm getting pretty sick and tired of this bullshit," he admitted. He sank down on the bed to yank his shoes off. "What the hell are we doing? We're not investigators... We're soldiers-for-hire. Maybe we don't know how to ask the right questions. Hell, maybe I ought to just say screw it and turn myself in. I don't want you getting caught in my mess."

Scarlett frowned. "We're not quitting. The answer is out there and we'll find it. Besides, Conrad is an investigator and he'll come through with something we can use."

"The same man who is now charged with hunting me down? Yeah, I wouldn't expect much more help from him unless it's the gift of metal bracelets."

"Connie will do what he can from his end," Scarlett said. "But we need to keep the faith and do what we can on ours."

"And what would that be?" he asked with a touch of sarcasm. "Because right now I don't have much faith to spare. At some point, we'll have to admit defeat. Whoever wanted McQuarry dead did their homework and we're not likely to find a bread crumb."

"Well, you came back a ray of sunshine, didn't you?" Scarlett said with a hard scowl. "Get yourself together. I don't have time for whiny-man bullshit."

"It's not bullshit—it's reality. We've got nothing."

Scarlett fell silent. She couldn't argue facts. Their leads had dried to nothing and they had zero chance of finding who McQuarry's secret lover was before the FBI managed to lock on to their location and haul Xander in on trumped-up charges.

Orange had never been his color, but he supposed he'd better get used to the idea because the promise of a lengthy prison sentence was looming.

Xander yanked his shirt off and tossed it. "I need to shower," he muttered, disappearing into the bathroom so he could get his head on straight.

Turning the water on, he stripped and climbed into the hot spray. The motel was a dump but the water pressure was surprisingly good. He stood under the pelting water for a long moment, letting it scald his skin. If only he could wash away the stain of his addiction, none of this would be happening.

If he hadn't been looped out of his gourd, he would've been sharp enough to see someone rigging the amphitheater. He would've been able to stop the senseless murder of innocent civilians.

But that's not what had happened, and he couldn't change that—no matter how many hot showers he took.

Chapter 14

Scarlett had never seen Xander so broken down. Xander was the perennial smart-ass, the one who always had a joke or a flippant comment to share.

He didn't lose hope or sink into despair.

Hell, Xander went high-flying into terrible odds with a wink and a robust *huzzah*!

She didn't recognize the beaten-down man Xander was becoming. To even suggest turning himself in? That comment alone showed he wasn't thinking clearly.

There was something vulnerable about Xander that she'd never seen before and it tugged at a secret, private place she didn't like to give much light.

Her phone buzzed but she ignored it. She knew what she wanted to do and if she didn't do it right now, she'd talk herself out of it. It was something they both needed right now.

Zak or Conrad could leave a message. Whatever they had to say could wait an hour.

Pulling her shirt free, she shimmied out of her jeans and walked naked into the steamy bathroom. She pushed aside the flimsy plastic shower curtain to find Xander in all his magnificent, scarred-up glory, hands braced against the wall, standing beneath the water.

She stepped into the shower and gently slid her hands up his back, pausing to trace each scar left behind from past injuries before pressing her lips to the raised skin.

Xander stilled at the touch of her lips, his body tensing.

Scarlett thrilled at the power bunching beneath his skin, reminding her of how easily this man could bend and twist her into a sexual pretzel.

"What are you doing?" he asked quietly.

"What we both need."

Xander turned, shielding her from the spray. His gaze lit up with a hard light and an expression of need so stark it took her breath away. No man had ever looked at her the way Xander did—as if she were necessary for his very breath—and her knees threatened to buckle.

"Are you sure?" he asked.

In response, she rose on her toes and pulled him closer, brushing her lips across his, her tongue darting in invitation. He answered without hesitation, drawing her into the cove of his embrace, lifting her up and holding her against his body, his hands sliding down to grip her ass.

"God, Scarlett," he groaned, their bodies fitting together like puzzle pieces. Their tongues twisted against one another as the heat in the shower intensified. Steam swirled around them as they kissed, and Scarlett was lost in the sensation of skin against skin until Xander pulled away, a look of worry crossing his features. "Are you sure about this? Why'd you change your mind?"

Scarlett chuckled. "Are you really going to look a gift horse in the mouth right now? Don't worry. I want this." To illustrate, she pulled his mouth back to hers and kissed him deeply while her free hand reached down to firmly clasp his hardened shaft. She thrilled at his sharp intake of breath when she tightened her grip as she warned in a silky tone, "If you're getting cold feet, you should tell me now."

"There's nothing cold about my body right this second," he growled against her mouth, "And yeah, this is happening."

She sucked in a wild breath as he flipped her around, his hands coming up to fill his palms with her generous breasts, teasing her nipples with a soft touch for such a big hardened man.

She wanted to feel him inside her, to lose herself in the simple pleasure of being filled by a man who knew how to make a woman squirm.

Scarlett already knew from experience that Xander knew what he was doing and she was impatient to get on with it, even though shower sex wasn't her favorite.

With Xander, that could change.

Xander paused long enough to direct the spray away from their bodies and then turned her around, gently pushing her against the wall and spreading her legs. She bit her bottom lip against the smile threatening to happen as he knelt down and buried his face between her thighs. Scarlett closed her eyes and gripped the shower curtain rod for support with one hand and the handicapped access rod with the other, lifting her leg to give him better access.

His tongue made a slow, sensual slide in the most intimate places and he followed it with his fingers, massaging and pressing in all the right spots. Her nipples pearled as her breath quickened and within moments, Xander had her shaking. Her knees weakened as a sweet orgasm washed over her, a nice primer for what would come later.

He rose and kissed her, swallowing his name on her breath as pleasure continued to shimmy through her body.

He shut the water off and they climbed from the shower, wrapping scratchy cheap towels around themselves as they fell onto the bed. "We're going to leave a wet spot," Scarlett warned with a playful smile.

"Hell, yes, we are," he said, climbing her body to gaze into her eyes. She could lose herself in those incredible hazel eyes. There was an air of mystery that clung to Xander and reflected in his stare. Sometimes his eyes were green, other times a murky blue with mottled bits of brown flecks added to the mix. He was a beautiful, dangerous man and he turned her crank in ways no one ever had before, which made him the worst possible option in her love life.

But then that was her MO—find the worst guy in the bar and then screw his brains out because she wasn't about forever, just for the night.

Except with Xander. God, she wanted more than a night, more than a few nights and that scared her.

But she wasn't going to think of that right now.

Xander rolled her on top and she gladly straddled

those hips, loving how his dark hair traveled from his bare chest and narrowed to a single trail leading to his groin. She also loved that he didn't shave like some men. She preferred her lovers to be untamed, not manicured and trimmed like androgynous models.

Sinking onto his shaft, she closed her eyes on a groan as pleasure rippled through her. Scarlett took a greedy moment to thoroughly enjoy the sensation of being impaled on his solid length before she began grinding her hips, finding the rhythm that would send her into orbit for a second time.

Xander anchored his hands on her hips, guiding as he thrust against her motions, driving himself deeper with each movement.

She hated clichéd sayings but there was sexual poetry in the way their bodies fit together as if made for one another.

God, so dangerous. Everything about Xander was an exercise in total personal annihilation and it was exhilarating.

As she found her climax, she fell forward, shuddering and crying out, totally weak for a blessed moment.

But Xander hadn't found his and quickly flipped her onto her stomach before driving himself back in, losing himself in hard, savage thrusts that sent her hurtling toward another release.

Gasping, almost begging for mercy, she rode the wave as her orgasm crashed all around her and she briefly lost all sense of time and reason.

A good orgasm was the cure to overthinking because it stalled all thought for a blessed heartbeat.

In that heartbeat, they weren't on the run, breaking rules and heading toward certain death—they were just two people lost in the pleasure that two human beings could create with one another and it was heaven.

After a long moment, trying to catch her breath, she slowly roused herself to roll to her back, staring at the water-damaged ceiling, realizing that there was no way they could stuff the genie back in the bottle this time.

No way in hell.

And Xander knew it, too.

Xander tried to catch his breath as his heart hammered and his brain began to operate again.

He shouldn't have caved.

It wasn't right.

But he'd wanted to feel Scarlett in his arms again; it was all he'd been able to think about since that first night but he'd known it wasn't going to happen.

Before getting framed and going on the run, Xander would've happily enjoyed an illicit relationship with his TL but that was child's play in comparison to the obstacles in their way now.

And what had changed? Scarlett had been pretty clear in her stand that she wasn't going to sleep with him again.

Of course, her change of heart would have to happen on the same day that he felt like a total piece of lying shit.

"Why do I get the feeling you're going all deep and philosophical on me?" Scarlett teased, looking like a beautiful, savage warrior goddess with her sex-mussed red hair and flushed cheeks. She rolled to her side and nudged his shoulder. "If I promise to respect you in the morning, will that make you feel better?"

He chuckled. "Only if you buy me breakfast, too."

"So much for the rumor that you were a cheap date," she grumbled but followed with a genuine smile. "The sex was fantastic, by the way. And you were totally right—I needed that." She sighed happily and returned to her back, her near-perfect breasts inviting his mouth for some more playtime. "Sometimes I wish I understood why I'm such a stickler for the rules. Breaking the rules is so much more fun."

"Yeah, until you find yourself on the run, holed up in a shitty motel, chasing down impossible leads that inevitably turn out to be nothing."

Her smile faded and she sat up, grabbing her shirt to slip it over her head. "Something is going to shake out," she assured him, concern wrinkling her brow. "You can't lose faith."

"Faith is something I've never had in my supply shed."

"Well, you'd better find some because I can't carry you the whole way," she said.

"I don't want you to carry me," he said. "I didn't want you to stay at all. If you were smart, you'd distance yourself from me now. Hell, you should've done that from the start."

"Where's this coming from? Where the hell did you go this afternoon? You came back different."

He wanted to sink to his knees and confess every dirty little secret he was harboring in his dark heart, but he couldn't do that and it was tearing him in two. God, when did he turn into such a coward?

Two tours in Iraq and Afghanistan, shot innumerable times during his tenure as a military man, and yet he'd never been more afraid than he was right now.

Wasn't sex supposed to relax you?

He felt more tightly wound than ever.

"I'm just saying you should probably walk. I don't want the responsibility of your screwed-up career because you chose to put your chips in with me. It's looking like I'm a bad bet."

"Jesus, Scott, I've never seen you so maudlin. Where's the smart-ass genius that never plays by the rules but still gets shit done? I want that guy back. This guy is a poor imitation."

Xander scooted from the bed and scooped up his jeans to slide them on. "What you see is what you get," he said, shrugging. He was being an asshole and she didn't deserve it, but he was dangerously close to spilling the beans and that wouldn't help anyone. "Look, the sex was fun but I think you were right in the first place. We probably shouldn't do that again. Messes with the natural order of things."

"You're a piece of work," Scarlett muttered, swinging her legs over the bed and snatching her own jeans. "You really are a narcissist. I feel bad for any woman who's had the misfortune of falling in love with you."

"Don't worry, honey. I don't let them get close enough to let that happen." He knew he ought to shut up but the drugs in his system had a hold of his mouth and he was on a self-destructive path. Besides, it was better for Scarlett to be free and clear of the shit storm that was coming for him. Truthfully, he didn't want Scarlett to see him run down like a dog. He already knew he wouldn't be taken into custody alive.

Maybe it was selfish of him but if he was going out, he wanted it to be on his own terms and he wouldn't put that burden on Scarlett.

So, what he was doing was a mercy.

"Call Zak and arrange transport. I really don't want you here anymore."

"Screw you."

"Look, I'm not trying to be a dick—"

"And yet, you're so naturally good at it."

"But this has made me realize that we're spinning our wheels and this only ends one way. You still have a career to save, Scarlett. My story doesn't have a pretty ending. You need to start thinking of saving yourself and stop worrying about me."

"Where did you go?" she asked, stubbornly latching on to the detail he wanted to ignore. "You came back different and now you're pushing me away."

"C'mon, Scarlett, don't make me be a total jerk. I'm trying to nicely tell you that you need to get the hell out of here because I don't want you here anymore. You're slowing me down. The answers I need aren't here in Tulsa."

"And where do you think the answers are?"

"Not here." He held his ground. "And not with you."

If his cutting remark hurt, she hid it well and he would have expected nothing less but he felt like crap for going this route.

Unfortunately, there wasn't time for playing nice.

Scarlett shook her head. "Screw you, Xander," she said, grabbing her purse and leaving, slamming the door behind her.

He sank down on the edge of the bed. The bittersweet smell of sex lingered in the musty room. It was the right decision he told himself when he was tempted to run after her.

But suddenly Scarlett was back and this time it wasn't as his pissed-off lover—it was as his TL and she meant business.

"Get your stuff. The FBI is here."

Chapter 15

She was pissed as hell—Xander's thinly veiled rejection attempt was an obvious deflection—but she didn't have the time to beat the truth out of him because the FBI had just pulled up.

It was sheer luck she'd seen them before they'd seen her. She'd have to find out later why Conrad hadn't been able to warn her first.

"They'll be at our door in less than three minutes," she said, grabbing her bag just as Xander grabbed his. They were always prepped to leave at a moment's notice, which came in handy when the law was on your tail.

"Can we make it to the car?"

"Negative."

"Borrowing a car it is then," he muttered, shouldering his bag. "Let's go."

They slipped out, went in the opposite direction of their rental and the agents beginning to make their way toward the room, quietly hot-wired a newer sedan and left the motel in the rearview mirror.

As soon as they hit the freeway, Xander said, "I can drop you off at a bus station." Scarlett responded by punching him in the leg hard enough to cause a charley horse. He grunted but otherwise didn't give away that her punch had to have hurt. "I'll take that as a no."

"You're damn right it's a no and since we're on the road and I have a captive audience, your little act back at the motel was total bullshit and I didn't buy any of it."

Xander surprised her with silence.

"Look, whatever you're hiding, I can deal with, okay? But I can't deal with this lying, deflective crap. Are we clear?"

"Did it occur to you that I have a very good reason for being private about what I'm going through? Maybe I just don't want to share and I'm having a hard time dealing with the fact that I'm likely going to eat shit on this situation because luck is definitely not on my side. Maybe I don't want an audience to what is going to be the worst moment of my life."

"Boo-freaking-hoo. Cry me a river. So you've had a bad hand dealt to you. That's when you need your friends the most and you don't push them away, jackass."

"Are you my friend, Scarlett?" he shot back. "Because I'm a little confused as to what we are."

He had a point. They'd blurred lines and that was something that made for discomfiting times for people like Xander and Scarlett who appreciated the symmetry of rules and tradition. "I don't know what we are," she shot back truthfully. "But I know I'm not about to let you face this storm alone. I believe you're innocent and I'm going to fight alongside you until we prove it."

"That's just it, Scarlett, what if we can't prove it? The end result will be the same, except, it'll be two careers instead of one being trashed."

She refused to listen to his reasons, even if they were semi-valid. If she dug too deep into her motivation, she might find something scarier than the threat of a federal prison sentence.

For now, she was content with her mission objective—prove Xander's innocence and leave it at that.

"One crisis at a time," she said, bolstering her own argument. "Don't go accepting defeat before we've exhausted all options."

"That's just it. We have."

"No, we haven't. We need to find out who McQuarry was sleeping with on the side. Once we find out who he was banging—and who Williams was protecting—I think our luck will turn."

"Oh, that's all we need? Why didn't you say so in the beginning?" Xander said with a derisive chuckle. "And here I thought it was going to be something difficult to find."

"Damn it, Xander, are you going to be a giant wet blanket or are you going to actually use that brain of yours and think of solutions? I've never seen you act like such a whiny baby. Remind me to never call you if I'm ever on the run from the FBI."

That actually made him laugh and his laughter broke the tension between them.

God, she was glad.

She didn't like being on the outs with Xander. She'd long since lost her objectivity, which was a bigger problem than she wanted to admit, but she couldn't let one of her team go to prison for a crime they hadn't committed.

End of story.

At least that was the end of the story for now.

"We need to ditch this car and get a new one," Scarlett said. "They'll have an APB on the plates as soon as they discover it's been stolen."

"Roger that." Xander paused, thinking, then said, "You think Williams knows who McQuarry was seeing on the super down low?"

"Yeah," she answered, "But he's not talking."

"Correction—he didn't want to talk to you."

She barked a short laugh. "And you think he's going to want to talk to you?"

"Well, I find people are more inclined to spill their guts when they have a gun pointed at their head."

Scarlett narrowed her gaze. "True, but do you think that's wise? To attack a US senator? Don't you think you have enough charges sitting on your docket?"

"Hey, the more the merrier," Xander returned. "Besides, time to get reckless. Go big or go to the big house, where in spite of what the media would have you believe, is not all free cable and lobster dinners and much more like don't drop the soap or you'll be someone's bitch."

Scarlett bit back a smile. Maybe Xander was right. They'd been playing it safe, trying to do everything the nice and tidy way. But things were already messy as shit in this kitchen so at this point, breaking a few eggs probably wasn't going to make things worse.

"Fine. Let's pay the good senator a visit. Take the next exit."

Within an hour, they were making their way into the senator's house. In an unexpected stroke of good luck, Williams was alone—and enjoying what appeared to be very expensive scotch in his living room while watching reruns of *Jeopardy* in his silk puppy-print pajamas.

Here goes nothing...

The plan was for Scarlett to hang back in the shadows while Xander subdued the senator. There was no need for the senator to know that Xander wasn't acting alone. If things ended up going south, Scarlett could still walk away from the nightmare, which was something Xander was adamant about.

Within seconds, Xander had Williams tied tight and then motioned for Scarlett to enter the room, which she did with great stealth, hanging behind the senator so he couldn't see her. Her job was to act as a silent lookout and to let Xander handle the interrogation.

"I have money," Williams said, his voice quivering with fear, visibly shaking. "Whatever you want... I can get it for you. *Please*. Don't kill me."

"Look, Senator, I'm going to cut to the chase. I'm Xander Scott, the man being framed for McQuarry's murder and I'm damn tired of being accused of something I didn't do."

Williams cocked his head to the side, confused as he focused his gaze more intently. "Xander Scott... I don't understand... What do you want with me?" he asked.

"I need answers and I think you've got what I'm looking for."

"You're in some serious trouble, son. Don't make

things worse. Turn yourself in. Let the law work. If you're innocent, the evidence will exonerate you."

"The evidence has been jerry-rigged to point straight at me, even though there's no reason why I'd have motive to kill McQuarry, much less innocent people. Whoever did this wanted to make sure McQuarry remained silent about something and I think you know who wanted McQuarry to shut his piehole forever."

Williams sputtered. "Me? How would I know? We weren't friends, only colleagues. I didn't poke around in his personal life."

"But everyone knows politics is incestuous, and whether or not you were purposefully listening to gossip, you still heard it. I need to know who McQuarry was banging on the down low and you're going to tell me."

"I already told your friend, I'm not about to smear the name of a good man based on flimsy, mean-spirited gossip."

"And under normal circumstances, I'd consider that right neighborly of you but right now I couldn't give a shit about your ethics because I need a name and I'm not leaving until I get one."

"Son—"

"I'm not your son and quit acting like you care." Xander cut the senator's patronizing statement off. He was serious about leaving with information, one way or another. "I want a name."

True nervousness replaced the senator's bluster. "I can't."

"And why is that?" When Williams remained silent, Xander shared a look with Scarlett. Was Williams protecting the identity of McQuarry's lover out of loyalty or fear? Xander nudged Williams's foot with his booted one. "Were you lovers, too? Is that what this is about?"

Williams's face turned florid. "I am not gay."

"No shame, Senator. C'mon, out with it. Who was McQuarry sleeping with?"

"I support gay rights and I'm not homophobic, but I already told your friend to stop barking up this tree… It's dangerous for everyone. I have a family to protect."

Fear kept Williams silent. *Interesting.*

Xander leaned forward to whisper in Williams's ear. "What makes you think *I'm* not dangerous?" Xander trailed the tip of his gun down Williams's cheek, giving the man time to realize what a precarious position he was in. "Here's the situation, Senator. I've been framed for a job I didn't do and my life is pretty much in the shitter right now after serving my country and the thanks I've gotten for my sacrifice has been less than encouraging. If I were to give the US government a Yelp review, it would be scathing right about now and I'm not feeling particularly forgiving. So I don't give a shit about your family or the fact that you're scared of whoever you're trying to protect because I'm leaving with a name, one way or another. Are you feeling me?"

"Thank you for your service," Williams whispered, swallowing hard. "I have the utmost respect for our servicemen and women."

"Yeah? Prove it. Give me a damn name."

"Can't you understand that I *can't*?"

Xander didn't have time to care about Williams's problems. "A name."

"It's pure gossip," Williams tried to say, shaking his head. "But gossip of this nature can ruin careers and some people will do anything to protect what they've spent a lifetime building. This person has the resources to make problems go away."

"Was McQuarry shacking up with the Illuminati?" he joked, half serious but curious as hell as to who this powerful person was that had everyone shaking in their loafers.

"Unlike the Illuminati, this man is very real."

"So give me a name and let me take my chances." When Williams remained buttoned-up and silent, Xander knew with a sinking heart that Williams would rather eat a bullet than face the potential wrath of whomever he was protecting. He really didn't want to shoot an old man in puppy pajamas. He sighed and looked to Scarlett, shaking his head. She'd come to the same conclusion as well. "If you can't give me a name, give me a direction to head into. Look, for a politician, you seem like a decent guy. Give me a fighting chance to save my own ass before this corrupt shadowy figure manages to get away with murder."

Williams nodded, seeming to understand Xander's position. "I want to help you, I really do…"

"Then help. Pretty simple." Xander sighed dramatically, adding, "How's that saying go? 'All that is necessary for the triumph of evil is that good men do nothing.' Yeah, that seems appropriate here, right?"

That seemed to hit a chord, just as Xander had hoped it would. The thing was, Xander could sense that Williams was a good man in an arena filled with snakes. It almost made Xander feel bad for manipulating the senator, but he didn't have the luxury of a conscience right now.

"I can't give you a name but I can give you a solid lead," Williams said, relenting. "The person you're looking for is in Washington, DC, top brass. That's all I can say."

"If you're saying that McQuarry was screwing the president…"

"It's not the president," Williams said quickly. "But that's all I can say. I hope you can understand that I've given you all I can."

"Yeah, sure. I understand," he said, motioning for Scarlett to go so he could release the senator. Once Scarlett was gone, he untied the man. "Sorry we had to meet under these circumstances," Xander said, shrugging. "But being on the run and all, it's hard to make lunch reservations."

Williams rubbed at the chafing on his wrists, eyeing Xander. "I'm real sorry you got swept up in all this. McQuarry never should've played with fire, but he had a thing for anything taboo. No matter whose life was at stake, including his own, apparently."

"I'm innocent," Xander said bluntly but Williams's sad expression said it all. It didn't matter who knew that Xander hadn't planted that bomb; he was the convenient patsy and no one was willing to stand by the truth out of fear that they might face the same end as McQuarry.

"Good luck. You're in my thoughts and prayers," was all Williams could say.

With a derisive snort, Xander let himself out and joined Scarlett who had the car running and ready to go.

"Ready to get the hell out of Tulsa?"

"More than ready," Scarlett answered.

"Amen to that," he muttered. If he never set foot in Tulsa again, it would be too soon.

Chapter 16

"A grown man in puppy pajamas," Scarlett murmured, settling into her seat beside Xander on a redeye out of Tulsa. "Just because your pajamas are made of silk doesn't make it okay to put whatever print you want on them."

"I don't know. I was tempted to ask where he bought them. I thought they were pretty sweet."

Scarlett knew he was joking; Xander slept in the nude. "You're getting soft in your old age," she said, smiling. "You were never going to shoot that old man."

"Not soft, just practical," he scoffed. "Shooting people is messy work. I didn't want to deal with the spatter. Besides, as much as I hate to admit it, Williams is probably one of the good guys."

"Yeah, he seems like it. And here I thought all politicians were self-serving assholes. Now I can't just lump them all in one box. Pretty inconvenient."

"Right?" Xander agreed, shifting in his seat. "I hate coach."

Scarlett grinned. "Yeah, your long legs aren't much for economy travel. You could've sprung for first class."

"People pay attention to first-class passengers," Xander replied with a grimace. "The least amount of attention we attract, the better."

Just when she thought Xander couldn't surprise her more, he did something else to make her see him a little differently.

"You're damn smart," she said.

"Should I be insulted by the surprise in your voice?"

Ahhh, confession time. "When we first met, I thought you were like many super soldiers—capable of following orders with extreme prejudice but not a deep thinker. Since getting to know you better, I've realized that you're much more capable than I first thought."

"I'm flattered—I think."

"No, seriously, you have what it takes to be a supervisor or a team leader of your own unit if you wanted."

"I don't want," Xander returned. "Being the boss has never been on my bucket list. Too many headaches, too many responsibilities. Plus, all the admin crap gives me a gut ache."

Yeah, she could relate to that. "Paperwork is a giant drag," she agreed. "But good leaders are hard to find. Sometimes our calling comes to us when we least expect it."

"Cute," he said, dismissing her suggestion. "You might want to get some shut-eye while you can. Stepping into Washington is going to be far more dangerous than Tulsa."

And then Xander closed his eyes, prepared to follow his own advice. Within moments, he was lightly dozing.

Scarlett sighed. Why was she trying to give Xander career advice when neither of them knew if Xander was going to have a career to go back to? Maybe she just needed to believe that they were going to be successful.

She couldn't stomach the idea of Xander going to prison.

Especially for a crime he hadn't committed.

Damn corruption. Why did politicians have to be so shady?

Xander was right about Washington being a different ball game than Tulsa. There would be heightened security, more sharp-eyed law enforcement and FBI crawling all over the place.

They'd need someplace safe to hole up. Red Wolf had a few safe houses but she wasn't sure if it was wise to use them. Another shithole motel was an option, but it would only be a matter of time before the FBI found them. With all the street cams and the FBI's facial recognition software, it would be a miracle if they weren't made simply going into a McDonald's.

Aside from Conrad, her contacts in Washington were slim and she didn't want to involve anyone else in case things went sour.

She glanced at Xander. Why did men look like angels when they were asleep? Scarlett wasn't a delicate flower in her sleep. She drooled and probably snored, too. Funny, though, Xander didn't seem to mind.

Xander just curled his big arm around her waist and pulled her into the cove of his body and that's where she stayed, cozy as a bug in a rug.

And she'd never been a cuddler. *Ever.*

But somehow, being pressed against Xander was the most relaxing feeling she'd ever experienced.

They fit together. Not sure how that had happened but there was no denying it. The sex was epic—her cheeks flushed at the memory as her thighs twinged—and she didn't want to give that up.

But if Xander was found guilty? She rubbed at her temple where a headache was threatening to form. They were up against impossible odds. A sane person would walk away, cut their losses and wish Xander luck. Clearly, Scarlett was crazy because the idea of walking was anathema to her.

So that meant one thing—she had to double her efforts to find whom McQuarry had been seeing behind closed doors.

Whoever this person was, they were powerful. Powerful enough to stage a bombing and place the blame elsewhere and cruel enough to consider innocent civilians as collateral damage.

She'd seen enough war to know that men and women in power often thought little of the lives it took to achieve their objective.

Which was why she'd gotten out of the military. At least in the private sector, the job was about the money and there was no subterfuge about motivation. Politicians were loath to admit that half the time they attacked another country it was for financial gain, preferring to wrap their reasons up with patriotic causes that were really an afterthought.

Xander was right; she needed to shut her brain down and get some sleep while she could. There was no telling what was going to happen once they reached DC.

For all she knew, all hell could break loose.

* * *

They arrived in DC at four in the morning, which was a benefit because they didn't have as much traffic to deal with but it was cold and snow threatened in the forecast.

Hailing a cab, Xander decided in the short term it was best to find an out-of-the-way motel to hole up for the day until he could secure something else.

Scarlett nodded, agreeing, but they were both on edge. It was hard not to be paranoid. DC wasn't exactly criminal-on-the-run friendly.

They checked into a seedy motel on the edge of town with an ironic name, The Presidential, and after securing the room, he suggested that they catch a few more hours of sleep.

His legs were stiff from being bent in one position for four hours and his back was killing him. He went into the bathroom to wash down a few pain meds away from Scarlett's watchful eye but even as he swallowed the pills, his gut churned.

He wanted to be honest. God, if he could, he'd rather sit across from Scarlett and lay himself wide open but he couldn't afford the luxury of penance. Not yet. Maybe if this all shook out the way they were hoping, he'd get that opportunity to spill his terrible secret but for now, he had to man up and soldier on.

Love these pep talks, man. Doing great.

Yeah, sure, if by doing great, he meant he was about to fall flat on his face in a mud puddle then, yep, doing *fabulous.*

Xander splashed some water on his face to rinse away the stale airplane air and returned to find Scarlett already curled up in the bed, lightly snoring.

His breath caught in his chest. He'd never tire of seeing her in his bed. She was hard as granite and yet, she had a tender side that he'd only caught stolen glimpses of. It was the stolen moments that pulled him in harder, even though he ought to be pushing back.

If he weren't such a coward, he'd walk right now. Scarlett didn't need his problems becoming hers. He leaned against the doorjamb, watching her sleep. As much as he knew the right thing to do would be to cut her loose, he also knew he wasn't going to do it. Well, he'd already tried but she'd seen through his act and called him out on it.

Who wouldn't fall for a woman like her?

He climbed into the bed and pulled her close, loving the smell of her hair as she nestled against him in her sleep.

Who would've thought that badass Scarlett Rhodes would be his cuddle bunny?

Certainly not him.

He allowed himself this moment of simple happiness. He was starkly aware of how precarious the moment was, especially since the FBI was now actively chasing them.

Well, chasing *him*.

An urgent need to make love to Scarlett nearly had his hands moving downward but he curbed his impulse. He wasn't stupid. He knew why he felt desperate for a connection and he wasn't going to subject Scarlett to his chaotic neurosis.

He closed his eyes and forced himself to relax, to drift.

Half asleep, his mind went to Tulsa the day of the bombing. Of course, his memory was sketchy because of his stupid mistake but there had to be something he had overlooked.

Something that might help them find what they needed to bust this phony scam of a case wide open. The reality was neither he nor Scarlett were investigators—they were the hired guns—but they needed to think like detectives if they were going to come out the other side with anything worth saving.

What purpose would it serve to make a public spectacle out of closing a loose end?

Assuming that whoever was behind the bombing was the same man McQuarry had been seeing on the sly and was a powerful person in Washington, why draw attention to McQuarry's murder?

Unless he was killing two birds with one stone?

What was currently happening in world events?

Xander mentally flipped through his mental cache of details that were hitting the headlines: gun control, Russian influence on American politics, smartphones destroying kids' abilities to concentrate, street gang violence, international terrorism, the polar ice caps melting at an alarming rate... The list was endless.

But what did any of those have to do with McQuarry?

A bomb sent a message.

A bomb spread fear.

Fear caused people to react without thinking.

Creating fear was the most effective way to push an agenda that otherwise might've failed.

When the Twin Towers fell, the Patriot Act rose from the ashes like a phoenix, casting its eagle eye on the American people under the guise of offering protection against further terrorism; but in reality what it did was give the government carte blanche to spy on anyone it chose without needing proof of wrongdoing.

Bye-bye right to privacy. But hey, that's the price of safety.

And the people, still shaking from the terror of the 9/11 attacks, gladly sacrificed their freedom for the illusion of safety because, let's get real, there was nothing that could truly protect people from any and all threats.

However, people needed something to cling to and the government had been only too eager to provide that protection for the tiny price of sacrificing one right that they'd never even notice was taken.

So, if someone were trying to push an agenda what possible benefit could anyone have in creating fear in the American people, yet again?

Instability was a potent motivator.

Xander gently climbed from the bed, his mind fighting against the lethargic pull of the meds in his system.

There was something there—a tiny spark—that wouldn't let him shut down, even though he desperately wanted to close his eyes and sleep for a few more hours.

Maybe they'd been thinking too small because the idea of a bigger threat was too overwhelming.

If McQuarry had been a pawn in a dangerous game of politics, the corruption could very well go straight up the chain.

Xander shivered at the implication. Only someone with deep resources could've framed Xander so neatly, using his past against him, transposing his fingerprints onto the explosives and accomplishing his objective with so little blood on his own hands.

Xander brewed a cup of subpar coffee and slugged it

down to chase away the cobwebs in his brain. The bitter sludge made him chuckle silently. Scarlett wouldn't touch this swill. For a tough soldier, she was surprisingly picky about her coffee.

Donning his jacket, he slipped out of the motel room. He needed to poke around and Scarlett needed quality coffee. Time to do as the politicians did and kill two birds with one stone.

Chapter 17

Zak frowned at the intel in his hand, pursing his mouth at the disturbing information. CJ walked into the briefing room and caught Zak's expression.

"Did you just find out that I was right and the lunar landing was filmed in a sound stage in Anaheim?"

Zak looked up briefly. "You gotta lay off the conspiracy theories. The lunar landing is well documented."

"That's what they *want* you to believe," CJ countered with a wry grin. "Don't be a sheeple, man. The truth is out there if you look for it."

Zak groaned and shook his head, choosing instead to slide the printout toward CJ, saying, "Read this."

CJ picked up the paper and scanned the contents, his brow furrowing as he finished. "What the hell is this?"

"Scarlett told me to chase down something and I did. This is the result."

"You gonna tell Scarlett?"

"Of course. She needed the information for a reason."

"Seems kinda of messed up to be digging into his personal business when we should be trying to save his ass."

Zak nodded, feeling the same but, like Scarlett must've felt, something was off. He hated to think that Xander was lying to them all but hell, the bread crumbs were leading straight back to Xander and that didn't sit well.

"Might as well get it over with," Zak muttered, grabbing the burner to dial Scarlett. "Just like ripping a bandage off—quick and neat."

"Yeah and with it, several layers of skin and hair."

Zak agreed. "Sometimes."

Scarlett picked up on the second ring. "Yeah?" The scratch in her voice told Zak she'd been sleeping but she was instantly into work mode. "What do you got?"

"I looked into that facility you wanted me to, Crossroads Medical." He paused a beat, then said, "Yeah, so, I'll just come right out and say it… Dr. Yarrow is known for being generous with his scripts for the right price. He prescribed a pretty high dose of OxyContin almost a year ago but according to records, the last prescription Xander filled with Crossroads was four months ago."

The heavy silence that followed as Scarlett digested the information told Zak that Xander was still medicating in spite of the doctor cutting him off.

"Is he still using?" Zak asked, almost reluctant to know the answer.

"Yes."

Zak swore under his breath. "That means he's getting the drugs on the street and once you start paying for black-market pills, you're paying through the nose to get them."

CJ's expression dimmed as he followed Zak's end of the conversation, shaking his head with disappointment.

But maybe it wasn't as bad as all that. Zak said, "Look, just because he's getting the meds elsewhere doesn't mean he's an addict or anything. Legislature is cracking down on narcotic scripts and a lot of legit people are having to play fast and loose with the rules. It doesn't make Xander a bad guy. How does he seem to you? Does he act like a junkie?"

"No," she answered but there was hesitation in her tone.

"TL, now's the time for honesty. Do you think Xander is a junkie?"

This time her voice was more sure. "No, but I think he's hiding something and I think what he's hiding is his drug use."

"Well, to be fair, it's not something most people would share for funsies."

"I'm his boss. It's my job to know if one of my team members is compromised—in any way."

Zak could hear the recrimination in her tone and he knew she was beating herself up for Xander's supposed bad judgment. "You're going to have to triage this," he said. "If he doesn't seem like the drugs are affecting his reasoning skills, you got bigger problems. You can always tackle the drug issue once his ass is off the line. For now, your objective remains the same."

"If he's lying to me, it calls into question his integrity. If he could hide a drug problem from me, *from us*, what else is he hiding?"

She had a solid point, but he couldn't bring himself to believe that Xander had any part in that bombing, no matter if he were a junkie. Besides, blowing up McQuarry, literally, made no sense from Xander's side. No, the answers were elsewhere. The drug use was a personal problem—the bombing, a bigger issue.

"Do you believe that Xander could kill those innocent people?" Zak asked, going to the heart of the dilemma.

Scarlett didn't hesitate. "No."

"Then focus on clearing his name and then kick his ass later for the lying."

It was a solid plan and Scarlett agreed, promising, "I'll kick his ass so hard I'll risk losing a shoe."

"Something to look forward to," Zak said, grinning. "In the meantime, try to save his ass first."

Scarlett clicked off and Zak looked to CJ, saying, "If they manage to pull off the impossible and uncover who is actually behind all this, I almost feel sorry for the misery that Scarlett is going to rain down on Xander's head for lying to her."

CJ nodded. "Yeah, he might even wish he were in prison. At least then there'd be bars between them."

Scarlett looked up as Xander opened the motel door and walked in holding a coffee in his hand. She accepted the coffee without a word and waited for him to speak first.

"Been awake long?" he asked.

"Long enough," she answered, sipping her coffee.

"Long enough for what?"

"Long enough to get some information that I need to sort before we go any further."

Xander dropped onto the bed, spreading his hands as if he had nothing to hide. "Okay? I'm assuming this has something to do with me?" At her nod, he said, "All right, hit me."

"I'm just going to cut to the chase because we don't have time to mess around with this anymore. I asked Zak to look into something for me and he came through with some information that I need explaining."

"Okay?"

"Why'd you lie to me about your prescription?"

"I didn't," he said.

"Your last legal prescription was prescribed four months ago."

"Yeah? What's the issue?"

She pointed at the pills she knew he kept in his pocket. "Where are you getting your pills if you're not getting them legally?"

Xander opened his mouth but closed it, his lips firming as he cast his gaze to the matted motel room floor. "I, uh, get them from an acquaintance. But I told you, I'm weaning myself off. It's just taken longer than the doc was comfortable with because of all the new state regs. It's nothing."

"If it's nothing, why have you been hiding this from me?"

"Because I'm not proud of it," he admitted.

"We don't have time for your pride," Scarlett said, annoyed. "Just out with it."

"Look, I told you, I hurt myself on my own time. I didn't want to go to the Red Wolf facility because I didn't want it on my record. I wrenched my back pretty good and Dr. Yarrow prescribed some pain meds. It's not a big deal."

"It is a big deal because you've made it a big deal," she said, not budging. "Let me see if I've got the facts correct. You were cut off from your legitimate source and now you're buying your stash from a drug dealer?"

He forced a chuckle. "Sounds so sordid when you say it like that."

But she wasn't laughing. Scarlett held out her hand, demanding, "Let me see your pill bottle."

He stiffened. "Why?"

"If you've got nothing to hide, let me see."

"This is ridiculous. You're not my mother or my parole officer so let it go."

Scarlett saw the sweat beginning to build on his hairline, the fidget he was trying to contain and her misgivings grew. "Give me your pill bottle right now or I walk and I give the FBI your location."

She wasn't messing around anymore.

"I told you to walk before now," Xander said with a seemingly unconcerned shrug. "I've never asked you to stay. I mean, calling the FBI seems a little shitty but if you feel that's what you need to do—"

"Cut the crap, Xander." Scarlett slammed her fist down on the small table so hard it stung her hand. "I've proven to you that I'm on your side, but you've been lying to me about something and I think it has everything to do with these goddamn pills so just come clean!"

The tension between them grew.

"Scarlett, why can't you just let this go?" he asked with a short groan, as if her questions were inconvenient as hell, which only pissed her off more. After all she'd done for him—and continued to do—he didn't have the right to be irritated for her calling him on the carpet.

"Because I don't like being lied to," she returned with a hard look.

One way or another she was going to have the truth, even if it destroyed her faith in him.

They held each other's gaze, neither willing to back down. If Xander was thinking he could win a test of wills, he'd be sorely mistaken.

Finally, Xander rose with an expletive, shoving his hand through his hair as he paced with angry short strides. "This is bullshit and none of your damn business. Let it go."

"No."

"What do you want me to say?"

"The truth."

"What is the truth?"

Scarlett narrowed her gaze. "I'm not going to play this stupid game. You know what the truth is. Stop pussyfooting around and just spit it out."

"Fine, Scarlett." Xander stopped. "You got me. I'm a damn drug addict. Is that what you want to hear? Want to know the reason why I'm sketchy about my pill use? Because the day of the bombing I accidentally overdosed and passed out. I have no friggin' clue what happened with McQuarry because I was knocked flat-out on my ass. How's that for some friggin' truth!"

Scarlett stared, shocked. "What?" she managed, her mouth dropping open for a moment. "What do you mean? Knocked out?"

"I mean *exactly* that," he answered, his anger leaching into a flat tone as he sank back down on the bed, almost seeming defeated. "The plane ride jacked up my back and I could barely walk. It was a struggle to hide the fact that I was practically crippled. I took more pills than I should've and it knocked me out. So there's no possible way I could've pulled off the bombing because…I was dead to the world. It's a miracle I survived the blast with only a few cuts and scrapes. I was too close to the blast radius and should've been crushed by debris, but I guess my guardian angel was on-duty that day because I managed to walk away."

Scarlett couldn't believe what Xander was telling her. How had she completely missed the fact that Xander wasn't 100 percent physically? What kind of TL was she that she missed that kind of crucial detail?

Bewildered and embarrassed by her own failing, she asked with confusion, "Why'd you lie?"

"C'mon, what was I supposed to say? That I have a slight drug problem and that I shouldn't have been on the job but I was anyway because I thought I could handle myself? You and I both know how that sounds and I guess my arrogance was louder than my common sense. Plus, once I'd made my statement, I couldn't very well take it back. I had to ride it out."

"You could've told me," Scarlett countered quietly, stung that he hadn't trusted her enough to be honest.

"Scarlett, you were my boss. I didn't want anything to come back on you. Honestly, I never thought this would come back on me the way it has. If I'd known someone was going to try to frame me for the bombing, I would've come clean the minute we had a private moment but that's not how it played out and I had to roll with the cards that'd been dealt."

She could understand his reasoning and his logic

but it didn't stop the hurt. The fact that it did hurt was more troubling than Xander's confession. Why did it matter so much? She couldn't afford feelings for Xander. She was his TL. Even if he weren't being framed for murder, there was no future between them.

Swallowing the lump in her throat, she refocused. "Where did you go when I was talking to Williams?"

"You already know."

She did but she needed him to admit it. When she stubbornly held her silence, Xander sighed and said, "I knew I had to replenish my stash. I went to score but I have already made the decision to check myself into rehab or whatever else I have to do once this situation is sorted and I'm not being chased by the FBI."

"Easy to say. Why did you wait this long?"

"Arrogance, I guess. I thought I could handle it on my own. I was embarrassed. I didn't identify with a drug addict. It wasn't until I found myself supplementing on my own that I realized I had a problem and even then I thought it was manageable on my own. I was wrong."

Xander was humbling himself. It had to be excruciating for someone like him—for anyone. She couldn't imagine.

Now she had a decision to make. Trust Xander and take him at his word, even though he'd broken her trust, or simply walk because once trust was broken it was never the same.

"Xander," she murmured, exhaling a shaky breath. "This is bad."

"Why do you think I've been hiding it?"

"This only makes you look ten times more guilty."

"Trust me, I've come at this from every angle possible. If I could prove that I was passed out at the time of the bombing, I could exonerate myself but then I'd lose my job and no one would ever hire me again. If I hold to the lie that I was on the opposite side of the amphitheater when it blew, I remain a wanted man. Either choice sucks."

"Yes, but being a free man is better than an incarcerated one, even if you're unemployed, right?"

"Not for me," he answered with a definite shake of his head. "I need Red Wolf. Keeps me sane."

She understood where he was coming from and knew he spoke the truth. The reason they were so good at their jobs was because Red Wolf was practically tailored for people like them.

It wasn't as if they could take a regular civilian job and make it work.

"Is there anything else you need to spill?" she asked. "You're not a secret spy for Russia or anything are you?"

"No," he said, but a hint of that damnable grin threatened as he added, "But I guess I should come clean about coveting that ass from the very first time we met."

Scarlett didn't want to laugh but she couldn't help the smile as she grudgingly admitted, "Ditto, asshole" before settling against the chair, thinking through the situation. So, she knew Xander's dirty secret and assuming he was being completely honest this time, she had to decide whether or not to walk or keep helping him clear his name.

The odds were stacked against them—they were likely going to fail spectacularly.

And yet…she knew she wasn't going to walk.

Hell, going up against crappy odds was kinda her thing.

Besides, no one lived forever, right?

Right.

Decision made.

Chapter 18

Xander knew the minute Scarlett decided to stay. He felt the shift in the air and he didn't know whether he had the right to be grateful or if he should feel guilty, but he was definitely happy.

It was selfish of him but he didn't want her to leave. Hell, he never wanted to let her go but that was an issue for another day. For now, he just wanted to savor the moment because only God knew how long it would last.

He took a bold step toward her and when she didn't stop him, he dropped to his knees in front of her, parting her legs so he could position himself between them.

"You should've told me," Scarlett said, gazing down at him, her eyes darkening as he popped the button on her jeans and slowly unzipped them.

"I know," he acknowledged as he pressed a gentle

kiss to her exposed belly, smiling against her skin as she shivered. "What can I say? I'm an idiot."

"Yes, you are." She lifted her hips so he could shimmy her jeans down to pull them free. He pressed a trail of kisses from hipbone to hipbone before sucking at her slit through the thin cotton shield of her panties, taking great pleasure in teasing with his tongue and mouth. The impatient thrust against his mouth was exactly the encouragement he needed. Scarlett threaded her fingers through his hair and pushed his face deeper, whimpering when the tiny slip of cotton prevented his tongue from going straight to her swollen nub. "You're a tease," she growled.

He laughed and rose, pulling Scarlett with him. In a quick movement, Xander hoisted her over his shoulder like a sack of potatoes—a delicious, yummy and delectable sack of potatoes—and she yelped when he lightly smacked her perfectly sculpted ass with the flat of his palm before tossing her onto the bed.

"I've always wanted to do that," he admitted with a grin as he pulled his shirt off.

"Savor it because it's never happening again," Scarlett replied but the high flush in her cheeks told a different story.

"You are the hottest woman I've ever seen," he said, his gaze drinking in the sight as she tossed her shirt and removed her bra. Those breasts... If he weren't already as hard as a rock, he would've split in two. He could lose himself between her thighs and sleep forever beside her and be a happy man forever.

Scarlett slowly let her legs open, revealing his favorite place in the entire world. "I believe you have a job to finish," she said and his heart nearly stopped.

"Hell, yes," he said, wasting no time in burying his face between her folds, until her legs started to shake and her head to thrash as if he were exorcising a demon.

He'd never been so into a woman that he wanted her in his life on the daily.

He wanted that with Scarlett.

Helluva time to figure that out when you're on the run.

His hands shook as he levered himself above her, taking a rare moment to simply gaze down at the woman who complicated and completed his life in ways he couldn't even begin to put into words. He swallowed, loving the slight haze in her eyes, partially hidden by her half-mast lids. Her lips were parted as her tongue teased her bottom lip, inviting his mouth. How could he ignore such a sweet invite? His mouth claimed hers at the same moment that he pushed himself inside with one slow, measured motion until he was completely buried inside her hot body.

"Let's forget the world and stay here in this shitty motel, just like this," he said on a gasp, squeezing his eyes shut as Scarlett gripped him tight and pleasure cascaded though him. "I'm not going to last long if you keep doing that."

Scarlett's deep-throated laugh sent shivers walking down his back. They fit together like a custom lock and key. She grinned and said, "You mean stop doing *this*?" And the woman clenched hard, squeezing her internal muscles, clamping down around him so that he saw stars. He groaned and rose up onto his knees to toss her legs over his shoulders, bending her in half as he buried himself deeper. This time it was her turn to moan as he thrust against her and he loved every gasp.

"*Xander...*" she breathed, her nipples hardening to tiny pebbled roses, begging for his mouth but he was too close to his own release to stop to play. He rammed against her like a wild man, loving how eagerly she took everything he had to give.

And then he came hard. Losing himself like never before.

Scarlett stiffened as she found her own release. "Jesus..." the word rattled from his mouth as he withdrew and collapsed beside her, both breathing hard as they recovered.

The silence was broken only by their breaths, his mind blissfully empty for the first time since this nightmare had begun.

The weight of his secret had leached all of the happiness from his life, even when he should've been having fun. But this time had felt different, more freeing. He'd never experienced anything so wonderful.

Goddamn, he was turning into a sap but he didn't care.

Xander turned to catch Scarlett regarding him with a slow smile and a sweetness spread across his chest. He opened his mouth and she silenced him with a finger across his lips. "Don't ruin it," she advised and he nodded.

Good thinking. This was why she was the TL and not him. Instead of speaking, he pulled her into his arms and they drifted to sleep with the ease of honeymooners rather than two people on the run facing an uncertain future.

And it was pretty damn awesome.

* * *

As much as she wanted to hide in this crappy motel and avoid the problem, Scarlett wasn't hardwired to run.

Rousing herself from the bed, she went to the bathroom, washed up and emerged to find Xander awake and dressed.

Something had shifted between them but it wasn't awkward. Her heart rate quickened at the sight of Xander, the suspicious frequency enough to send warning bells clanging but she didn't want to analyze her feelings. Not right now.

Instead of talking about what was happening, she chose to focus on the case.

"I've been doing some thinking, and it occurred to me that whoever killed McQuarry wanted to make a splash, something over-the-top, and why would someone want that unless they had an agenda?"

Xander snapped his fingers, pleased with her train of thought. "I was thinking the same thing. When the Twin Towers fell, what followed immediately after under the guise of protecting the American people?"

"The Patriot Act," Scarlett answered, nodding. "Which likely never would've passed without the foundation of 9/11 to build upon."

"Exactly. So maybe McQuarry's death was secondary to the true agenda of whoever is pulling the strings."

"Something terrorist-related, I would imagine, right?"

"That was my first thought but if that were the case why would they pin the blame on an American hero? Let's get real. If they wanted to serve a terrorist angle, they would've picked a Middle Eastern patsy not a decorated white male veteran."

Xander had a point. "Okay, so perhaps stiffer laws of some sort? Deeper background checks? Maybe we should look into pending legislature and see if there's anything that sounds remotely close to what we're seeing."

"That should be easy enough," Xander said, going to her computer and handing it to her. "Just do a Google search."

Scarlett scooted onto the bed and logged in, quickly typing the search perimeters. She frowned as the results popped up. "The list is endless. It could take weeks to wade through this crap."

"Narrow the search perimeter, try using the Department of Defense in the search," Xander suggested.

Scarlett typed in the search and several pending bills popped up. One in particular caught her eye. Department of Defense Appropriations Act, H.R. 720. "Hey, this might be something," she said, paraphrasing as she skimmed the details. "Looks like a DOD spending bill that would allow organizations access to the FBI's fingerprint database with the intent of disclosing criminal records for employment or volunteer purposes."

"On the surface, seems like a good idea. Maybe that way fewer pedophiles would find their way to positions of authority with kids."

"Yeah, I agree but it's another bludgeon to right to privacy, which is something the Patriot Act has already taken a whack at."

"I don't think people care about their privacy anymore as long as they feel safe," Xander said, shrugging. "Let's keep looking."

Scarlett scanned the pending bills but nothing else popped. "H.R. 720 is essentially a spending bill, allocating more money to the department with the additional provisions provided, maybe as a sweetener."

"How so?"

Scarlett warmed to her own theory, sitting up, she said, "Look, anytime a politician comes up with a bill that requires more spending people are automatically against it, because they're tired of paying for a bloated system. However, appeal to their bleeding hearts—kids in danger, old people, et cetera—they suddenly become more forgiving, more willing to listen."

"Good point," Xander said. "And honestly, how much money could it take to make channels accessible with the right servers?"

"Exactly. Little investment for a potentially bigger reward."

Xander's wheels were turning, too. "But the only way to get the bill to pass is to create a spectacle that calls into question public safety."

"In this case, set up a scare to get the people riled up, feeling unsafe and a bill that proposes *additional* safety at the right time, and it's a sure thing."

"The only way to know if we're on the right track is to ask around but I can't exactly walk up to anyone in this town and ask them about their motivation behind H.R. 720."

Scarlett nodded. "No, but Red Wolf can. I'll send Zak and CJ."

Xander looked down at his hands. "Are you sure we should keep putting Red Wolf in the middle of this? It's bad enough that I've got you involved. I don't want Zak and CJ getting caught in the crossfire, too."

"They want to help. I couldn't tell them to back off if I wanted to. They've got just as much skin in this game."

"How so?"

"If someone had the balls to frame a highly decorated veteran working for a classified-clearance PMC, they can come after anyone. We all have a vested interest in seeing this through so that it doesn't happen to anyone else."

Scarlett knew she'd made her point when Xander nodded quietly and moved on but there was another reason none of them would walk—they were a team and they never left a man behind.

But Xander knew that, too, because she caught the sheen in his eyes before he glanced away.

"While Zak and CJ are chasing down this lead, we'll follow up the angle of McQuarry's secret lover."

"We don't even know where to start," Xander said, frustration lacing his tone.

Scarlett knew it was a shot in the dark and a wild card at best but she had a hunch.

"Let's start with the DOD," she suggested and Xander cast a curious look her way. "Secrets have a way of spilling. We just have to ask the right people the right questions," she explained with a small smile.

"The DOD…" he repeated with a quizzical smile. "And how do you suggest we get access to anyone worth talking to in that department? They've got security on top of security."

"I didn't say we'd just walk in and flash our badges, but even the DOD personnel have personal lives, right?" At Xander's slow nod, Scarlett ended with,

"Well, I'm sure there's someone out there looking for a date and I haven't had a good glass of wine in too long."

"You're going to go out on a date?"

"Undercover."

Xander scowled. "I hate this idea."

Scarlett rose and wrapped her arms around his neck. "Sometimes you have to get your hands dirty. Trust me, I can handle this."

Xander's muttered, "I know *you* can. The question is can *I*?"

His words sent a thrill straight to her heart. She laughed, kissed him hard and then went into TL mode.

They had work to do.

Chapter 19

It was the first time in a while Xander had talked to his buddies Zak and CJ and it hit him in the feels.

Using a dark-web video chat program, Xander patched in with Zak and CJ while Scarlett went off to see if her friend Conrad could help them narrow the target list from the DOD for her date.

The grainy video feed was crap but it felt good to see them again.

"Hey, jerk-face," Zak said by way of hello. "Long time no smell. How's life on the run?"

Xander gestured grandly to the shithole they were staying in and replied, "As you can see, it's the friggin' Ritz. How are you?"

"I'd be better if I wasn't running interference so that the FBI didn't catch your bony ass."

"My ass is not bony," Xander said. "Grade-A Choice

beef right there. Don't be jelly. It's not your fault you weren't graced with perfection."

CJ popped into the frame. "Hey, dickwad, TL pay you back for that whack on the head you gave her back at the warehouse? She was *pissssssed*!"

"Yeah, that was unavoidable and she understands," he said, pretty sure of himself, but the idea of Scarlett whacking him upside the head as payback once this was all said and done was a real threat. He'd think of that possibility later. "Thanks for believing that I didn't blow up McQuarry."

CJ shrugged. "No problem. We wolves gotta stick together, right?"

"Yeah," Xander agreed, but then looked to Zak with nothing but true friendship and said, "Thanks, man. I appreciate all the help. I owe you one."

"You don't owe me nothing," Zak said.

But then CJ piped in with, "Bullshit. Drinks on you when you come home," and Xander laughed.

"You got it, buddy. Full round on me. I promise."

"So how's it being locked in a room with TL 24/7?" Zak asked, half serious. "Neither one of you are the easygoing type."

"What are you talking about? I'm chill as shit," Xander disagreed. "But yeah, it's been fine. Nothing, uh, I can't handle. I mean, she snores but beyond that... Yeah, it's, uh, great." He sounded like an idiot with something to hide. Time to change the subject. "So Scarlett is going to see if her FBI buddy can get us the schematics to the Department of Defense. At this point, it's the best lead we have."

"Yeah, this case hasn't been exactly easy to chase down. I think I prefer dropping down into an Afghani war zone than all this cloak-and-dagger shit. I wasn't cut out to be a spy, that's for sure," Zak said, echoing Xander's own feelings. "Give me a gun and a target and I'll sleep like a baby at night."

"You probably shouldn't say that out loud," CJ advised in a low whisper, which was comical as shit because CJ was as crazy as a circus clown.

"So what do you think you're going to find in the DOD?" Zak asked.

"There's a pending bill that might need a little grease and we think that McQuarry's death was the grease."

"What bill?"

"H.R. 720."

Zak shook his head. "Total Greek to me. I don't follow that shit but I'll keep an ear to the ground and see if I can't find anything that shakes out."

"Thanks, man. In the meantime, Scarlett is going to go on a *date* to get intel."

"TL is going on a *date*?" CJ repeated, incredulous. "Like at a gun range or something?"

"No, at a fancy restaurant where they serve decent wine, apparently."

CJ shared a look with Zak, then asked, "Has TL ever worn a dress?"

Xander tried to remember if he'd ever seen Scarlett in a dress. He came up empty. He'd seen her in camos, jeans and a T-shirt, and even a ghillie suit but never a dress. Hell, he wasn't sure if he was ready to see her in a dress for someone else.

He tried to hide his discomfort but he wasn't a very good actor.

"You okay? She can handle herself," Zak said, misinterpreting Xander's reaction. "No one's going to get the jump on Scarlett."

Xander had no worries there. Scarlett could break a man's spine without a struggle but what if she had to play the part of an interested date? What if she had to kiss the man? Yeah, he hated that idea with a passion. He forced a smile for Zak's sake. "Yeah, sure, of course. I just hate that she has to go through this stupid farce on my account. Not used to having others fight my battles."

CJ and Zak commiserated with understanding nods. "All right, man, you sit tight, stay out of sight and let us see what we can make happen on our end. We're gonna figure this out, you'll see. Have faith, brother."

Xander nodded and clicked off, leaning back with a sigh. His gut was unsettled, churning the fast food he'd wolfed down earlier. If he managed to get through this ordeal without losing all his muscle and gaining twenty-five pounds, it would be a bigger miracle than clearing his name.

Scarlett returned, opening the door, carrying a shopping bag. He ignored the bag, knowing full well it was for her date, and said, "Did you get ahold of your FBI friend?"

"Yes, and he managed to send me the schematics. He also did me a solid and actually managed to get me a blind date with the man who might be able to give us some intel on the DOD bill."

Xander perked up. "Wow, that's definitely a solid. He must be a pretty good guy to go through all these hoops for an ex. How serious was this again?"

"I already told you, it was serious for him, not so much for me. Move on."

He knew that dance. Too many women had been on the opposite side of that equation when it came to him. Being tied down to one person… It just didn't track with his personality or his career choice.

But to hear Scarlett echoing his own situation made him realize that maybe they were too much alike to make anything real work.

Why was he even thinking about this? He needed to focus.

"What's in the bag?" he asked, deliberately changing the subject.

"Oh! Yes, check it out." Scarlett pulled the slinky black dress from the bag along with the accompanying black heels and Xander forced his expression to remain neutral. She was going to wear that sexy dress… for someone else. "What do you think?" she asked.

"I think it's…uh, great."

Scarlett laughed. "Ye of so little words. I'm going to start getting ready. I opted for an early dinner with drinks so I need to get moving."

"Drinks? Do you think that's a good idea?" Xander asked with a scowl. "Not sure mixing alcohol in an already tense situation is a recipe for success."

Scarlett leveled a pointed look his way. "This coming from the man who lied about his drug addiction and ended up getting framed for a bomb he didn't plant? Sorry, but I think your opinion on this particular matter is invalid."

Ouch. Couldn't argue with her logic. Besides, if he pushed things much further, he'd have to admit that the only reason he was throwing a fit was because he didn't like the idea of Scarlett getting dressed up for someone else.

And neither of them were ready for that level of honesty.

"Fair enough," he conceded, shrugging off his attitude for her benefit but inside he was still churning with discomfort. "Do what you think is best."

"I will." She disappeared into the bathroom and emerged a half hour later transformed into a smoking goddess with unbelievable curves. It was all he could do not to drool like a Saint Bernard.

"How do I look?"

Like a goddamn vision. He unstuck his tongue from the roof of his mouth and nodded. "Uh, good. Decent."

"Decent?" she repeated wryly. "Excellent, that was exactly what I was shooting for. Do you think if I change my earrings I might pass for slightly above average?"

He tried not to stare at the curve of her hips and the nip of her waist because he'd surely give himself away if he couldn't stop fixating on the fact that she was dressed to impress for another man. Xander cut his gaze away and pulled an earpiece from his duffel. "Make sure you wear these. They are equipped with GPS and I'll be able to hear everything that's being said."

"What else you got in that bag of tricks?" Scarlett accepted the earpiece and pushed it into place. "Did you raid the tech closet before going on the run?"

"Can't go on a picnic without a fully stocked basket," he quipped with the flash of a grin.

She chuckled, saying, "Testing, testing," and Xander gave her a thumbs-up when it came through loud and clear on his end. Her cell dinged and she checked the notification. "My Uber is here. Cross your fingers that this leads to something," she said, moving to the door, but he couldn't let her leave just yet.

"What are you doing?" she asked with a frown as he caught her arm and pulled her to him.

"Something stupid," he muttered before closing his mouth over hers, her tongue immediately darting to dance with his. They were playing with fire but he was coming to realize that he was more than willing to burn for Scarlett.

Scarlett entered the swanky restaurant and was immediately ushered to a table reserved by a lanky man with a Roman nose and large owlish glasses in a suit.

The man, James Doakler, rose to greet her, his eyes lighting with obvious surprise at his good fortune. "I have to say, you're not the usual blind date that I get stuck with," he said, giving her a lingering once-over. "You do not disappoint in the least. My only question is…where have you been my entire life?"

Scarlett pretended to appreciate his awkward praise when in reality she wanted to stomp on his insole. She forced a light laugh as he helped her to her seat, pulling out her chair like a gentleman, which was, at least, a point in his favor.

James took his seat opposite Scarlett, his gaze still undressing her to the point where she had to demurely look away on the pretense of laying her linen napkin across her lap.

He'd taken the presumption to order red wine, which fortunately for him, Scarlett enjoyed but she didn't like anyone making assumptions on her behalf.

"If I'd known you were going to be so hot I would've ordered their best Cabernet."

He chuckled as if he were funny and she merely smiled as she sipped the wine. It was no mystery why this man was single. She felt sorry for any woman who hitched her wagon to this numskull.

"Mmm, delicious," she murmured, realizing she was going to need an entire bottle to get through a night with James Doakler.

CJ had managed to copy the man's cell contacts and use a coworker's contact information so that Zak's texts looked as if they were coming from his buddy, then rerouted any responses to CJ's server so that their cover wasn't blown.

The end result? James had no idea his buddy Carl was completely clueless about this supposed blind date and it would stay that way. Once the subterfuge was discovered, she'd be long gone.

James adjusted his tie and gestured to the waiter with impatience. Scarlett recognized right away that James felt more important than he was, which was something that would work in her favor. Men like James fed on the adoration of others and their egos were insatiable. All she needed to do was play to his appetites and he would sing like a bird in his attempt to inflate his own worth.

Scarlett suffered through an appropriate amount of excruciating small talk before she inched her way into sensitive territory. "James, I find it so fascinating that you work for the Department of Defense in such an important position. How long did it take to work up to being the Secretary of Defense's right-hand man?"

"Five years," James answered, proud of himself. "It's not an easy position but it's worth it. I'm doing something that matters. I truly believe that." Scarlett nodded as if she agreed, which only encouraged James to keep sharing. "We're on the precipice of major change and it's exciting times, especially when someone who knows what they are doing is at the helm."

Scarlett pretended interest. "How exciting. What an incredibly interesting job you have."

James puffed out his chest. "Indeed. I could tell you some things but I wouldn't want to scare you away. *Classified* things."

Scarlett pretended to be aghast. "Now you're scaring me. What kind of things?" she teased with mock seriousness.

"Oh, you have no idea. But it's not all bad. We have some real smart people putting things into play that will not only help this nation but will help take care of some of the social problems that have been running amok in this country. Too much liberal nonsense if you ask me."

Ahh, the clichéd liberal versus conservative argument. Honestly, Scarlett was neither. She liked to think of herself as more well rounded and leaned neither to the right or the left. She liked to reside somewhere in the middle because that's where common sense was usually found.

However, she wasn't going to say that to Mr. Doakler. She was going to play to his cues. As such, she agreed vigorously, seeming to appreciate his viewpoint. "That's incredibly good news to hear. The world has gone to hell in a handbag. Honestly, I would love to see a return to faith in our lives."

James nodded, pleased. "It is so refreshing to hear a beautiful, intelligent woman say what needs to be said. Yes, let's just come right out and say, we need

God back in our lives. The minute the Almighty was
no longer allowed in our classrooms out went the good
strong morals and ethics that built the foundation of
this great nation."

Scarlett held a dim view on all organized religion
but it seemed an easy jumping off point, particularly
for people who clung to certain belief structures. All
it took was a small tidbit of bait for James to snap it
up, revealing the way he leaned.

James waited for the waiter to leave after taking
their orders, then said, "Don't you worry. Like I said,
big change is coming and it's going to be good."

Scarlett smothered the shudder at the implication
but she had to stay on task. If this were a real date, she
would've shut him down within seconds of meeting.
But if somehow the date had managed to progress to
this point, she would've reminded him that their fore-
fathers were big proponents of separating church and
state. Furthermore, she'd fought in way too many coun-
tries against people who committed atrocities in the
name of religion and wanted no part of it.

But she was playing a part and affected a confused
expression while toying with the rim of her wineglass
with her finger. "So tell me, what does the Department of Defense have to do with the current political
climate?"

James clucked his tongue as if finding her ignorance
adorable but needing correction. "Politics are played
on many different stages," he explained with a wink.

"Interesting," she murmured, wondering what the
hell that meant. "Care to elaborate?"

But clearly he wanted to talk about something else.
"Enough about me. I want to know how is it that a

beautiful, sexy woman like you is still unattached?" he asked, his gaze dipping to her cleavage before returning to her eyes. "I mean, you are a *ten*. I have to be honest, it's not often that I find another person at my level."

Scarlett nearly choked on her wine. The man was aspiring to be a five, at most, but men like him were blind to their own faults.

"I guess I just never met the right person," Scarlett answered with a coy smile, glancing up through her lashes.

"I guess that's lucky for me." He grinned, revealing uneven, slightly stained bottom teeth from either too much coffee or too many nicotine breaks.

With her flirtiest smile, Scarlett said, "Tell me, what's it like working for the Secretary of Defense? I must confess I'm so intrigued by what you do and the fact that you're the right-hand man of such a powerful person in this country. What an honor."

If there was a hint of suspicion in his eyes that she kept steering the conversation back to his job, it was gone once he had the opportunity to keep talking about himself and his importance.

"The security clearances alone would make your head spin." He shrugged as he said, "I know where they hide the nukes and you'd be shocked at some of the locations."

Scarlett tried not to laugh. This man was following the self-important blowhard playbook to the letter. "Nukes? Just saying the word scares me. I don't like to think of a world where we live in fear of nuclear weapons."

James reached across the table to grasp her hand

as if protecting her. "Don't worry, honey, you're safe. There's no one more powerful than the good ol' US of A. Not even Russia."

Now she really wanted to gag. *Stay on topic.* "You know, it's so funny that you should say that. I ran across some pending legislature that really caught my eye but I confess I don't really understand all of it. Maybe you could help put it into terms I can understand."

She gently withdrew her hand to place it in her lap, surreptitiously wiping away his damp touch with her napkin.

James didn't seem to notice and was more than happy to educate her with his knowledge. "I'm at your service," he said.

She responded with a smile, saying, "You are so sweet," and he beamed, his gaze riveted on her as if she were the Virgin Mary on a world tour.

"Only with you. You bring out the sweetness in me. I feel this is fate. We were meant to meet. Do you feel that?"

All that Scarlett could feel was the pressure of a ticking clock and how she had to make this date seem somewhat believable so as not to raise alarms but she nodded as if she agreed with him. "I definitely feel we were destined to meet."

"You know I don't always say this but…this is kismet."

Not trusting herself, Scarlett drained her wine and James dutifully refilled her glass. If she weren't careful, she would be drunk by the end of dinner.

"So tell me, honey, what legislation is confusing your sweet little mind?"

She ignored the patronizing tone and said, "Actually, it's a spending bill, H.R. 720, I believe, and I just don't understand what the big fuss is all about."

James looked pleased by her knowledge. "Look at you, being informed. That's cute. Well, this bill is very important and we have a pretty good idea that it's going to pass the Senate."

"Oh? And why is that?"

"I don't know if you've been following the news lately but there was an incident in Tulsa that tragically took the life of a US senator."

Scarlett pretended to be horrified. "How did I miss that? How awful. What happened?"

He shook his head dramatically. "It's the saddest story really. One of our own—an American hero—went crazy and took out his anger with the world on an innocent man."

It took everything in Scarlett not to stab James with her fork. "That's horrible. What did he have against the senator?"

"Who knows? Unstable people rarely have logical motivations. However, I can say that this bill might ensure that something like this never happens again."

"I don't understand… How?" she asked with real confusion. "It's a spending bill. How would a spending bill prevent domestic terrorism?"

"On the surface, I know that's how it seems but this nation needs to funnel more money into our country's defense and the only way to do that is to make it matter to the American people. You might not know this but the Department of Defense is woefully underfunded. We need more money being funneled into protecting the nation and our people. That crazy unhinged fool who planted the bomb in Tulsa, that never would've happened if we'd had access to the man's background. He could've been put on a watch list and any purchase that could have been used to create a bomb would've been flagged. We could've prevented a tragedy simply by having the ability to monitor his purchases."

Scarlett felt sick to her stomach. *What a nightmare.* It was worse than a violation to the right of privacy—it was an evisceration.

She hid her true reaction and said, "That makes sense," even though she disagreed.

She had many more questions, but she pretended as if she were naturally losing interest in the subject. She couldn't seem too eager to pry or else she risked blowing her cover.

Seeing as James thought she was a bubbleheaded idiot with great boobs anyway, she decided to play the part a little more deeply.

"It's terrible of me but I heard some interesting gossip. I probably shouldn't repeat it but it's just so fantastically ridiculous that I can't even imagine that it's true."

James smiled, interested. "Oh? Trust me, I've heard them all. What is it?"

Scarlett pretended to blush as if it embarrassed her to even repeat the gossip, which only drew him in further. His smile widened as if she were the cutest thing he'd ever seen. *The man was an idiot.* Scarlett leaned forward to whisper in a conspiratorial tone, "I heard this *crazy* rumor that the secretary was having a secret affair. Can you believe that?"

James chuckled but his vibe changed. "You know, you can't believe everything you hear. The secretary is a good, solid family man. Just the kind of man who should be in charge of our nation's defense. Strong, solid morals. That rumor was just plain ugly gossip probably spread by liberals looking to topple the applecart."

Scarlett nodded, pretending relief. "I thought so. I mean he seems so virile and powerful, much like you. I can't imagine that he would be having an affair... with another man."

She let that last part drop and watched for James's reaction. She wasn't disappointed.

James coughed, fumbling with his linen napkin to press against his lips. "Yes, ugly gossip. Like I said, he's a solid family man. And I'm sure you can understand that there are many people who would use any means necessary to discredit him and his work."

"Of course," she said with a supportive nod. "Why do you think somebody would say that? It's just so mean."

James sighed, troubled by her comment. "That's the problem with today's country. People don't think before they speak. They don't realize how hurtful words can be. There are real threats out there. Threats to our way of life, threats to our families, to our loved ones. The secretary is trying to prevent any further threat and trying to preserve our way of life. If that's not heroic, I don't know what is."

Scarlett smiled, watching him closely. "You respect him," she said. "He must be a very good man."

"The best."

Was it hero worship? Or something else? James's posturing told Scarlet he actually did know something about the secretary's private life, but he wasn't going to give it up just because she kept poking here and there. He needed a little more persuading.

Perhaps from an unstable American hero.

Chapter 20

Scarlett walked through the motel room door and before he could say a word, she said, "That was excruciating," as she kicked off her heels and went to the bed to rub her feet.

He gestured for her to lie down and he took over. It had been equally excruciating for him to listen to that hellish blind date but he couldn't quite help but bust her chops a little bit for the part she'd played. "Can you do me a huge favor?" he asked, grinning as she groaned with pleasure while he rubbed away the torture of a night spent in high heels.

"Yeah? What?" she asked, propping herself up on her elbows to meet his gaze.

"Can you, maybe, talk in that super sexy airhead voice you used with the super important Mr. Doakler? It kinda did something for me."

"Eat me."

"If you say so," he said, ready to follow orders, but her dead glare stopped him. "Okay, so that was not a suggestion."

"No, it was not."

So it was back to business then. "What did you manage to get out of that, aside from an expensive dinner and an awkward goodbye kiss from the sounds of it."

"Ugh. Don't remind me. He slobbers like a Great Dane." She rose and lifted her foot free from his hands, turning so he could unzip her dress. Scarlett let the dress drop to the floor, completely oblivious to his reaction as she walked to the bathroom in nothing but a black thong with a matching push-up bra. "I have to pee. Give me a minute and I'll debrief you on my findings."

The door closed and Xander stared down at his instant erection. *Yeah, calm down, buddy. She's not in the mood.* More's the pity. His back twinged and he reached for his pill bottle right as Scarlett emerged. Her gaze narrowed but she didn't say anything.

But he felt the guilt anyway. "As soon as my name is clear, I'm kicking these things," he said.

"Let's focus on the case," she said, ignoring his promise. It bothered him that she didn't give him at least a little hell. Was that a bad sign? Damn, but they didn't have time for his paranoia, either. Besides, Scarlett was already moving on. "I think James knows more than he's letting on about the secretary's private life."

"What makes you think that?"

"His body language."

He couldn't argue her hunch. Scarlett had always

been sharp when it came to deciphering hidden clues and agendas. "What are you thinking?"

"I don't know, but I think he might be more willing to share information if he had a visit from a certain unstable American hero who is pissed off at the world if you know what I mean."

"Oh, goody. It's my turn to take him on a date."

"Just don't let him kiss you. He's terrible."

Xander scowled, hating that the man had put his lips on Scarlett in any fashion. He wasn't cut out for this spy shit, either. "When are we going?"

Just then Scarlett's burner phone rang. She picked up on the first ring. It was Conrad. She hung up quickly and motioned with an expletive. "We have to go."

"Damn FBI," he growled, shouldering his duffel while Scarlett stuffed her dress and shoes into her bag, removing any sign that they were there. "Don't they have better things to do than chase me down like a rabbit?"

"Someone is hungry for your head," Scarlett reminded him as they booked it out of the room and headed under the cover of night to the car parked on the opposite side of the motel.

They climbed into the car and managed to get out of the area before the FBI showed up this time.

As much as he didn't like the fact that Scarlett and Conrad had history, his intel was saving their asses.

They found another shithole motel, The Starlight, and checked in under false names, using cash as always.

The mint-green and mustard-yellow decor was enough to make an interior designer lose their lunch but it seemed clean enough and the bathroom had a tub and shower, which was a plus.

Scarlett dropped her bag and tested the bed, frowning when it barely budged. "This bed is going to be like sleeping on a plank."

"The Japanese say that sleeping on a plank is good for your back," he said but when he tested the bed himself he held back the grimace, adding with a chagrined tone, "But I'm not sure that applies to someone with a jacked-up back."

Scarlett nodded, understanding what he wasn't saying. Sleeping on that piece of crap was going to aggravate his condition, which would only force him to medicate more, which was exactly what he didn't want to do.

Especially now that Scarlett knew his dirty secret. Each time he popped a pill, he felt he was letting her down.

"I'll push it as far as I can," he said, trying to make some kind of effort to show that he meant what he said about quitting but Scarlett wasn't interested in listening to his promises. "Are you tired?" he asked.

"Yes," she admitted, quickly stripping and climbing into the bed, snuggling down into the blankets, then pausing to sniff at the comforter before announcing, "Smells like an old lady."

"And by 'old lady' do you mean, sweet old granny who bakes cookies and pies and always smells like powdered sugar or the kind of old lady who shuffles along in her wheelchair and randomly spits at strangers?"

"The latter."

"Wonderful."

He stripped and climbed in beside Scarlett, hesitant to reach out to her. Sometimes Scarlett was approachable and other times she wasn't. He waited to see if she scooted closer to him. When she remained where she was, staunchly on her own side, he sighed and rolled over.

There would be no cuddling tonight.

It was a long time before sleep found her, even though she was exhausted.

Watching Xander take his pills was a stark reality check each time she started to slip into the fantasy that there could be something real between them.

She'd even started thinking about future plans, if and when they managed to clear Xander's name. One of them would have to find a different job. Conrad was always saying she had a job with the Bureau if she wanted, but she loved her work with Red Wolf and didn't want to start over somewhere else.

It wasn't fair to ask Xander to find something else, either.

But if they wanted to make things work…

Hell, that was the question, wasn't it? What if Xander wasn't interested in a relationship? Maybe she was jumping the gun. She didn't even know if she wanted a relationship.

She just knew that she felt things for Xander—real feelings that she couldn't ignore—which made his addiction all the more troubling.

She couldn't be with a drug addict.

She just couldn't.

In spite of her father's penchant for spouting scripture when it was convenient, he had been a lousy addict with a mean streak and she swore she'd never fall for someone with the same problem.

One could argue Xander was nothing like her father but addiction changed people.

Each time she watched him pop that pill...she was reminded of her father and how much she loathed the man.

But they had bigger problems right now and that was their saving grace. Her heart actually hurt when she thought of walking away from Xander. There was no way she could deal with that when they had much bigger issues to solve.

Xander had rolled to his back and begun to snore. She smiled, recalling an old joke her bawdy grandmother used to tell.

Do you know why men snore when they're on their back?

No, Nana, why?

Because their balls cover their butthole and create a vacuum!

Of course, at ten years old, she hadn't understood the joke but her grandmother had always told inappropriate jokes that'd gone way over her head. She missed that chain-smoking, loud-laughing old broad, though.

She'd been the only one who had been able to keep Scarlett's dad in line. When Nana died, that's when things had gotten bad.

In so many ways.

She hated thinking about the past. Xander's situation had inadvertently brought up bad memories. It wasn't Xander's fault that she had a shitty childhood; but she was mad at him anyway for putting himself in this situation.

If he'd just trusted her enough to be honest, things would've been so different. She could've done more to protect him than Xander had done for himself. Hell, all Xander had done was mess things up worse.

She nudged Xander with her foot when his snore went up a notch and he snorted and rolled to his side. Scarlett had never enjoyed sharing a bed until Xander.

Another point that made it abundantly clear that her heart was involved on a level that made her want to run.

Yet running from Xander wasn't an option because she simply couldn't bring herself to do it.

Not even when she should've earlier on.

Ahh, screw it. She scooted close and wrapped her arms around his solid body, inhaling the scent that was uniquely his. As if that were the magic element missing, her eyelids began to droop and within minutes, she was finally asleep.

Troubles, for the moment, forgotten.

Chapter 21

They decided to scope out Doakler's house during the day while he was at work and then come back at night to do the interrogation.

"So we'll follow the same plan as with Williams. You stay out of sight while I do the dirty work. No sense in blowing up your game if we don't have to."

Scarlett nodded. "He's pretty soft. He should cave easily. Probably faster than the senator."

Xander cracked his knuckles, ready to do this, but he was a little apprehensive of the outcome, too. "What happens if we're right and the Secretary of Defense has something to do with McQuarry's death? How do we prove it? He's pretty high up the food chain."

Scarlett shared his concern but she was in TL mode. "Focus on the objective," she said. "We need to find out if Doakler knows anything. If something turns up, we'll move to the next objective. One step at a time."

Xander nodded, breathing a little more easily knowing they had a plan. "All right, are you ready to do
this?" he asked.

Scarlett gloved her hands and pulled her dark beanie
over her bright red hair, her smile painted on. "More
than ready."

"You just want payback for that slobbery kiss he
planted on you," he teased as they climbed into the car.

"Don't front. You want payback for that kiss, too."

Ohhh, the woman knew him well. No sense in lying.
He hated the idea of anyone touching Scarlett aside
from him. Instead, he just gave her a cocky nod and
left it at that. Their feelings for one another were an
additional complication that they didn't have time to
confront. *One crisis at a time.*

They rolled up to Doakler's neighborhood, cutting
the engine a block away and parking in a dark alley
away from the main road.

Doakler lived alone with his cat in an upscale neighborhood but nothing quite as fancy as the senator. The
block was made of newer construction, an upwardly
mobile subdivision filled with young families and
middle-aged couples in the prime of their adulthood.

Xander pulled the black ski mask over his head and
they made their way silently into the house, quickly
bypassed the alarm system and found Doakler asleep
in his bed, clutching a small ratty teddy bear.

Xander shared a look with Scarlett before she melted
into the shadows and then scared the ever-loving shit
out of the man by dragging him out of the bed and
dropping him to the floor.

Doakler yelped like a kicked puppy, terrified as
Xander hauled him to his feet and tossed him into the

ornate chair in the corner. Tying him easily to the chair, Xander blindfolded him with a pair of Doakler's own underwear and then once he knew Doakler couldn't see, he removed the ski mask and motioned for Scarlett to join him.

"I have money..." Doakler pleaded, scared out of his mind. "I know important people!"

"I'm not interested in your money. I just want some information."

"Information?" Doakler repeated, confused. "What kind of information?"

"The classified kind," Xander answered, grinning when Doakler's bottom lip began to tremble. "Word on the street is you're an important man."

"No, I'm no one. I—I—I'm just a glorified clerk. I push paperwork. I don't know anything."

"I think you'd be surprised what you know."

Doakler shook his head. "I don't understand... Who sent you? Oh my God, are you...*Russian*?"

"Do I sound Russian?" Xander asked dryly. "No, I'm not Russian, you idiot. I need answers and I think you're going to give them to me."

"I honestly don't know anything about anything. I'm just a paper-pusher, a gopher. I get coffee and lunches and file papers... Truly, I don't know anything of real value."

"Don't sell yourself short, Jimmy," Xander said, amused at how quickly the man lost the bravado he'd put on display for Scarlett's benefit. "I think you know more than you realize. How about I make you a deal..."

"Anything," Doakler promised with a fervent nod. "Whatever you want."

"If you answer my questions like a good boy, I'll

leave all your parts exactly as I found them—attached to your body."

Doakler gulped. "And if I can't answer your questions?"

"Then I'll have to take out my frustration on your fingers and toes and *other* extremities. You don't want me to do that, do you?" Doakler shook his head. Xander smiled. "Good. Then let's start."

"But what if I don't know what you're asking?"

Xander answered in a dark tone, "Well, let's just hope that you do." Doakler swallowed and jerked a nod. Xander was surprised the man hadn't pissed himself yet. "Okay, let's start with something easy. How closely do you work with the Secretary of Defense, Mark Bettis?"

"I'm his clerk," Doakler answered, licking his lips. "I prepare the paperwork, send emails, handle his social and business calendar."

"So, is it safe to say you keep him organized?"

"Yeah. I guess so. Yes, that's accurate."

"Would you say that no one gets an audience with the secretary without your knowledge?"

Doakler bobbed a nod. "Y-yes."

"Good, good. Okay, so being that you're pretty much in charge of his comings and goings, it's probably safe to say that you know quite a bit about his personal life."

"I guess so."

"Tell me what you know about Bettis."

"What do you mean?"

Xander provided as an example, "His wife's name, favorite golf course, foods he likes and dislikes, people he associates with socially... Those kinds of things."

Doakler paused and Xander tapped the man's knee

with his gun to remind him that his patience had a limit. "H-his wife's name is Janet, he doesn't golf and he's allergic to shellfish. I—I don't know what you mean about people he associates with. P-please clarify."

"Sure thing, buddy. What I mean is who's he sleeping with aside from his wife?" Xander asked, putting it bluntly.

It was dark so Xander couldn't see if the man had just paled but he was willing to bet Doakler had. "I don't know what you mean?"

"Jimmy, you have to ask yourself if protecting the secretary's secret is worth your kneecaps. I mean, would the secretary protect your secrets with the same dedication? I don't think so. All you have to do is tell me who he was sleeping with and then I'll let you go."

"I—I don't know," Doakler squeaked but Xander wasn't buying. Xander moved the gun from Doakler's knee to his groin, purposefully pushing the gun against his junk. Doakler yelped and tried to scoot away but he was tied tight. "Please! I want to have kids someday!"

"I understand, but I have to have answers. I can't leave without them, so either you fess up or I'm going to have to turn you from a rooster to a hen, my friend, and you'll spend the rest of your life pissing in a bag."

Now Doakler was sobbing. "Man, I don't know. I don't. I'm not lying. I swear to you. Please don't shoot my penis!"

Maybe the man was as useless as he said. Xander looked to Scarlett who motioned for Xander to keep trying. A thought occurred to him. He returned to Doakler. "Okay, stop your crying. For God's sake, you're a man. Act like one." He paused long enough for

Doakler to stop blubbering, then said, "Okay, tell me who Bettis was *rumored* to be sleeping with."

"Rumor? But…that's just office gossip."

"Let me be the judge of that. You know what they say, within every rumor lies a kernel of truth."

Doakler shook his head, adamant. "No, the secretary is a good man."

"Good men can make bad judgments," Xander said with a small shrug. "Humor me. Tell me who Bettis was banging on the side, according to the water-cooler gossip."

It was obvious Doakler hated even letting the words fall from his mouth but he answered, "When you hear it, you'll know it's a total lie."

"Out with it."

"An Oklahoma senator."

Both Xander and Scarlett perked up, straightening as they held their breath. "Yeah? Which one? The dead one? McQuarry?"

Doakler shook his head. "No. Sheffton."

Holy friggin' shit.

Sheffton?

"Are you sure?"

"That's the name that was tossed around but like I told you, it's a total lie. For one, Bettis has been married for thirty years to the same woman—clearly not gay—and for two, Sheffton was only ever on the secretary's calendar once."

"When? Was it before or after Senator McQuarry was killed?"

Doakler paused to remember, then said, "Before. A month or so before."

"And why was Sheffton visiting Bettis?"

"Sheffton came to voice his concerns over H.R. 720 but by the end of the meeting, he'd changed his mind and decided to support the bill."

"Why? McQuarry was still alive. Sheffton would've had no pull on the Senate floor."

Doakler seemed stumped as well, as if he hadn't thought about that reasoning. "I...I don't know," he admitted.

What if McQuarry hadn't been sleeping with anyone but his gold-digging mistress and the story of him sleeping with some high-powered official was simply a smoke screen?

And if that were true, was Sheffton the one who had orchestrated McQuarry's death for his own gain?

"I swear that's all I know," Doakler said, swallowing hard. "Please don't shoot me."

Xander patted Doakler on the head like a dog and said, "You did good. I'm not going to shoot you, but I am going to leave you tied up so I can leave without you calling the cops."

Doakler sagged with relief. "Thank you. Thank you!"

"Don't mention it. Thanks for your help."

"You're welcome?"

Xander and Scarlett cleared the house and jogged back to the car. Only when they were safely driving away did Scarlett say, "You know he could starve to death and then his damn cat will eat him."

He shook his head. "Naww, I didn't tie him up that tight. If he struggles long enough, he'll break free."

Scarlett grinned. "You enjoyed that a bit too much."

"I did," Xander agreed. "God, I miss my job. Can

we hurry up and solve this so I can go back to torturing and killing people for a good cause?"

"I think that psych doc was right—you are a sociopath," Scarlett joked with a shake of her head.

"You say that like it's a bad thing..."

They laughed and detoured for ice cream before heading back to the motel.

"Your intel was good. James Doakler gave up some information," Scarlett said to Conrad over the phone. "He said that Sheffton came to the Secretary of Defense before McQuarry died to talk about H.R. 720 and that prior to the meeting, Sheffton opposed the bill but after the meeting, was supportive."

"Why would Sheffton's influence matter?"

"That's exactly the question, right? Unless Sheffton already had plans to make McQuarry go away and he had deep enough connections to ensure that the governor would appoint him in the event of McQuarry's death."

"A workable theory. Any proof?"

"Aside from the frightened ramblings of a man about to piss himself? No."

"That's not admissible in court," Conrad pointed out dryly. "Even if your theory is right on the money, if you've got no way to prove it...you've got nothing."

"Yeah, I know." She sighed. "Thanks for the tip on the raid, too." Conrad exhaled heavily and Scarlett knew her friend was treading on thin ice for her. "I'm sorry you're in the middle."

"It's a place I put myself in," he replied, but Scarlett knew he was doing this all for her. The guilt sat heavily on her shoulders but they were all in too deep to pull back now. "Platt said something that was a little weird last night when he called me in the dead of night to drunk ramble at me."

"Does your boss make a habit of making those kinds of calls?" she asked.

"Not before this case started. I think someone is doing more than putting a little administrative pressure on him for the sake of making the Bureau look good. I think someone is blackmailing him."

"Really? Any idea who?"

"My guess is that whoever offed McQuarry is the same person putting the squeeze on Platt."

Scarlett let that sink in for a minute. "It would have to be someone in a position of power...or someone with really damaging dirt on Platt. How much do you know about your boss?"

"I know he's a thorough investigator on the job but I don't know shit about his private life and frankly, I was okay with that. He's not the kind of man I would hang out with after hours."

"No? Why not?"

"His personality is shit and he's a little awkward. Platt has just always given me a weird vibe. But he's good at his job and up until this point, he never gave me any grief. Now that he's riding my ass, I'm about ready to transfer to a different branch."

Scarlett frowned, uncomfortable with the position Conrad was in because of her. "Maybe you should pull back. I don't want you getting caught in the crossfire."

"I'm fine. You just worry about finding the evidence you need to get us all out of this mess."

"I'm trying," she said, frustrated by the incredibly slow amount of progress they'd made. "Seems each time we go a few steps forward, we take even more steps back. It's hard not to lose faith, you know?" She trusted Conrad, otherwise she never would've revealed how she was struggling with the situation. But again, she realized it wasn't fair to Conrad to lay her problems on his table. "I'm sorry. I'm just cranky today."

"You don't have to apologize, Scarlett. I care about you. I'm here if you need someone to listen."

"I know." Scarlett bit her lip, knowing that Conrad had feelings for her that she could never reciprocate. If she were smart, she would've felt something more than friendship with Conrad when they'd dated. He was a good man—but she felt absolutely nothing when they kissed. Not a spark, not even a tiny zap unlike the way her body lit up like a Disney light parade when Xander so much as looked her way. Attraction was a funny thing and almost always inconvenient. "Thank you, Connie. Be careful out there, okay? You never know who could be watching."

Again, Conrad promised he'd be fine and they clicked off.

That unsettled feeling refused to leave her gut. If Platt was being blackmailed by someone high up the chain of command, say the Secretary of Defense, how the hell were they going to find the evidence they needed to take down a giant in government like that?

And even if they did manage to find some shred of evidence that connected McQuarry's death with the secretary, would anyone care or listen?

The current administration seemed a little lax in the alarm department when it came to potential treason or international sanctions. Would they even care if the secretary had orchestrated the death of a US senator if he spun the story with the angle that he was protecting the American people?

There was a reason she hated politics.

Everyone had a secret face and an even more covert agenda.

Sussing out the truth was going to take an act of divine intervention and Scarlett was fresh out of patron saints to pray to for help.

Maybe Xander was right—they ought to cut their losses, pack up and leave for Mexico. Xander had the cash to make it happen. They could live comfortably for a while before the money ran out.

Even as the thought of fleeing was appealing for a brief moment, she knew it would never happen. Neither Xander nor Scarlett were hardwired to run away from a crisis.

Sure, Xander split before getting arrested, but that's because he'd known the only person who'd care about his innocence was himself and he wasn't going to rot in prison for a crime he hadn't committed.

He may joke about running off to another country but he'd never actually do it.

And neither would she.

No, it was either prove his innocence…or die trying.

That was the cold hard truth, the one she'd been trying to avoid.

She knew Xander would never go to prison.

He'd rather put a bullet in his own skull before he'd let that happen.

And the thought of Xander dead was more than she could handle.

Time to double down. The answers were out there, waiting to be found.

Chapter 22

Scarlett frowned and opened her laptop. "Hey, I just got something from Conrad." Xander peered over her shoulder as she clicked on an attachment and Carl Sheffton's details unfolded in front of them. She smiled and murmured appreciatively, "Nice job, buddy," as she perused the contents.

When she was finished, she turned to Xander who mirrored her quizzical expression. "Was that the most sanitized, bullshit background detail you've ever read?"

Xander nodded, agreeing. "Not even a single parking ticket. Is this guy for real?"

"No one is that squeaky clean. Not even politicians with big dreams."

"I don't trust perfect people because perfect doesn't exist, which means someone went to great lengths to make sure anything unflattering or questionable was removed from his record."

"Who has that kind of power?" she asked.

"You'd have to go pretty high up the chain to reach that level of access."

"Like Secretary-of-Defense level?" Scarlett supplied and Xander had to agree it was a solid theory. She groaned. "Is it bad that I was really hoping we could get away from pointing the finger at the Secretary of Defense?"

"No, I was hoping we'd skate past that possibility, too."

"I guess we're not that lucky."

He smirked. "Tell me about it."

Scarlett leaned back in the chair, propping her feet against the opposite chair. "So how do we go about finding the evidence we need to take down the man in charge of the nation's defense? It might be easier to prove that Santa Claus is real."

Xander felt the flutter of Scarlett's panic as if it were his own. The odds had always been shit but they'd just gotten so much worse.

"We could go straight to the source…"

Her eyes bugged. "Uh, no. Roughing up the secretary is not going to happen. For one, he's going to have major security, far more than we can handle, and two, even if we managed to pull off getting information out of him, confessions made under duress are inadmissible in court. Not to mention, once we played our hand, chances are we'd be dead a few days later. If the man is willing to blow up a US senator, he's not going to blink an eye at taking down you and me."

No argument there. He moved to her laptop, gesturing, "May I?" and when she nodded and slid the computer toward him, he looked into the government calendar, scanning for any event the secretary might be in attendance.

Bam. Xander snapped his fingers and pointed. "Here it is—and damn, if our luck isn't turning. Sheffton is going to be in attendance, too. There's a preliminary hearing on H.R. 720 happening in two days' time. That's our best time to put some surveillance on the two and see if one leads us to the other."

"They'd never be so obvious," Scarlett disagreed, shaking her head. "If anything, they'd probably avoid any contact with one another so as not to raise any suspicion."

"You could be right but we don't have the option of turning our noses up at any possible lead."

Scarlett nodded, even though he could tell she hated this plan. To ease her fears, he suggested, "We can have Zak and CJ take care of surveillance under the guise of providing additional security if anyone asks. They have the credentials. No one will second-guess them being there."

"I don't want to involve Red Wolf in this. Feels too dangerous."

"Which is exactly why Zak and CJ will friggin' jump at the chance to do it."

She knew he was right. The thrill of doing something covert was like a drug to them. They liked the danger.

"Fine," she conceded and reluctantly made the call. As expected, Zak and CJ were all in. While they worked the appropriate credentials needed to gain access to the federal building, Xander closed his eyes and tried to recall every detail from the night of the bombing, but from a different angle.

From Sheffton's angle.

"You know, there's a term psychologists use for people who say and do something and then attribute their actions and words to someone else…"

"Yeah, it's called transference. Where are you going with this?"

Xander straightened, his gears moving fast. "We can both agree that Sheffton's record is plastic as shit. His politics are also firmly planted in family values soil. If the rumors are true and it wasn't McQuarry but Sheffton who was having an affair, it would serve Sheffton to redirect those rumors away from himself."

"Yeah, a family values platform doesn't usually leave much room for adulterous affairs with members of the same sex."

"Exactly. What if McQuarry found out about Sheffton and threatened to go public with his findings? That's some serious motive, don't you think?"

Scarlett agreed. "I think someone who is willing to go to such lengths to ensure his record is squeaky clean is willing to go to any length to keep it that way."

Xander thought so, too. For the first time since this nightmare began, he thought he saw a glimmer of hope.

Out of habit, he began to reach for his pill bottle but stopped. Scarlett caught his action and quickly looked away.

There was nothing he could say that would convince her that he was serious about going clean, and he got the impression that the more he insisted, the less she believed him so he said nothing.

Instead, he just showed her by his actions that he was serious and that meant going longer between pills, even if it killed him, because he had to start somewhere.

* * *

It was late and Scarlett's eyes burned with fatigue but she didn't want to stop, not when they were getting closer and the urgency was becoming more intense.

Rubbing at her eyes, she tried focusing harder but Xander took control of the situation and gently closed her laptop. She looked up at him with a frown but he just shook his head and grabbed her hand, saying, "Look, we're both seeing double at this point. We need to get some sleep."

She didn't want to argue. In fact, it felt good to let someone else call the shots for once. Nodding, she followed Xander's lead, quickly stripped and climbed into the bed.

As was becoming their norm—Xander's arms closed around her and she snuggled against his solid warmth. His soft breath on the back of her neck soothed her nerves and she relaxed almost immediately.

"Do you have any brothers or sisters?" she asked sleepily.

His low chuckle rumbled through his chest as he answered, "Why? Are you thinking of trading me in?"

She smiled. "No, I was just curious."

"No. I'm an only child. You?"

"Same." She smiled wider, even though there was nothing remotely funny about her next quip. "Dad only got the opportunity to screw up one kid."

But Xander got it and chuckled, too. "Same."

"Why does this work?" she asked, too tired to guard her tongue. Everything about this moment felt wonderful, even if it was ill-fated. "We shouldn't work. Nothing about this should work."

"Yeah, I know. But somehow it does. And works pretty great, too. We're a good team, Rhodes."

"Yes, we are, Scott," Scarlett returned with a sleepy giggle but there was more happening between them than seamless teamwork. She couldn't imagine snuggling with Zak or CJ. Hell, she hadn't even enjoyed cuddling with Conrad. Up until now, sex was fine but snuggling had been a no-go.

But being here with Xander, she couldn't explain it. It was simply everything she never knew she wanted.

That was some deep shit.

Probably too deep to discuss in their current situation. Her mouth didn't seem to agree. "Have you ever been in love, Xander?" she asked, very interested to know his answer.

She felt his deep sigh in her soul. "I don't know… maybe once. It didn't last. Couldn't last. I'm just no good at that stuff."

She could relate. "Me, neither."

His arm tightened around her, as if to say he understood and he didn't hold it against her. "Scarlett…" he ventured, hesitant.

"Yeah?"

"Can I tell you something?"

She stilled. "Sure."

"It was never about just scratching an itch. I want you to know that."

She closed her eyes, knowing what he meant. Scarlett jerked a nod to indicate she'd heard. When she found her voice again, she admitted, "It wasn't for me, either."

His entire body relaxed as if he'd been holding his breath until she answered. "Good."

"Goodnight, Xander."

"'Night, baby girl."

She silently thrilled at the small endearment. In this moment, she wasn't the badass TL, the ball-busting boss or the broken girl who couldn't seem to let anyone in. She was simply his.

And no matter how messed-up their situation or how wrong it was to cling to something so fleeting, it felt right.

So right.

And she'd deal with her feelings later.

Chapter 23

Scarlett had left several messages for Conrad and he hadn't called back yet. Something felt wrong.

"Conrad hasn't returned my calls," she told Xander, pacing the motel room while Xander methodically cleaned his gun. "Something's wrong."

"He'll call. He's probably just lying low. Maybe he's getting some heat and has to play it careful."

Maybe, but Conrad always returned her calls. It was just one of those things that happened because he still had feelings for her, and her gut was saying something wasn't right.

"I need to see if he's okay."

Xander looked up. "That could backfire," he warned. "By now, the FBI has to know you're with me, which makes you a potential accessory. If you get caught…"

"I know," she said, understanding the risk and the

consequences but she couldn't shake the terrible feeling in her gut that something had gone wrong. Conrad lived in DC. "We can go tonight, sneak in when everyone is asleep. Conrad lives alone so we don't have to worry about anyone being in the house."

"Are you sure you want to take this risk?" he asked.

"He's done so much for us. I feel we have to."

He nodded, accepting her answer. "Okay, we'll go at twenty-two hundred."

"With any luck, he'll call before we head out," Scarlett said, clinging to a single thread of hope that her gut was wrong and Conrad was simply lying low as a precaution.

But as the day wore on and Conrad's silence grew, Scarlett was agitated and ready to bounce as soon as nightfall hit. Somehow she managed to wait until the agreed upon time but was out the door at 22:01.

Following the same plan, they rolled up to Conrad's neighborhood and she was hit with memories that she'd forgotten.

Conrad had just purchased the house on Howitzer Lane and had been eager to show her.

Leading her by the hand, he gave her the grand tour, ending with the large master bedroom with the beautiful granite countertops and full-size state-of-the-art Jacuzzi tub.

"What do you think?" Conrad had asked, his gaze beaming with hope. "Nice, right?"

"It's more than nice. It's gorgeous," she'd answered, glancing around, impressed. "This is quite the pad, man. You've done well for yourself."

Conrad reached for her and she went with a wary smile. "But do *you* like it?"

Scarlett knew with a sinking heart where he was going with his question. She'd worried for a few weeks that Conrad was getting closer than she was comfortable with but had hoped that she was overreacting.

Apparently, her instincts were spot-on—Conrad was in love with her.

"It's a lovely house for you. You should be proud of your accomplishment."

Conrad frowned, knuckling her cheek softly as he said, "Scarlett, can't you see that I'm crazy about you? I want to build a life together."

Scarlett knew she would never feel that way about Conrad and it was cruel to keep him living in hope that she might someday. Gently tugging herself free, she took a step back, saying sadly, "But I don't."

"What do you mean?" Conrad asked, confused.

"I mean, I don't want to settle down in the 'burbs with you…or anyone for that matter. I'm just not into that scene and never will be. I'm sorry."

Conrad's crestfallen expression was one she had to live with but breaking his heart then had been a mercy. Shortly after, she'd taken the job with Red Wolf and hadn't looked back.

When Conrad had contacted her a year later, she'd been wary but she'd missed their friendship. As long as he stayed in the friend zone, Scarlett was happy to remain in contact.

Now, as they rounded the backside of the darkened house, she wished she'd never accepted that phone call because then he wouldn't be caught in the middle of this mess.

Xander went to jimmy the side-door lock but she stopped him with a silent shake of her head, knowing where Conrad kept his spare key. For someone who worked with cutting-edge technology every day, Conrad was endearingly old-school about certain things.

Quietly letting themselves into the garage, Scarlett saw Conrad's Mercedes sedan and her misgivings grew.

They gained access to the house and Scarlett couldn't help but relive some of the memories, the hope and the possibility that Conrad had entertained when he bought this place and how awful it had been when she let him down.

Honestly, she was surprised he'd kept the house but he'd admitted that right after their breakup the housing market had crashed and he'd been forced to keep it, which had turned out to be a blessing because now the house had tripled in value and he had plenty of equity to play with.

Shaking off the memories, Scarlett and Xander slowly checked the house but as they approached Conrad's office, Scarlett stopped, her sensitive nose catching the faint odor of copper.

Xander could smell it, too.

They entered the office and Scarlett flipped the light, casting an eerie glow on the macabre scene.

Dried blood splatter on the walls.

Xander caught Scarlett as she stumbled back, horrified.

Conrad, slumped over his computer, a bullet through the back of his skull and the cloying smell of decomposition starting to tease the air made Scarlett want to vomit.

She was no stranger to death. Dead bodies didn't

usually phase her but then she'd never been witness to a former lover's dead body like this.

"I'm going to be sick," she whispered and backed out of the room, needing to get away from the scene.

Xander nodded grimly and she couldn't get out fast enough. Drawing deep gulping breaths, she tried to steady her nerves, tried to think straight but all she could see was Conrad dead because of her.

Because she'd roped him into this mess when she should've left him out.

Someone had killed a good man to hide their corruption. She swallowed and wiped at her mouth, feeling numb.

Xander joined her and she went straight into his arms, needing some kind of comfort before she fell completely apart.

"It's my fault," she whispered against Xander's chest, wanting to sob but her brain was too stunned to process anything but the pure guilt and agony of Conrad's death. "He's dead because of me."

But Xander wasn't going to let her throw a pity party, not yet. He grabbed her by the arms and gave her a sharp shake. "You did not do this. You hear me? Whoever did this is going to pay. I swear to you. We're going to find out who killed Conrad. I promise."

"We don't know what we're doing," Scarlett lamented, her grief quickly melting into rage because that was something she understood. "We're stumbling around in the dark like a couple of amateurs and we've gotten someone killed. Who's next? Zak and CJ? I can't do this, Xander. I can't have more people dying because we're playing detective when we're not trained like that. I don't know what I was thinking. We ought to just cut our losses and leave for Mexico while we still can."

"What the hell is wrong with you? The Scarlett I know doesn't tuck tail and run just because things are tough."

"Don't lecture me on tough," she hissed, wiping at her eyes. Irritated that the tears had started. "If you'd been tougher on yourself, checked your damn ego and gotten help before the Tulsa job, none of this would've happened!"

She knew the answer wasn't to start attacking the one person they were trying to save but she couldn't help the rage that was beginning to percolate inside over Conrad's senseless death.

But Xander didn't lash back and it only made her feel worse.

"You're right," Xander said, bowing his head under his own guilt. A beat of heavy silence passed between them and Scarlett's chest felt ready to cave in. Xander lifted his head and grasped her hand, holding it tight. "I promise you we will find who did this and make them pay. Even if we make them pay the old-fashioned way…"

"An eye for an eye?" Scarlett asked, her grief and rage needing a victim.

And only Xander could understand and not judge her for it because he felt the same. "Hell, yes, baby. We'll pluck the son of a bitch's eyeball out and make him choke on it."

That was a promise she would count on.

We'll avenge you, Connie. I swear it.

Xander knew the moment his TL had returned to beast mode because she snapped back into forward action. Ignoring Conrad's body, she began a methodical search of the room, going through papers, looking for clues that Conrad might've left behind.

In their line of work, they saw a lot of messed-up shit—it just came with the job—and sometimes it left a person jaded but nothing ever prepared them to see someone they knew or cared about splayed out like human garbage.

Whoever had done this had been cowardly, shooting Conrad in the back of the head.

The bullet had gone through Conrad and right into the computer, killing the hard drive. Whatever Conrad had been working on was lost to them. They didn't have the time or the resources to have the hard drive recovered by forensics. But whatever Conrad had been investigating must've been damaging enough to send someone after him.

As much as he hated to point out a painful truth, they were getting close to the answers and someone was trying to stop them.

Scarlett said, "Conrad said he thought someone was blackmailing his boss, Platt, which was why he was riding his tail so hard. Knowing Conrad, he would've bugged Platt at some point to get more information."

Xander nodded, impressed. "Maybe he heard something that he shouldn't have and Platt found out?"

Scarlett stopped to think, then said, "Conrad loved his gadgets. He was always trying to outdo himself with the newest tech. Whoever did this killed the computer but they probably didn't think to take his phone. Conrad always sent a backup of his computer to his cloud. If we can find Conrad's phone, we can find who Conrad was listening to."

But Conrad's phone was gone, too.

"Damn it," Scarlett cursed, pacing as she racked her brain for another solution. Then she remembered something that she'd always teased Conrad about but hoped against hope he'd continued to do. Going to his closet, she threw open the doors and rummaged through his sock drawer where she pulled out a single key. Then she went to the bottom drawer, shoved aside the neatly folded shirts to reveal the false bottom with the single keyhole. Xander watched as she unlocked the secret drawer and pulled out a metal fireproof box. She explained as she opened the box, "Conrad was always paranoid of losing important information so he kept everything he wanted to keep safe in here, including a backup phone that automatically updated through the cloud so if he ever lost his main phone, he never lost any speed."

Just as she'd hoped, a duplicate phone, powered and ready, sat alongside important paperwork and a few pictures.

She handed the phone to Xander but paused as she retrieved a single picture of her and Conrad during happier times. Conrad had her wrapped in his embrace, his smile shining brighter than the sun.

Scarlett rubbed at the tingle in her nose. "Why couldn't I have loved him like I should've?"

Xander knew that torment. He'd broken hearts of good women just as Scarlett had broken Conrad's, but they were a different breed of people and sometimes that heartbreak was a mercy.

And she knew this but sometimes the guilt of doing what needed to be done was something that remained with you. He gave her a look of understanding and she let it go. Stuffing the picture in her back pocket, she returned the box and locked the drawer.

"Whatever Conrad was working on will be on this phone," she said, sniffing back unshed tears. "We should go."

Xander agreed but before they left, he called 911 from the landline with gloved hands. They weren't going to leave Conrad there to be discovered by the neighbors after the smell had gotten so bad someone finally noticed.

Scarlett wiped at her eyes and nodded her gratitude. Without saying another word, they slipped from the house, closing everything up as they'd found it, driving off into the night with the hope that Conrad didn't die in vain.

Back at the motel, Xander took a moment to hug Scarlett hard, knowing in his heart that he couldn't push the broken pieces back together again but he could show her that she wasn't alone.

Scarlett pulled away, needing to focus on anything other than what she was feeling, which was something he understood. Avoidance was a tried-and-true method of dealing with emotional pain, at least for the time being, and he was going to follow her lead.

"Hand me Conrad's phone," she said, sitting at the small table and firing up her laptop. Xander complied and she hooked her cord up to the phone, downloading the contents of Conrad's hard drive to her own.

It took a few minutes but finally the laptop dinged softly and she unhooked the phone, winding up her cord and putting it away before opening the files.

She scanned quickly, bypassing anything that seemed unimportant. "Ah-ha," Scarlett murmured, double-clicking on a file marked TEMP. At Xander's confusion, she explained, "Conrad always dumped everything into the TEMP file until he could sort it later. It was a digital catchall but he was a little OCD about things and always wanted everything as organized as possible. That little fact might just work in our favor."

Xander nodded. "Let's hope."

Scarlett opened file after file until she came across the jackpot, her mouth dropping open as she turned to Xander, unable to believe their luck. "I think we just found the evidence we need to link Platt and Sheffton together."

Xander leaned forward, his heart rate quickening. "What does it say?"

"It's the transcription of the bug Conrad planted in Platt's office. Sheffton was blackmailing Platt."

"With what?"

Scarlett turned the laptop so Xander could read for himself.

"If I'd known you were this incompetent, I would've handled this myself."

"Scott is a specially trained soldier, not your average citizen on the run. I told you to be patient."

"I've been patient and my patience is at an end."

"Please, I got this. I have some new leads—"

"Bullshit. You've got nothing. You think I don't have eyes and ears in all the right places? You're sitting with your thumb up your ass and we're finished with your lack of results."

"Please... It was one time... A mistake. I swear I never did it again..."

"You and I both know that's not true but we'll let the courts decide."

"No!"

"Senior Director Paul Platt caught with child porn... has a certain ring to it, don't you think?"

...

Xander's gaze widened at the intel. Platt must've found out that his office was bugged and realized it was Conrad. He would've done anything to keep that secret quiet. "Why do I get the feeling Conrad's murder is going to get pinned on me, too?"

Scarlett shared Xander's grim assumption but she placed her hand on his. "Not if we stop Platt first," she said.

"But does Sheffton say anything that links him to McQuarry specifically?" he asked.

Scarlett scanned the transcript, stopping with a grin. "Right here. It's weak but it's definitely shady."

Xander leaned in to read.

"Don't make the same mistake McQuarry did and underestimate my influence. I can make you go away just as easily."

"Of course, of course... I'm on your side. Please, trust me. I can get the job done. I'll take care of any loose ends. Just give me another chance. Please."

"Even on paper, this guy sounds like a pussy," Xander said with a frown. "I'm almost willing to bet my liver that Platt was the one who killed Conrad. Shooting someone in the back is cowardly as shit."

Scarlett agreed, her gaze darkening. "I think we ought to pay Senior Director Platt a visit tomorrow."

Tomorrow Zak and CJ were tailing the secretary and Sheffton to see if they scuttled off together for some private time. They were armed with high-powered cameras to photograph anything interesting and/or salacious.

That part CJ had been excited about.

So while CJ and Zak were chasing after Sheffton and the secretary, she and Xander would pay Platt a visit and see what they could shake out of the fat bastard.

Both Scarlett and Xander shared the same thought—morning couldn't come soon enough.

Chapter 24

The following morning after Scarlett uploaded the transcript to Red Wolf servers for safekeeping, she and Xander loaded up and went to seek an audience with Platt.

He wasn't hard to find—predators had a tendency to flock where they could find or be close to prey.

There was a children's park near to the federal building. With precious little digging, they discovered Platt liked to take his lunch at the park, watching the kids play.

Platt, planted on one of the benches across from the play structure, was mid-sandwich when Xander and Scarlett flanked him on both sides, sitting uncomfortably close. Xander yanked the sandwich from Platt's hands and tossed it. Before Platt could say anything, Scarlett pressed the barrel of her gun into his fat side with a charming smile edged with glass. "Good afternoon, Senior Director Platt. Lovely day, isn't it?"

"Who are you?" he demanded, his lips compressing as Xander relieved him of his sidearm and recognition dawned. "You're making a huge mistake. Turn yourself in, son, before you make things worse."

"Thanks for the heartfelt advice but I'm not your son so shut the hell up," Xander returned with a cool smile. "But seeing as you're fond of advice, let me return the favor. Be careful of the company you keep."

Platt's lips thinned. "What do you want?"

"So many things," Scarlett answered, her tone hard. "But what I really want is to watch you fry. I'm Scarlett Rhodes, by the way, and I'm your worst nightmare. Did you know there are twenty-seven bones in the human hand, not counting the wrist, and it's possible to break each one with a certain Muay Thai strike to the center?"

Platt paled and swiveled his gaze to Xander, knowing he was in serious trouble. "You have a lot of nerve," Platt bluffed, trying to seem in control of the situation. "But you've saved me a lot of trouble by coming to me."

"Here's the deal. You're going to come with us and you're going to do it nice and quiet like a good boy or else things are going to get ugly for you real quick," Xander said.

Platt scoffed. "And why would I do that?"

Scarlett shoved the gun hard against his flab, causing him to grunt in pain. "Because if you don't I'm going to take real pleasure in gutting you like the pig you are."

"You wouldn't do that. Not here. There are kids everywhere," Platt said.

"Why? Because I'm a woman and I'm hardwired to care about kids?" Scarlett mocked, then leaned in closer to whisper in his ear, "I'm not that kind of woman. Right now, you better listen and cooperate."

But Platt wasn't so easily intimidated. They were in broad daylight and he knew they were limited in their power unless they wanted to go balls-out and shoot him in plain sight of everyone. "You're not very bright, are you?" Platt said to Scarlett. "Throwing your lot in with this criminal… You could've had a bright future. Griggs always thought highly of you."

"You don't have the right to say his name," Scarlett hissed, fighting the rush of tears. *No crying, not now!* She'd cry for Conrad later. "We know why you killed him."

Platt stilled and Xander took up the conversation.

"Sucks when our dirty laundry is out for everyone to see. I mean, you probably think you did a decent enough job hiding yours but the thing about dirty laundry, it always seems to surface no matter how well you think you've stuffed it away in dark corners."

"You're not only a criminal, you're insane."

"If only I were. Would've made framing me so much easier."

Scarlett jumped in. "Seems you've got a thing for young boys and girls and someone found out. That someone was Carl Sheffton and he's been blackmailing you. Now before you go and try to deny it, don't waste your time. We have the transcripts from the bug Conrad planted in your office."

Scarlett could feel Platt begin to tremble, his body jiggling with tiny rumbles that were impossible to hide. A slow cruel smile formed as she said, "You killed my friend to keep your secret but now you have to deal with me and I'm a goddamn avenging angel, you hear me, Platt? You're not only going to pay for what you did to Conrad, you're going to prison for a very long time for being a friggin' pervert."

"I didn't have a choice," Platt said, dropping his bravado, his tone flat. "Griggs overheard my conversation with Sheffton. I had to take care of the problem or Sheffton was going to leak my indiscretion to the press and then have me killed so I couldn't talk."

"Well, lucky for you we found you first. What makes you think that Sheffton isn't already planning to get rid of you?" Xander said. "You're a loose end he can't afford."

Platt licked his dry lips. "I've done everything he told me to," he said. "*Everything.*"

"But you're sloppy and that's something Sheffton discovered too late," Scarlett supplied. "But cheer up, you're going to help us put Sheffton away and in return, we won't put a bullet in your brain like you did Griggs. You don't deserve a quick death. You deserve something slow and painful, you pile of shit, for killing a man better than you'll ever be."

Xander jerked Platt up. "Enough talk. We have statements to give, don't we, Senior Director?"

"If I do that, he'll kill me," Platt said.

"You should have some measure of protection in prison," Scarlett said with a shrug. "But not my problem."

"Make me a deal or I don't talk."

They ignored Platt and stuffed him in the back seat of the car, while Scarlett slid in beside him so he didn't get any crazy ideas like trying to make a run for it.

Even though he was big, she'd seen bigger guys run faster than people gave them credit. Scarlett wasn't going to underestimate Platt's desire to get away.

"Why me?" Xander asked as he navigated traffic. "How'd you single me out for this frame job?"

"You fit the profile," Platt answered dully. "Have you read your psych eval? You read like the poster child for disenfranchised military. Highly skilled with a few screws loose and a loner without family to care if you went AWOL."

Scarlett wanted to smash the butt of her gun into Platt's nose. That could've described any one of Red Wolf's team. "How'd you get Xander's DNA?"

Platt sighed as if she were stupid. "Who said I did?"

Sudden understanding dawned and Scarlett said, "You doctored the evidence."

Platt shrugged. "Easy enough to do if you know what you're doing. I never figured he'd have the balls to try and figure this shit out. That was my mistake."

"That wasn't your only mistake," Scarlett growled, hating him more with every breath. "You're a disgrace."

"We all got demons, bitch. Even you. Even your lover-boy."

Xander scowled. "Stay on topic. No one is interested in your bait-and-switch tactics."

"Oh, so you know about your lover-boy's addiction to pills?"

Scarlett swallowed, narrowing her gaze. "I do. Now shut up."

Platt said, "A bit of good luck we stumbled on when lover-boy was caught passed out on the surveillance footage from the south side of the amphitheater. Made it ten times easier to pin the job on Scott. We knew he wouldn't come clean about being drugged up and once he made his statement, he couldn't take it back. Doctoring the forensics report was the final nail in the coffin."

Both Scarlett and Xander asked, "What surveillance footage?"

"Don't get excited, it's long gone. Erased. Blamed it on the blast."

"But—" A sharp pop interrupted her next question and Platt slumped over her, falling like dead weight against her, and another pop followed as the entire back window shattered.

Xander yelled, "Get down!" and swerved to lose the tail that was shooting at them.

Scarlett shoved Platt's dead body off her with a grunt to return fire, ignoring Xander's instruction to take cover.

"Damn it, Scarlett!" Xander shouted, accelerating through traffic, fishtailing around sharp corners as he tried to ditch whoever was shooting at them.

But Xander should've known better. She wasn't going to cower while they were under fire. She wasn't capable of hiding when bullets were flying.

Scarlett rose up, fired at the car behind them, killing the driver and sending them swerving into a brick building where the car exploded on impact. She slid down in the seat, reloaded in case there was another car behind that one, but they were in the clear. Whoever had sent that car had figured one was enough.

Their saving grace seemed to be everyone's penchant for underestimating them.

Scarlett looked at Platt, bloody drool dribbling down his slack chin, and swore under her breath. Platt had gotten off way too easily. She'd really been looking forward to sending him to prison, knowing how well pedophiles were treated on the inside.

He wouldn't have lasted a week.

"Asshole," she muttered, shoving Platt's inert body until he slumped like a lumpy sack of potatoes against the opposite window.

With Platt dead, they'd lost their ability to easily pin the conspiracy on Sheffton. But now that they had proof with the transcripts, Xander had a bold idea.

An idea that meant asking for help from a politician.

"Senator Williams," Xander said from the burner phone so it couldn't be traced. "This is Xander Scott."

"How did you get this number?" Williams asked, a slight catch in his tone that made Xander feel bad for tying him up and interrogating him in his puppy pajamas, but they hadn't known he wasn't a bad guy until after the fact. Maybe after all this was said and done, he'd send Williams an edible arrangement or something. "What do you want?"

"Look, I'm real sorry for the last time we met but I need a favor."

"A favor? That's bold."

Xander knew it was but hard times called for desperate actions. "You have no idea. I'm about to lay some shocking news on you, but I can promise you that the information is legit. You might even be in danger so it's imperative that you do what I ask."

"You're a fugitive. You broke into my house and terrorized me. Why would I do anything for you?" Then he caught the second half of what Xander had said. "What do you mean *danger*? Are you threatening me?"

"No, not me. You've got nothing to fear from me. I

only go after the bad guys and I'm sorry I thought you were one of them. I actually really liked your pajamas."

"Get to the point," Williams said. "What kind of danger are you talking about?"

"I'll just cut to the chase—Sheffton killed McQuarry and he's a raging psychopath in a designer suit. I think he also just had Senior Director Paul Platt killed so he wouldn't talk."

"Hold on, what are you talking about?"

"I know this is a lot but trust me, there's more. Platt framed me for McQuarry's death. He said there was footage on the south side of the amphitheater that proves I couldn't have set the bomb. I was passed out from a drug overdose."

"And why would I believe you? You just admitted that you were high on drugs when the bomb happened."

"Because it's my alibi and it's what Platt didn't want anyone to see. He said the footage was damaged due to the blast but I think you have the resources to see if anything can be salvaged from the footage."

"Even if I did, that footage is long gone," Williams said.

"No, it would've been collected as evidence. Trust me, that camera is in an evidence locker. You just need to get it."

Williams sounded flustered. "I don't understand. What would Sheffton have to gain from McQuarry's death?"

"Everything. Look, you're going to have to trust me like I'm trusting you to do the right thing—and be careful. Only trust this information with people you know for sure you can rely on. Sheffton has spies everywhere."

Xander could feel that Williams was questioning if Xander was insane and he totally understood his hesitation but before he could try another tactic, Scarlett took the phone.

"Senator Williams, this is Scarlett Rhodes. Xander is telling the truth. Platt was just killed right in front of me. We were being chased and shot at in downtown DC. I returned fire and killed their driver. The vehicle crashed into a brick building on Hapsberg Avenue. The incident should be all over the news by now. If you don't believe me, just check the newsfeed. We need your help. Sheffton is dangerous. Please tell us you'll help us. We can't do this alone." She handed the phone back to Xander and they climbed from the car, leaving Platt behind.

"We can't do this without your help." Xander put all his cards on the table.

"Why is Scarlett Rhodes with you?"

"Because I'm innocent," Xander answered bluntly.

Williams sighed, as if reluctant to help Xander but Scarlett had tipped the scales. "I'll see what I can do but I'm not saying I believe you," Williams said.

"I'll take it," Xander said.

"What are you going to do now?"

"Now we're going to try and stay alive long enough to catch Sheffton and his accomplice before they manage to push through a spending bill that will make the Patriot Act look like a walk in the park."

"H.R. 720," Williams guessed correctly, concern in his tone. "But Sheffton is going to oppose the bill. We talked about it before he left for DC."

"Whatever he told you was a line of bullshit. Sheffton is going to support the bill. He's in tight with the

Secretary of Defense and my guess is Sheffton is going to use whatever leverage he can to get what he wants in the future from Bettis."

"This is a nightmare," Williams said, and Xander couldn't disagree.

"Try living it for the past few weeks."

"If what you're saying is true, I'm sorry you've gone through all of this." After a heavy sigh, Williams said, "I'll see what I can do."

Relief followed as Xander said, "Thank you, Senator. And I really mean it about those pajamas. Pretty swag if you ask me."

"Stop talking about my pajamas," Williams growled and said, "I'll be in touch," before clicking off.

Scarlett looked to Xander. "Is he in?"

"Yeah, he's in but very touchy about his sleeping attire."

"I told you to stop mentioning them. It's just weird."

Xander shrugged. "What? I truly liked them."

"You don't even sleep in pajamas."

"Maybe if I had those sweet silky ones, I'd start."

Scarlett shook her head, looking ready to pistol-whip him. "Get focused. We need to ditch this car and *him*," she said, gesturing to Platt's cooling body, "and then we have a Senate hearing to crash."

"Is now an inappropriate time to tell you how turned on I am?"

"Very."

"Okay, I'll table that for now but just know, you are hot as shit when you're in badass mode."

Scarlett rolled her eyes but he caught the hint of a smile. Inappropriate or not, *oh, yeah*, she liked it.

Chapter 25

Scarlett and Xander paused after they parked in the Capitol Building parking lot in a different car they'd boosted. Scarlett looked to Xander with an arched brow. "Any idea how we're going to break into the Capitol Building without getting our asses shot?"

"Not a clue. Still working on that minor detail."

"Work faster."

Instead, Xander wrapped his hand around the back of her neck and hauled her in for a kiss. Their tongues danced and twined against one another and even though there wasn't time for messing around, he wanted to drag her into the back seat and screw her senseless.

He pulled away slowly, both breathing hard. "It must be that whole impending-death thing that gets the blood moving," he said with a crooked smile. "Or you're incredibly hot and I'm ridiculously horny."

She laughed and kissed him again. "You're impossible."

Just then her burner phone rang and it was Zak.

"Hey, still alive?" he said, joking.

"Barely," Scarlett replied, quickly recounting what had happened in the last twenty-four hours. At the news of Conrad's death, Zak quieted and it revived all the feelings she was trying to stuff down. She swallowed and shared a quick look with Xander. "Where are you?" she asked.

"At the Capitol. Where are you?"

"Same." She twisted around in her seat, looking for Zak and CJ. Of course, the odds of finding them were slim. "What are you doing here?"

"Following up like you asked me to. But I've done you a solid that you're totally going to owe me for. I got you some credentials. Fake name for Xander, of course, because he's still on the run but your name hasn't been flagged yet so we're good to go."

"I could kiss you," she said, smiling. "Good job. Meet us at the service entrance. No sense in drawing unnecessary attention," and then she hung up. To Xander, she said, "Zak has solved our problem on how to get in. He has credentials for us. We're going to meet him at the service entrance."

"By the time this is over, I'm going to owe Zak and CJ my firstborn."

Scarlett chuckled. "Let's go."

They met Zak and CJ, and she was momentarily struck by how emotional the guys' meeting was. They'd all been close but it took a screwed-up frame job to realize that they were truly bonded at the hip.

Zak handed out their credentials, but then CJ pointed out that she had some blood spatter on her shirt.

"Crap," she said, knowing she couldn't walk into a Senate hearing with blood as an accessory. Or could she? If they were going to crash the party, maybe the blood was appropriate. "Screw it," she muttered, pushing forward. "Let's do this."

They made their way past security and headed toward the hearing. They received some curious stares but otherwise they were left alone—*so much for the security of our nation*—and after flashing their credentials, made it onto the floor.

"Ready for nothing?" Scarlett asked, a bit apprehensive that everything was going to blow up in their faces.

"It's now or never."

"Here we go." She looked to CJ and nodded. *Do your thing, tech wiz.* Suddenly, the large screen used for projections began flashing, catching everyone's attention. Members of Congress began to shift, confused by the interruption and Xander took the opportunity to jump to center stage.

"Ladies and gentlemen, if I can have your attention…we are going to take a small break from your regularly scheduled programming of passing laws and shit to bring you a conspiracy worth paying attention to. If you please, direct your attention to the screen."

CJ had put together a tidy little show, starting with big pictures of Senator Carl Sheffton and the Secretary of Defense, Mark Bettis, in a tight embrace. Granted the pictures were a little grainy, but it was clearly the senator and the secretary. The ripple of gasps through the crowd echoed through the room. "I know, right? Naughty, naughty," Xander commented. "But that's only a tiny part of this story and you might ask why I'm coming to you instead of the authorities and that's an interesting story, too. I'm here because here is the safest place for me right now."

Sheffton, florid in the face, tried to edge his way out of the room but Zak barred his exit and forcefully redirected the man to his seat, saying, "You don't want to leave yet, Senator. Things are just getting juicy."

"Get this man out of here!" the secretary roared but everyone seemed frozen in place. Everyone loved a good conspiracy and it was probably the most excitement they'd had in years.

"Hold on, Mr. Secretary, this is important stuff," Xander called out, holding sway with the crowd like a charismatic master of ceremonies. More pictures of Bettis and Sheffton clearly being more than colleagues flashed on the screen and both the secretary and Sheffton looked ready to vomit. But then the transcripts popped on the screen, showing the conversations between Platt and Sheffton and the crowd gasped again; nervous shuffling followed as people whispered.

Scarlett joined Xander. "Senator Sheffton was blackmailing Senior Director Paul Platt into framing Xander Scott, a decorated military war hero for the Tulsa City bombing, which took the life of Senator Ken McQuarry. Platt changed the forensics saying Xander's DNA was found on the explosives, which wasn't true." She drew a deep breath before saying, "We have recovered video surveillance footage from the south side of the amphitheater that previously was believed lost that proves Xander couldn't have set that bomb."

That last part was a total bluff. It was too early to tell if Williams could find the camera or the footage, but no one else knew that. Just watching Sheffton sweat was worth the lie.

"Platt killed Special Agent Conrad Griggs—" her voice caught and she had to clear her throat before she could continue "—when Griggs found out Platt's secret. Then Sheffton had Platt killed to cut loose ends. We've given all of our evidence to someone we trust and right this minute he is packaging all of our collected evidence and sending it to the authorities and the press."

"I didn't have anything to do with this," protested Bettis as Capitol police entered the room.

The Speaker of the House gestured for the police to escort Sheffton and Bettis out of the building and said, "Thank you for your information. If you wouldn't mind releasing our feed, we'll take it from here."

Xander gave the Speaker a thumbs-up and watched as Sheffton and Bettis were removed, both squabbling at each other and promising legal action against the Senate for this embarrassment and obvious gross level of slander.

Scarlett, Zak, CJ and Xander looked at each other and Xander asked, "Am I in the clear?"

"Well, we just proved you didn't kill McQuarry, so I think you are," Scarlett said.

"Good. I'm ready to go home. I've missed my damn bed."

He slung his arm around her shoulders and they began to walk from the building. And then they were promptly arrested.

Sitting in lockup, Xander, CJ and Zak were in one cell while Scarlett was on the other side of the building where the women prisoners were kept.

"Do you think we're going to prison?" CJ asked.

Xander thought about it for a minute before answering, "Well, depends on what they decide to charge y'all with. Aiding and abetting a federal fugitive is generally frowned upon."

"Even when the fugitive is innocent?" CJ asked with a wink.

"Yeah, not sure about that just yet. I mean, I lied through my teeth about the camera footage. We have no idea if any of it was actually salvageable and honestly, that was my best bet for getting off on the murder charges."

"Sounds like shitty odds," CJ said, shaking his head, then looked apologetically to Xander saying, "Sorry, buddy. You might be screwed."

Xander chuckled, "Yeah, you think?" It'd been several hours since they were hauled into custody and they hadn't received any word. No one had called them into questioning or taken their statements. They were just sitting, like ducks waiting for the shotgun blast and it wasn't a great feeling.

His back started to protest his position and he tried to shift to relieve the pressure. Zak noticed and commented.

"Why didn't you say something, man?"

The question was real, no joking around, and Xander answered with the same seriousness. "I thought I could handle it. My ego got the better of me. I was embarrassed."

"We could've been there for you," CJ said.

"I know."

"So what are going to do about it?" Zak asked.

He sighed. "Assuming we get out of here? I'm going to check myself into rehab and get clean."

CJ sat up and said, "You know, if you'd trusted us, or at least trusted me because I'm less judgy than that guy over there—" he gestured to Zak with a grin "—I could've told you that I know a guy who's doing some cool stuff with stem cell shit. It's the real deal. You remember my shoulder injury when I jacked it up during that Iraq mission? Well, I didn't want no narcotics so I went the alternative route. *Bam*, stem cell rejuvenation therapy. Good as new." He flexed to demonstrate. "Hell, I think it's in better shape than before. This is serious sci-fi futuristic stuff, you know? But it works. You could do that with your back injury and get off that shit."

Xander nodded, touched that his buddies had his six even though he'd shut them out. "I'll check it out. Thanks, man."

CJ nodded, leaning back against the wall, sighing with boredom. "Someone either needs to book us or let us go. This is bullshit. We've got rights. Right?"

Zak ignored CJ's whining and said, "So what are you going to do with Scarlett?"

"What do you mean?" Xander asked, on guard. He didn't want to reveal anything that Scarlett wasn't ready to share.

"You guys have been practically living together under stressful circumstances. That can create a false sense of connection. I just wondered how you guys got through it."

"It was fine." A beat of silence followed and then CJ shared a knowing look with Zak, prompting Xander to ask defensively, "What was that look about?"

"You guys are banging. We can tell. But it's cool, man. You two have had chemistry since day one and frankly, we're glad you finally got it over with," Zak said.

Xander started to protest but it was stupid to even try; they already knew. He let out a long exhale and admitted to it. "Yeah, she's special. I like her. I mean, I think I love her. Shit, yeah, no, I love her. I didn't mean to but it just sort of happened and before you start spouting psychology babble, I felt this way before all this crap happened."

"Like I said, what are you going to do about it?" Zak repeated, staring him down. "You know, nothing will ever be the same after this. You have to make a choice."

Xander knew Zak was right but he didn't have an answer just yet. He had to get the drugs out of his system first. "My head's not on straight yet. I don't have the right to be thinking past getting clean."

Zak nodded, seeming to agree but they both knew the situation was far more complicated. Xander couldn't remain with Red Wolf and date Scarlett if Scarlett was his TL. Scarlett had worked her ass off to get her position within Red Wolf and Xander would never ask her to step down for him.

Which meant he would have to leave, but if he left… what chance did they have of making it work?

Hell, he was jumping the gun. He didn't know if Scarlett wanted to be with him—if they managed to get their asses out of jail.

The jailer, a stout, stern man with a permanent scowl, gestured to the three men and said, "You're being released."

Surprised but not about to look a gift horse in the

mouth, they happily left the cell behind to find Joshua Handler, owner of Red Wolf, standing there waiting for them.

Ahh, shit. The real boss man. They rarely interacted with Joshua but they knew who he was.

To CJ and Zak he said, "I trust you can find your way home?" They nodded and thanked him for his intervention on their behalf and then cut out of there like they were on fire. To Xander, he said, "Ride with me."

Either he was about to be fired or... No, that was probably it.

They climbed into the sleek dark town car and Xander had no idea where they were going.

"I'm impressed with how you handled yourself," Joshua said in one breath but ended with, "But you screwed up big-time and gave Red Wolf a black eye in front of some very important people."

Xander wouldn't make excuses, not anymore. "I'm sorry," he said. "I screwed up."

"Yes, you did." Xander waited for him to say the words but Joshua didn't. Instead, he said, "You're a good man. We've all made mistakes in life. You're going to go to rehab." It wasn't a question; it was a statement of fact that left no room for arguing. "Red Wolf will take care of it." He paused and looked to Xander, his pale blue eyes intense. "Is there anything else I need to know?"

"I'm in love with Scarlett."

There, he let it drop.

Joshua nodded, absorbing the information. "Does she feel the same?"

"I don't know. I hope so, but I don't know. She's

dedicated to Red Wolf and I would never ask her to change that."

"Good."

And that was all he said for the rest of the ride, which ended up being to his hotel. As Joshua exited the car, he said, "The car will take you to the airport where you'll go straight to a private Red Wolf facility to detox. When you finish, I'll be in touch."

Before Xander could say anything, Joshua closed the door, and he was on his way to the airport.

He didn't even get a chance to talk to Scarlett first, but he supposed that was the way it had to be.

Maybe it was even better this way. Guess it didn't matter, because that's what was happening.

Chapter 26

It'd been three months since their arrest at Capitol Hill and three months since she'd seen Xander. According to Joshua, Red Wolf was handling the issue of Xander's addiction and everyone else should get back to business.

Even though Scarlett desperately wanted to pepper Joshua for answers about Xander, she knew better. As much as it killed her, she swallowed her tongue and tried to focus on her job, which wasn't easy.

Sleepless nights where she flipped and flopped, staring at the ceiling, assaulted by the myriad of questions and memories that she couldn't sort; the grief over losing Conrad and attending his funeral; the need but utter lack of desire to process her feelings about Xander and how things had abruptly ended.

She wasn't the kind of woman who pined for a man but for the first time in her life, yeah, she was pining.

The only saving grace had been the rosy outcome following Sheffton's arrest for the murder of McQuarry and four civilians in the Tulsa City bombing.

Gotta hand it to Williams, he really came through when they'd needed him to. Williams was able to recover the surveillance footage from the amphitheater that Sheffton had been certain was deleted. Seems Sheffton hadn't followed through and made sure that the footage was gone. In his arrogance, he hadn't thought to double check and simply left the job to someone else and it had been overlooked. His sloppy work had worked to their benefit.

In light of the overwhelming evidence against him, Sheffton rolled over in the hopes of getting a more lenient sentence.

It hadn't worked.

Sheffton was currently awaiting sentencing and legal analysts were predicting that Sheffton would likely die in prison before he was eligible for parole.

Sheffton had been squeezing Platt, forcing him to dance to his tune, but that day that Xander and Scarlett had intercepted Platt at the park, Sheffton's men had already been en route to snip the loose end. Scarlett and Xander had only delayed the inevitable. Not that Scarlett could work up a tear for Platt's death.

Scarlett had zero empathy for pedophiles and even less for the man who had killed her friend. The world was a lot less safe without Conrad Griggs in it, that was for sure.

Even though Sheffton deserved what he got, Scarlett definitely got the impression that the government had tried to make an example out of Sheffton to show that they were serious about rooting out deep corruption but everyone knew that it would take more than a grand gesture to drain the so-called swamp.

However, it made for good press and no one was interested in fixing the real problem so life went on.

Ironically, the bigger scandal was Secretary of Defense Bettis resigning from his position in the wake of his affair with Sheffton, even though Bettis had been unaware of Sheffton's level of deception and depth of ambition until after everything had been revealed.

If there was anyone Scarlett had felt mildly sorry for, it was the secretary. He'd been clueless as to how Sheffton was manipulating him for his own purposes.

As it turned out, the Wakefield deal had simply been a business deal McQuarry had been pushing for his own gain and Bettis owning shares in the company had been coincidence.

It might've been refreshing to learn that money had been at the root of all the evil but, alas, ambition had been the catalyst.

Sheffton had been planning to use his relationship with Bettis to further his own career, knowing that the secretary would've said and done anything to keep their relationship quiet. Talk about some long-range, big-picture planning. She had to hand it to Sheffton for putting together a plan that would take years to put into play.

But poor Bettis was screwed. That man would end up paying for his indiscretion for his entire life.

Nothing was more titillating than a publicly disgraced politician. Shortly after the scandal broke, the secretary's wife, Janet, filed for divorce. *My, how people loved to watch the mighty fall.*

Speaking of mighty…

She knew Xander had finished his rehab three months ago but he still hadn't come back around. When his notice came across her desk, she'd fought the urge to cry silly tears.

She had to accept the realization that Xander wasn't coming back.

He was moving on and he hadn't said a word to her. Maybe she'd read too much into their time together but she thought they'd both felt something equally. It wasn't like her to fill in the blanks with her own interpretation of feelings. She was pretty blunt with her needs and desires but Xander had left her feeling tongue-tied.

The first night sleeping alone had been awkward. By the time morning broke, she was cranky, sleepy and her eyes felt filled with grit.

She figured all she needed was time to adjust to sleeping alone again—hell, she preferred the option to starfish in the bed—but it'd been months and she still reached for him in her fitful sleep and woke when her grasping hands clutched at nothing.

Zak found her in the break room pouring a second cup of coffee, grabbing a granola bar from the snack box. "How you holding up, TL?" he asked.

"Fine."

"One-word answers usually indicate the opposite," Zak said, winking as he tore into his granola bar. "Seriously, though, are you okay?"

Scarlett forced a smile. "I'm fine. Just tired."

Zak nodded, knowing she was full of crap but didn't

press further. They all knew that her disposition was because of Xander and she didn't want to talk about it.

"Well, I have something that ought to cheer you up."

Scarlett looked up from her coffee mug. "Yeah? What?"

"There's someone waiting in the briefing room to talk to you. Seems important."

Scarlett frowned, trying to remember if she had a meeting scheduled that she'd overlooked. Dumping her coffee down the sink and quickly rinsing her mug, she went to the briefing room to find Xander standing there.

Her breath caught and for a long moment, all she could do was stare.

Questions bubbled up but tears threatened and her throat closed. Why hadn't he called? Why hadn't he at least said goodbye when he left Red Wolf? What the hell? Why was he here now?

Xander broke the silence first. "You look good," Xander said, smiling as if he hadn't just dropped off the planet without so much as a "screw you" for a goodbye.

She held her tongue. He looked good, too. Clean, sharp, *sober*. He'd kicked his habit. Even if she was pissed at him for bailing on her, she was glad he was sober.

Zak quietly closed the briefing door, leaving them alone. She narrowed her gaze. This smelled of a set-up and she didn't like being ambushed. "What can I do for you, Xander?" she asked, finding her voice. "Did you forget some personal effects?"

"You could say that," he said, walking toward her but she stopped him with an outstretched hand that

clearly warned *DON'T*. He frowned but didn't push
her. "I guess I have some explaining to do."

"No. I don't want to hear it. Whatever you came
to do, do it and go. You're no longer a part of the Red
Wolf team."

"Stubborn as always. Nice to see not much has
changed in the three months I've been gone."

"No, you're wrong. Plenty has changed," she said.

He sighed. "Can I please explain and then you can
make your judgments?"

She crossed her arms. "No."

"Please?"

"You don't get to come in here, look cute and beg
for forgiveness. I'm not that kind of woman and never
have been so if that's why you came, you can just let
yourself out the same way you came in."

"Scarlett, just do me a favor and shut the hell up for
a minute. I swear, if after I've said my piece, you still
want me to go to hell, I'll go without another word. But
I came to say something and I'm not leaving until I do."

What would it hurt to hear him out? She supposed
it would provide some kind of closure. She jerked a
short nod, indicating he should get to it before she
changed her mind.

Xander drew a deep breath before jumping in with
an earncst expression. "Right after we left the jail,
Joshua sent me to a private Red Wolf facility to detox
from the narcotics. He put it pretty plainly—go to detox
or get kicked out on my own. I knew Joshua was offering me a once in a lifetime deal and I couldn't say
no. The town car dropped Joshua off at his hotel and
took me to the airport. I didn't have a way of telling

you what was happening and I didn't have a choice—
I had to take the deal."

"Why didn't Joshua tell me?" Scarlett asked, confused.

Xander didn't know. "I'm sure he had his reasons
but I wasn't about to question his decision, you know?"

Yeah, she got it. Joshua wasn't the kind of man you
put under a hot bulb for his decisions. He was fair but
stern and a little intimidating.

"I was there for a month and then when I came out,
Joshua told me I needed to prove that I wasn't going
to go right back to using again. I needed to prove to
Joshua but also to myself that I could rise from the
mess I'd created of my life. It was important to me that
I come to you with a clear head."

Her lip threatened to tremble. "And why is that?"

"Because I never wanted to see you looking at me
the way you did when I was using."

"And what way was that?"

"With disappointment."

She blinked back tears. "And?"

"And once I was clean, I worked on figuring out how
I was going to make things right for the both of us."

Scarlett shook her head, confused. "What do you
mean? The both of us? You quit Red Wolf."

He took a step forward, reaching for her hand. "Because I knew we couldn't be together if you were still
my TL and I would never ask you to quit. You love Red
Wolf." He drew a breath before continuing, "I needed
a different job, but there are only so many positions
suited to what we do. I did a lot of soul-searching and
realized the reason I've always shied away from a lead-
ership role was because I was afraid of screwing up.

Well, I've already been to the backside of that equation and I realized fear is a cop-out. If I hadn't been so afraid of seeming weak, none of this would've happened. Of course, one could argue that if none of this had happened I wouldn't have had this epiphany, but that's not the point. The point is I decided I wasn't going to let fear drive the bus anymore."

He gently pulled her to him and she went, but she was still confused as to what he was rambling about. Was he unemployed? Was he starting his own business? She didn't know which way the wind was blowing.

"Do you have a job or not?" she asked, mildly exasperated because the man was taking forever to get to the point.

Xander smiled and lifted his badge to show her.

An FBI badge.

Her jaw dropped. "What?" she exclaimed. "I don't understand... You're an FBI agent now?"

Xander grinned, explaining, "After Platt's role was revealed in the corruption and Conrad's death, I was offered a job, provided I could pass the entrance tests."

Her brow arched. "You passed the psych tests?"

Xander winked. "Joshua might've helped grease the wheels a little." Scarlett was still processing the bombshell Xander had dropped when he said, "I wanted to come back to you a changed man. Clean and sober, and free and clear to do this..." Then he cupped her face tenderly and brushed a sweet kiss on her lips. She sank into him, savoring the feel of his mouth on hers. The months faded away and she gladly lost herself in the pleasure of his touch.

She glanced up at him with an amazed smile. "So are you saying…?"

"Do I have to spell it out, woman? I want you. I want you to be my girl. I want to have arguments over which is the best Chinese food restaurant and I want to fall asleep with you snoring in my ear. I want it all and I finally have what I need to make it happen if you'll have me."

Tears leaked down her cheeks as she sniffed and said, "I don't snore." Then she threw her arms around his neck like a lovesick teenager, unable to believe she'd fallen in love with Xander Scott—a man so wholly un-suited for her and yet so utterly perfect as well.

"So are you saying you're ready to rack up some frequent flier miles?" he asked with a charming grin as he hoisted her up, cupping her ass firmly. "Because I've already checked the flights. It's a thirty-minute flight from DC to West Virginia."

Scarlett nodded as she sealed her mouth to his. "I'm ready."

She was more than ready.

This was the love she never thought she'd find and she'd found it in the most unlikely of places.

Xander carried her out of the debriefing room and the Red Wolf team burst into applause with Zak and CJ high-fiving each other as if they'd been betting on this outcome.

She grinned as Xander put her down and said over her shoulder as they walked out, hand in hand, "I'm taking the day off. Try to stay out of trouble while I'm gone and don't call me unless the world is ending!"

* * * * *

*Be sure to look for the next book in
Kimberly Van Meter's
Military Precision Heroes series,
available in 2019 wherever
Harlequin Romantic Suspense books are sold!*

Read on for an exclusive sneak peek at
Fatal Invasion, *the next sizzling book in
the Fatal series from* New York Times
bestselling author Marie Force...

ONE

"THIS IS A classic case of be careful what you wish for." Nick placed a stack of folded dress shirts in a suitcase that already held socks, underwear, workout clothes and several pairs of jeans. Only Nick would start packing seven days before his scheduled departure for Europe next Sunday, the day after Freddie and Elin's wedding. "That's the lesson learned here."

"Only anal-retentive freakazoids pack a week before a trip." Sam sat at the foot of the bed and watched him pack with a growing sense of dread. "*Three freaking weeks*. The last time you were gone that long, I nearly lost my mind, and I don't have much of a mind left to lose."

"Come with me," he said for the hundredth time since the president asked him to make the diplomatic trip, representing the administration on a visit with some of the country's closest allies. Since President Nelson was still recovering—in more ways than one—from his son's criminal activities, several of the allies had requested he send his popular vice president in his stead.

Sam flopped on the bed. "I *can't*. I have work and Scotty, and Freddie is going on his honeymoon for *two* weeks and… I can't." No Nick at home to entertain her. No Freddie at work to entertain her. The next few weeks were going to totally suck monkey balls.

"Actually, you *can*." Nick hovered above her, propped on arms ripped with muscles, his splendid chest on full display. "You have more vacation time saved up than you can use in a lifetime, *and* you have the right to actually use it. Scotty will be fine with Shelby, your dad and Celia, your sisters, and the Secret Service here to entertain him. We could even ask Mrs. Littlefield to come up for the weekends."

Their son's former guardian would love the chance to spend time with him, but Sam didn't feel right about leaving him for so long. However, the thought of being without Nick for three endless weeks made her sick. His trip to Iran earlier in the year had been pure torture, especially since it kept getting extended.

"Why'd you have to tell Nelson you wanted to be more than a figurehead vice president?" She play-punched his chest. "Everything was fine when he was ignoring you."

He kissed her lips and then her neck. "You're so, *so* cute when you pout."

"Badass cops do *not* pout."

"Mine does when she doesn't get her own way, and it's truly adorable."

She scowled at him. "Badass cops are not adorable."

"Mine is." Leaving a trail of hot kisses on her neck, he said, "Come with me, Samantha. London, Paris, Rome, the Vatican, Amsterdam, Brussels, The Hague. Come see the world with me."

Sam had never been to Europe and had always wanted to go, so she was sorely tempted to say to hell with her responsibilities.

"Come on." He rolled her earlobe between his teeth and pressed against her suggestively. "Three whole *weeks* together away from the madness of DC. You know you want to go. Gonzo could cover for you at work, and things have been slow anyway."

There hadn't been a homicide in more than a week, which meant they were due, and that was another reason to stay home. "Don't say that and put a jinx on us."

"Come away with me. Scotty will be fine. We'll FaceTime with him every day and bring him presents. He'll be well cared for by everyone else who loves him." He kissed her neck as he unbuttoned her shirt and pushed it aside. "You'd get to meet the Queen of England."

Sam moaned. She *loved* the queen—speaking of a badass female.

"And the Pope. Plus, you'll need some clothes—and shoes. *Lots* of shoes."

"Stop it." She turned her face to avoid his kiss. "You're fighting dirty."

"Because I want my wife to come with me on the trip of a lifetime? I *need* you, Samantha."

As he well knew, she could deny him nothing when he said he needed her. "Fine, I'll go! But only if it's okay with Scotty and if I can swing it at work."

"Yes," her husband said on a long exhale. "We'll have so much fun."

"Will we actually get to see anything?"

He pushed himself up to continue packing. "I'll make sure of it."

"Um, excuse me."

"What's up?"

"My temperature after your attempts at persuasion."

A slow, lazy smile spread across his face, making

him the sexiest man in this universe—and the next.
"Is my baby feeling a little needy?"

She pulled her shirt off and released the front clasp
on her bra. "More than a little."

"We can't have that." Stepping to the foot of the
bed, he grasped the legs of her yoga pants and yanked
them off.

"Lock the door."

"Scotty's asleep."

"*Lock the door*, or this isn't happening." With Secret Service agents all over their house, Sam couldn't
relax if the door wasn't locked.

"This is definitely happening, but if it'll make you
happy, I'll lock the door."

"It'll make me happy, which will, in turn, make *you*
happy." She splayed her legs wide open to give him a
show as he returned from locking the door, and was
rewarded with gorgeous hazel eyes that heated with
desire when he saw her waiting for him.

"You little vixen," he muttered.

"I don't know *what* you're talking about."

"Sure, you don't," he said, laughing as he came
down on top of her and set out to give her a preview
of what three weeks away together might be like.

THEY BROKE THE news to Scotty the next morning at
breakfast. "So," Nick said tentatively, "what would you
think if Mom came with me to Europe?"

Thirteen-year-old Scotty, never at his best first thing
in the morning, shrugged. "It's fine."

"Really?" Sam said. "You wouldn't mind? Shelby,
Tracy and Angela would be around to hang with you,
and Gramps and Celia too. We thought maybe Mrs.

Littlefield could come up for a weekend or two if she's free."

"Sure, that sounds good."

Sam glanced at Nick, who seemed equally perplexed by his lack of reaction. They'd expected him to ask to come with them, at the very least.

"Is everything okay?" Sam asked her son.

"Uh-huh." He finished his cereal and got up to put the bowl in the sink. "I'm going to finish getting ready for school."

"Okay, bud," Nick said.

"Something's up," Sam said as soon as Scotty left the room.

"I agree. He didn't even ask if he could miss school to come with us."

"I thought the same thing."

"We'll have to see if we can get him to talk to us before we go—and not in the morning," Nick said.

"I'll ask Shelby to make spaghetti for dinner. That always puts him in a good mood." Sam's phone rang, and when she saw the number for Dispatch, she groaned. "Damn it. You jinxed me!" So much for getting out of Dodge without having to worry about work. She took the call. "Holland."

"Lieutenant, there was a fire overnight in Chevy Chase." The dispatcher referred to the exclusive northwest neighborhood that was home to a former US president, ambassadors and other wealthy residents. "We have two DOA at the scene," the dispatcher said, reciting the address. "The fire marshal has requested homicide detectives."

"Did he say why?"

"No, ma'am."

"Okay, I'm on my way." Thankfully, she'd showered and gotten dressed before she woke Scotty. "Please call Sergeant Gonzales and Detective Cruz and ask them to meet me there."

"Yes, ma'am."

Sam flipped her phone closed with a satisfying smack. That smacking sound was one of many reasons she'd never upgrade to a smartphone.

"You'll still be able to come with me, right?" Nick asked, looking adorably uncertain.

Sam went over to where he sat at the table and kissed him. "I'll talk to Malone today and see if I can make it happen."

"Keep me posted."

A RINGING PHONE woke Christina Billings from a sound sleep. Two-year-old Alex had been up during the night with a fever and cold that was making him miserable and her sleep deprived. Her fiancé, Tommy, had slept through that and apparently couldn't hear his phone ringing either. He was due at work in an hour and was usually up by now.

"Tommy." She nudged him, but he didn't stir. "*Tommy*. Your phone."

He came to slowly, blinking rapidly.

"The phone, Tommy. Answer it before it wakes Alex." He needed more sleep and so did she, or this was going to be a very long day.

Tommy grabbed the phone from the bedside table. Christina saw the word *Dispatch* on the screen.

"Gonzales."

She couldn't hear the dispatcher's side of the conversation, but she heard Tommy's grunt of acknowledgment before he ended the call, closing his eyes even as he continued to clutch the phone.

Christina wondered if he was going back to sleep after being called into work. She was about to say something when he got out of bed and headed for the shower.

Nine months ago today, his partner, A. J. Arnold, had been gunned down right in front of Tommy as they approached a suspect. After a long downward spiral following Arnold's murder, Tommy had seemed to rebound somewhat during the summer. But the rebound hadn't lasted into the fall.

In the last month, since his new partner, Cameron Green, had joined the squad, Christina had watched him regress into his grief. He'd said and done all the right things when it came to welcoming Cameron, but he was obviously spiraling again, and she had no idea what to do to help him or how to reach him. Even when lying next to her in bed, he seemed so far away from her.

Sometimes, when she had a rare moment alone, she allowed her thoughts to wander to life without Tommy and Alex at the center of it. She loved them both—desperately—but she wasn't sure how much more she could take of the distant, closed-off version of the man she loved. They were supposed to have been married by now. Like everything else, that plan had been shoved aside to make room for Tommy's overwhelming grief. It'd been months since they'd discussed getting married. In the meantime, she took care of Alex and everything else, while Tommy worked and came home to sleep before starting the cycle all over again.

They didn't talk about anything other than Alex.

They never went anywhere together or as a family. They hadn't had sex in so long she'd forgotten when it had last happened. She was as unhappy as she'd ever been. Something had to give—and soon, or she would be forced to decide whether their relationship was still healthy for her. She did *not* want to have to make that decision.

Only the thought of leaving Tommy at his lowest moment, not to mention leaving Alex, had kept her from making a move before now. She loved that little boy with her whole heart and soul. She'd stepped away from her own career as Nick's chief of staff to stay home with him and had hoped to add to their family by now. When she thought about the early days of her relationship with Tommy, when they'd been so madly in love, she couldn't have imagined feeling as insignificant to him as a piece of furniture that was always there when he finally decided to come home.

Christina hadn't told anyone about the trouble brewing between them. In her heart of hearts, she hoped they could still work it out somehow, and the last thing she needed was her friends and family holding a grudge against him forever—and they would if they had any idea just how bad things had gotten. Her parents had questioned the wisdom of her giving up a high-profile job to stay home to care for her boyfriend's child, especially when she'd made more money than him. But she'd been ready for a break from the political rat race when Alex came along, and she had no regrets about her decision. Or she hadn't until Tommy checked out of their relationship.

This weekend they'd be expected to celebrate at Freddie and Elin's wedding, and she'd have to pretend that everything was fine in her relationship when it was anything but. She wasn't sure how she would pull off another convincing performance for their friends. Tommy was one of Freddie's groomsmen, so she'd get to spend most of that day on her own while he attended to his friend.

Dangling at the end of her rope in this situation, more than once she'd thought about taking Alex and leaving, even though she had no legal right to take him. Another thing they'd never gotten around to— her adoption of him after his mother was killed. What would Tommy do if she left with his son? Call the police on her? That made her laugh bitterly. She'd be surprised if he noticed they were gone.

Tommy came out of the bathroom and went to the closet where he had clean clothes to choose from thanks to her. Did he ever wonder how that happened? He put on jeans and a black T-shirt and then went to unlock the bedside drawer where he kept his badge, weapon and cuffs.

She watched him slide the weapon into the holster he wore on his hip and jam the cuffs and badge into the back pockets of his jeans, the same way he did every day. Holding her breath, she waited to see if he would say anything to her or come around the bed to kiss her goodbye the way he used to before disaster struck, but like he did so often these days, he simply turned and left the room.

A minute later, she heard the front door close behind him.

For a long time after he left, she lay in bed staring up at the ceiling with tears running down her cheeks. She couldn't take much more of this.

TWO

SAM WAS THE first of her team to arrive on the scene of the smoldering fire that had demolished half a mansion in one of the District's most exclusive neighborhoods.

"What've we got?" Sam asked the fire marshal when he met her at the tape line.

"Two bodies found on the first floor of the house, both bound with zip ties at the hands and feet."

And that, right there, made their deaths her problem. "Do we know who they are?"

He consulted his notes. "The ME will need to make positive IDs, but the house is owned by Jameson and Cleo Beauclair. I haven't had time to dig any deeper on who they are."

"Are we certain they were the only people in the house?" Sam asked.

"Not yet. When we arrived just after four a.m., the west side of the house, where the bodies were found, was fully engulfed. That was our immediate focus. We've got firefighters searching the rest of what was once a ten-thousand-square-foot home."

"Any sign of accelerants?"

"Nothing so far, but we're an hour into the investigation stage. Early days."

"Has the ME been here?"

"Not yet."

"Could I take a look inside?"

"It's still hot in there, but I can show you the high-lights—or the lowlights, such as they are."

Sam followed him up the sidewalk to what had once been the front door. Inside the smoldering ruins of the house, she could make out the basic structure from the burned-out husk that remained. The putrid scents of smoke and death hung heavily in the air.

"That's them there," the fire marshal said, pointing to a space on the floor by a blackened stone fireplace where two charred bodies lay next to one another.

Sam swallowed the bile that surged to her throat. Nothing was worse, at least not in her line of work, than fire victims. Though it was the last thing she wanted to do, she moved in for a closer look, took photos of the bodies and the scene around them, then turned to face the fire marshal. "Anything else you think I ought to see?"

"Not yet."

"Keep me posted."

"Will do."

He walked away to continue his investigation while Sam went outside, carrying the horrifying images with her as she took greedy breaths of fresh air. As she reached the curb, the medical examiner's truck arrived. She waited for a word with Dr. Lindsey McNamara.

The tall, pretty medical examiner gathered her long red hair into a ponytail as she walked over to Sam.

"Fire victims," Sam said, shuddering.

"Good morning to you too."

"Hands and feet bound with zip ties."

"Here we go again," Lindsey said with a sigh. "Looks like it was quite a house."

"Ten thousand square feet, according to the fire marshal."

"I'll get you an ID and report as soon as I can."

"Appreciate it." Sam opened her phone and placed a call to Malone. "I'm at the scene of the fire in Chevy Chase."

"What've you got?"

"Two DOA, bound at the hands and feet, leading me to believe this was a home invasion gone bad. I need Crime Scene here ASAP."

"I'll call Haggerty and get them over there."

"I want them to comb through anything and everything that wasn't touched by the fire, and they need to do it soon before the scene is further compromised. We've got firefighters all over the place."

"Got it. What's your plan?"

"I'm going to talk to the neighbors and find out what I can about the people who lived here while I wait for Lindsey to confirm their identities."

"Keep me posted."

Sam slapped the phone closed and headed for her car to begin the task of figuring out who Jameson and Cleo Beauclair had been and who might've bound them before setting their house on fire. If the bodies were even those of the Beauclairs. Cases like this were often confounding from the start, but they would operate on the info they had available and go from there.

Her partner, Detective Freddie Cruz, arrived as Sam reached her car, which she had parked a block from the scene.

"I guess it was too much to hope our homicide-free streak would last until after the wedding," he said.

"Too much indeed. We've got two deceased on the

first floor of the west side of the home, hands and feet bound."

"Do we know who they are?"

"We know who owns the house, but we're not a hundred percent sure the owners are our victims," she said, passing along the names the fire marshal had given her. "Let's knock on some doors and then go back to HQ to see what Lindsey can tell us."

"I'm with you, LT."

"Any word from Gonzo?"

"Not that I've heard yet."

"He can catch up."

Don't miss Fatal Invasion *by Marie Force,
available now from HQN Books.*

Get 4 FREE REWARDS!

We'll send you 2 FREE Books plus 2 FREE Mystery Gifts.

Harlequin® Romantic Suspense books feature heart-racing sensuality and the promise of a sweeping romance set against the backdrop of suspense.

FREE Value Over $20

YES! Please send me 2 FREE Harlequin® Romantic Suspense novels and my 2 FREE gifts (gifts are worth about $10 retail). After receiving them, if I don't wish to receive any more books, I can return the shipping statement marked "cancel." If I don't cancel, I will receive 4 brand-new novels every month and be billed just $4.99 per book in the U.S. or $5.74 per book in Canada. That's a savings of at least 12% off the cover price! It's quite a bargain! Shipping and handling is just 50¢ per book in the U.S. and 75¢ per book in Canada.* I understand that accepting the 2 free books and gifts places me under no obligation to buy anything. I can always return a shipment and cancel at any time. The free books and gifts are mine to keep no matter what I decide.

240/340 HDN GMYZ

Name (please print)

Address   Apt. #

City   State/Province   Zip/Postal Code

Mail to the **Reader Service**:
IN U.S.A.: P.O. Box 1341, Buffalo, NY 14240-8531
IN CANADA: P.O. Box 603, Fort Erie, Ontario L2A 5X3

Want to try 2 free books from another series? Call 1-800-873-8635 or visit www.ReaderService.com.

SPECIAL EXCERPT FROM

⊕ HARLEQUIN®

ROMANTIC suspense

*A security breach has exposed Major Matt Riley and the
secrets he's kept for fourteen years, putting the woman
he's never stopped loving and their son in grave danger.*

*Read on for a sneak preview of the first book
in* USA TODAY *bestselling author Regan Black's
brand-new Riley Code miniseries,*
A Soldier's Honor.

She wasn't accustomed to sharing a bed with anyone.

"And what about us?"

"Us as in you and me?" His gaze locked on her, hot
and interested. "Is that an invitation?"

She backpedaled. "I meant us as in what are Caleb and
I supposed to do while you're fixing the problem?"

He watched her steadily as he took a long pull from the
beer bottle. Setting the bottle aside, he took a step toward
her. "Which part concerns you most? Sticking with me
for safety, or maybe just the idea of sticking with me?"

The last one, a small voice in her head cried out. But
she wasn't that overwhelmed nineteen-year-old anymore.
She was a grown woman, a mother with a son and an
established career. No matter the circumstance, Caleb's
safety was her top priority.

She planted her hand in the center of his hard chest.
His heart kicked, his chest swelled as he sucked in a
breath. He leaned into her touch, as though his heart

was drowning and she was the lifeline. Good grief, her imagination needed a dose of reality.

"Bethany," he murmured.

The blood rushing through her ears was so loud, she saw him speak her name more than she heard it. The blatant need in his brown eyes triggered an answering need in her. Any reply she might have given went up in flames when he lowered his firm lips to her mouth. He kissed her lightly at first, but she recognized the spark and heat just under the surface, waiting for an opening to break free and singe them both. Her hands curled into his shirt, pulled him closer. Oh, how she'd missed this. She'd thought time had exaggerated her memories and found the opposite was true when his tongue swept over hers, as he alternately sipped and plundered and called up all her long-ignored needs to the surface.

Our second first kiss, she thought. As full of promise as the first first kiss had been when they were kids.

"Oh. Ah. Sorry. Never mind." Caleb's voice, choked with embarrassment, doused the moment as effectively as a bucket of ice water.

She muttered an oath.

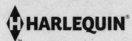

Love Harlequin romance?

DISCOVER.

Be the first to find out about promotions,
news and exclusive content!

Facebook.com/HarlequinBooks

Twitter.com/HarlequinBooks

Instagram.com/HarlequinBooks

Pinterest.com/HarlequinBooks

ReaderService.com

EXPLORE.

Sign up for the Harlequin e-newsletter and
download a free book from any series at
TryHarlequin.com.

CONNECT.

Join our Harlequin community to share
your thoughts and connect with other
romance readers!
Facebook.com/groups/HarlequinConnection

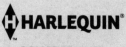

HARLEQUIN®

**ROMANCE WHEN
YOU NEED IT**

HSOCIAL2018

Reward the book lover in you!

Earn points on your purchase of new Harlequin books from participating retailers.

Turn your points into **FREE BOOKS** of your choice!

Join for FREE today at
www.HarlequinMyRewards.com.

Harlequin My Rewards is a free program (no fees) without any commitments or obligations.

MYR18